PRAISE FOR *A Field Guide To Murder & Fly Fishing*

"These stories bristle with energy and immediacy. The writing is spare and meticulous and packs a hefty emotional punch. I am not exaggerating when I say this collection kept me up at nights. I just couldn't stop reading." ***—Addison Independent***

"Tim Weed proves himself a skilled creator of a sense of place . . . each story deposits one definitively into a geography, of mind and map." ***—The Boston Globe***

"I found myself consuming [these] thirteen tightly wound tales with addictive delight." ***—Fiction Writers Review***

"From the mountain lakes of the Colorado Rockies to the cobbled streets of Spain, this fascinating collection of short stories never disappoints. *A Field Guide to Murder and Fly Fishing* is a collection you'll be happy to get lost in." ***—Ploughshares***

"If you seek a guide—on coming of age, lost love, temptations both resisted and surrendered to, and the need to both engage with and respect the planet—Weed's book is a good choice. It won't tell you which laws to obey and which to break—but it will show you, with simultaneous beauty and savagery, what will happen either way." ***—Colorado Review***

"Each story is a jewel, cracking open what matters most: love, family, and our big beautiful planet." **—Ann Hood, author of *The Book that Matters Most***

"Two young boys learn about death and mercy on a camping trip, a fishing guide contemplates and crosses a dark line during an excursion with a rich, entitled client and a teenager following the Grateful Dead for a summer tour plunges into a frightening drug addled spiral. These are just some of the characters searching for truth and meaning in life and death in the new short story collection by Vermont author Tim Weed." ***—Vermont Public Radio***

"I found myself parceling out the stories to make them last. These are stories that will live a long time both on the page and in your heart." **—Joseph Monninger, author of *The World as We Know It***

"Weed's stories . . . have their roots in the relationships between men and boys, and between men and nature, and they are colored by his long experience as a travel and adventure writer . . . His characters are fishermen, mountaineers, and teenagers all on a quest for self-discovery. From the title page to the last page, this is a book of gems." —***Big Sky Journal***

"Under the blue skies and dark waters of *A Field Guide to Murder & Fly Fishing*, readers can feel pain, empathy, and purpose bubbling out from the sharp-detailed mental images." —***Pleiades***

"Weed begins with the assumption that his readers are ready and able to see that the world is not as it seems. Things happen we cannot anticipate, and men change in surprising ways . . . Humans and their sometimes mysterious natures are all it takes for Weed to spin fiction of the first order." —***The Brattleboro Reformer***

"It's the book Hemingway and Salinger and Rick Bass would write if they traveled the world together and then got stranded in a canoe. But better!" **—Eleanor Henderson, author of *The Twelve Mile Straight***

"Many of Weed's stories have a hint of the mysterious, even the supernatural, but they are all grounded in sharply-rendered material worlds so fresh one feels one might step directly into the literary photographs he has created and stroll around for a while. A top-notch debut, not to be missed." **—Jacob Appel, author of *Einstein's Beach House***

"[In "Tower Eight"] Weed delves into adolescent friendship and the idea of being an outsider with great care for his characters. The tale begins and ends with one character musing on the reality of the other. The surreal ploy is subtle enough to bring the story into the realm of good literature, making the reader question perceptions of reality. Weed's prose is weightless, and weighty, all at once." —***Seven Days***

"The Money Pill" feels like essential literature—for its self-awareness, its bold impeachment of globalism, and its sultry, sticky atmosphere of arousal and shame." —***Necessary Fiction***

"["Steal Your Face"] is a short story that would make Mark Twain proud, as if Tom Sawyer or Huck Finn found themselves on tour with Jerry and the boys and culminated their eventful summers on a head full of acid in Colorado at the Red Rocks amphitheater." **—Roland Goity, Vagabondage Press**

"*A Field Guide to Murder & Fly Fishing* is more than a collection of adventure stories. It is a significant and moving collection of ideas, snapshots, and visions that leave a lasting impression. Never predictable, this collection is a must for travelers, adventure seekers, and anyone who cares to examine the depth of [Weed's] varied and flawed characters." ***—We Are the Curriculum***

"Gearing up or slowing down, these short stories are a great way to leap into summer reading." ***—Petoskey News-Review***

"As readers, we have been given passports into Tim Weed's fictional worlds . . . We cannot alter the fates of those we have joined but, if we give them a chance, they could alter ours." ***—Small Press Book Review***

"This collection of stories by Tim Weed is grounded in the specificity of its settings, all of which contain hazards of one kind or another. But it is also full of mystery, and much of the mystery is cosmic. Its stories are about transgression and karma, and a natural order that seems to render its characters uncertain of their own reality. It is written so deftly, with such a light touch, that suspense builds in each story like a gathering storm." **—Patrick Joyce, author of *One Devil Too Many***

"This is an outstanding story collection. And while the prose isn't exactly Hemingway-terse, it still brings Papa to mind: men fishing, men on skis, men climbing mountains. But there's also a magical element here that calls Borges to mind. Who is that strange woman at the bar? Who is that young climber's companion? It's altogether a satisfying read.." **—Clifford Garstang, author of *What the Zhang Boys Knew***

ALSO BY TIM WEED

Will Poole's Island

A Field Guide To Murder & Fly Fishing

STORIES

Tim Weed

GREEN WRITERS PRESS *Brattleboro, Vermont*

FIRST PAPERBACK EDITION BY GREEN WRITERS PRESS, APRIL 2018

Originally published in hardcover by Green Writers Press in 2017.

Printed in the United States

10 9 8 7 6 5 4 3 2 1

"The Camp at Cutthroat Lake." *Pooled Ink*, Northern Colorado Writers, LLC, & *Borealis*. "The Afternoon Client." *Writer's Digest* online (Winner of the Ninth Annual Writer's Digest Popular Fiction Awards, Crime Category), & *Sixfold*. "Tower Eight." *The Mountain* (anthology: Grand Prize Winner), Outrider Press, & *Gulf Coast*. "The Dragon of Conchagua" *Saranac Review*. "Six Feet under the Prairie." *Manifest West, Volume II*, Western Press Books, & *Colorado Review*. "Keepers." *MidCurrent* & *Boston Fiction Annual Review*. "Mouth of the Tropics." *Green Writers Press Journal* & *Victory Park: The Journal of the New Hampshire Institute of Art* (as "Specimen"). "A Winter Break in Rome." *The Flexible Persona*. "The Money Pill." *Everywhere Stories: Short Fiction from a Small Planet*, Press 53, & *Lightship Anthology 2*, Alma Books. "The Foreigner." *Polterguests* (anthology), MSR Publishing, & *Margin: Exploring Modern Magical Realism* (anthology), & *Compass Rose Review*.

Green Writers Press is a Vermont-based publisher whose mission is to spread a message of hope and renewal through the words and images we publish. Throughout we will adhere to our commitment to preserving and protecting the natural resources of the earth. To that end, a percentage of our proceeds will be donated to environmental activist groups. Green Writers Press gratefully acknowledges support from individual donors, friends, and readers to help support the environment and our publishing initiative.

Giving Voice to Writers & Artists Who Will Make the World a Better Place
Green Writers Press | Brattleboro, Vermont • www.greenwriterspress.com

ISBN: 978-0-9974528-4-6

Visit the author's website: www.timweed.net

PRINTED ON PAPER WITH PULP THAT COMES FROM FSC-CERTIFIED FORESTS, MANAGED FORESTS THAT GUARANTEE RESPONSIBLE ENVIRONMENTAL, SOCIAL, AND ECONOMIC PRACTICES BY LIGHTNING SOURCE ALL WOOD PRODUCT COMPONENTS USED IN BLACK & WHITE, STANDARD COLOR, OR SELECT COLOR PAPERBACK BOOKS, UTILIZING EITHER CREAM OR WHITE BOOKBLOCK PAPER, THAT ARE MANUFACTURED IN THE LAVERGNE, TENNESSEE PRODUCTION CENTER ARE SUSTAINABLE FORESTRY INITIATIVE® (SFI®) CERTIFIED SOURCING.

Contents

Acknowledgments

For their friendship, professionalism and matchless support in the editing and production of this book I thank Dede Cummings and John Tiholiz, along with everyone at Green Writers Press. For perceptive editorial reactions and advice on these and related stories over the years I thank Joseph Monninger, Alden Jones, Robert Stone, Russell Banks, Wilton Barnhardt, Antonya Nelson, Susan Neville, Tom Paine, Pablo Medina, Amber Dermont, Alexander Hogan, Elizabeth Cohen, Gary McKinney, Roland Goity, Cliff Garstang, David Crouse, Cris Freese, Whitney Scott, and Armand Inezian. Special thanks to the beloved guardians of my solitude, Julia, Roo, and Toby.

for Susan and Chuck

"Whosoever is delighted in solitude, is either a wild beast or a god."

—Sir Francis Bacon

The Camp at Cutthroat Lake

Two boys and a man in his late forties sit in an aluminum rowboat in the middle of a lake at the bottom of a broad mountain basin. The lake mirrors the sky of a calm summer afternoon, but tendrils of cold air coming down from the surrounding crags will soon dispel the fragile illusion of warmth. All around the rowboat the lake is pocked with rises, the fleeting perfection of circular ripples left by trout taking a dun mayfly hatch. The boys are freckle-faced and crew-cut. Each holds a spinning rod, and from the tip of each rod a length of transparent monofilament line leads out to the half-red, half-white sphere of a bobber floating on the still meniscus of the lake. Approximately eighteen inches below each bobber hangs an artificial salmon egg, a tiny maraschino cherry suspended in water so clear that if salmon eggs had eyes, each could see the glint of the hook impaling the other.

The man takes a match from a box in the pocket of his red flannel shirt and strikes it on the oarlock. He cups his hands around the flame and holds it over the cob of the pipe clamped between his strong white teeth. The boy sitting in the stern of the rowboat—the man's nephew—watches the flame dance high as the man puffs. With a whip of his wrist the man extinguishes the flame and places the smoking matchstick back in the box, and the box back in his pocket. His skin is tanned leather. Two days of gray stubble accent his handsome jaw. The only sound is the occasional whistle of a camp robber—a gray jay—from the spruce glades surrounding the lake. It is the summer of 1978.

"Okay," the boy sitting in the prow of the rowboat says. "I'll take a fly now." He is son to the man, cousin to the younger boy who watches from the stern. His hair is reddish-blond and cut uniformly at half an inch, so that the pale contour of his skull shows through.

"What kind, Jack?"

"You *know* what kind. Those little gray ones coming up off the water."

The man leans forward in the boat, offering the open fly-wallet like a dessert menu. Jack squints at the flies and then points.

"Good choice, Jack." Jack's father pinches the fly between his thumb and forefinger to remove it from the wallet while the boy reels in his line. He lifts the rod tip over his father's head so that the bobber swings back and forth like a pendulum. The man watches it swing for a moment, reaches for it, and tucks it under his arm while he bites the monofilament to remove the hook with the salmon egg, and quickly ties on the fly. Jack casts the bobber out, and Jack's father turns to his watching nephew.

"Want a fly, too, Tommy?"

"Sure, I guess." Tommy reels in his bobber and the man shows him the wallet, but before Tommy can pick out a fly Jack's bobber is dragged under the surface and he jerks it high, ripping the hook from the unseen trout's mouth. The bobber hits the side of the aluminum boat, a loud drumbeat echoing over the lake.

"Easy, Jack," the man says through his teeth that clench the pipe stem. "Not so hard next time."

Tommy picks out a fly and his uncle ties it on. A moment after his bobber hits the water it dives: two distinct tugs as if by a kind of prearranged signal. Tommy raises the rod's tip and the trout goes into a frenzy of runs and twists, a determined fight to flee, unhook, survive. Heart pounding, Tommy reels in, the taut line slicing to and fro through the water, the rod bending and jumping with powerful life. When the fish is beside the boat Jack's father leans over, nets it, and holds it up for Tommy to see—a luminous creature writhing in the hammock of black mesh.

"Wet your hands," the man says. "You should be the one to unhook it."

"Can we keep it?"

"I always release the first catch, but this one's yours, Tommy. It's up to you."

Tommy lays his rod down in the rowboat and leans over to wet his hands in the frigid water. He takes the net and holds it with one hand while he reaches for the fish with the other. The creature is cold and substantial and slippery, and there is something miraculous about it: the tense, streamlined musculature; the trembling, golden-brown skin with black and orange speckles under an opalescent sheen.

He looks up at his uncle. The man smiles and nods.

With both hands Tommy lowers the fish and cradles it in the cold water. For a moment, nothing happens. Then the trout pulsates, as if animated by a sudden charge of electricity, and darts away. There is a green-gold flash like fleeting shadow-lightning, and then it is gone.

Tommy looks up, bewildered. Somehow it feels as if more time has elapsed than the few seconds it has actually taken to release the trout. His uncle grins at him. The air on the lake is dry and fresh, with the Christmas-tree scent of spruce.

Jack gets another bite but he jerks the line too hard and dislodges the hook again. Tommy smells his own hands; the trout-scent is clean and pleasant mingling with the spruce.

As the sun sinks below the spur of the pyramid-shaped peak to the west, Jack's father assembles his fly rod and begins to cast. The yellow line rolls and unrolls over the lake in a long, neat loop, unfurling straight before settling lightly on the surface. The boys watch, awestruck. On the third cast a violent splash engulfs the fly just as it settles on the water. The boys watch as the man fights the big trout in and leans over the edge of the rowboat to net it. It's another beauty, slightly larger than Tommy's, with a stroke of bright scarlet on the throat.

"Cutthroat," he says. He mutters something under his

breath, brings the creature up to his lips like a sacrament, and lowers it to the water to free it.

A few minutes later, after the man has put away the fly rod, he takes up the oars and whistles the Battle Hymn of the Republic as he rows them toward the shore, where an old Jeep Willys and two army-surplus tents sit in a meadow next to a small creek that rushes down from the high country to feed the lake. Jack catches Tommy's eye and sarcastically pantomimes his father's act of kissing the fish. Tommy shrugs and looks away.

"What's the matter?" Tommy whispers, shivering under his gray-wool blanket. They're sitting in foldout chairs by the tents, looking out over the iron-colored lake. The whole basin is in shadow except for the peaks of a jagged cockscomb ridge to the east; these are bathed in alpenglow. Jack's father is out of sight in the spruce glades; in the distance the boys can hear the snap of dry branches. Jack's lips are turned down at the corners in an angry frown.

"He could've *told* us they would only take flies. Instead of letting us strike out with salmon eggs all morning."

"I think he wants us to learn for ourselves," Tommy says, pulling the blanket tighter over his shoulders.

"You don't understand, Tommy. Everything has to be done *exactly his way*. He gets these ideas in his head. I can't even watch *television* when he's around. He's always trying to *teach* me something."

"If someone knows a thing, why shouldn't they teach it? Don't you want to learn?"

There is a rustling in the shadows and Jack's father emerges with a bundle of broken twigs. He strides over and dumps the wood by the fire pit. He's wearing frayed khaki pants with red suspenders over a white V-neck undershirt. A streak of sweat runs down the center of the undershirt and his upper arms glow palely in the half-light.

"Know how to build a fire, Tommy?"

"Sure, I guess."

"Show him how to do it right, Jack. I'll go for one more load." He turns back in the direction he came and is soon swallowed in darkness.

"See what I mean?" Jack whispers. He gets up, wool blanket draped over his shoulders like a cape, and squats before the fire pit. He shows Tommy how to build a fire efficiently and without paper: a handful of dry spruce needles at the center, small twigs in a compact teepee, a layer of thicker branches around them leaving an opening for the match.

"Good," Jack's father says, dropping another bundle of sticks on the pile. He kneels to light the pine needles.

The wood is dry and the flames roar up, illuminating the three in the fading dusk. Their faces are pale and drawn in the firelight, the way human faces gathered around fires have looked for a hundred thousand years. The man heats up some chili and they use metal forks to eat it directly out of the fire-blackened pan. Afterwards he produces a chocolate bar and breaks it in three pieces. They savor the chocolate in the darkness, staring at the blood-red embers in the heart of the fire.

The sun rises over the cockscomb arête; it will be another clear and windless day. As they eat breakfast in the rich dawn light the camp robbers watch them, big solemn jays with clean, gray feathers and wise-looking whitish heads, perched on spruce branches at the edge of the meadow. Occasionally one of the birds emboldens itself to come forward for a scrap of egg or a crumb of last night's bread.

Tommy asks his uncle to teach him how to fly-fish, and after breakfast the man obliges, setting him up in the meadow beyond the tents to cast a line with no fly tied to the tippet. Jack watches for a while, then walks over to the Jeep to get his air-powered BB gun.

Later, out on the lake, Tommy's uncle ships the oars and lets the boat drift. "Careful not to slap the water with your line," he urges. Tommy casts, concentrating on the rhythmic motion he learned in the meadow—back-stroke, pause, forward-stroke, pause—letting the line straighten out fully before reversing direction.

"Very good, Tommy," his uncle says, grinning. "But don't forget to let the fly touch the water sometimes. If you want to catch any trout, that is."

Tommy lets the line settle and watches the fly drift on the glassy surface. It looks insignificant, a tiny fleck of lint on the shimmering expanse of lake. In the background is the periodic, muffled gasp of Jack's airgun.

Suddenly the water under the fly erupts and there is a live weight pulling on the line. The fly rod is suppler and more sensitive than the spinning rod; the connection to the animal feels less mediated, more direct. Heart pounding, he brings the fish up beside the boat. The man scoops it and hands Tommy the net with the thrashing trout.

"I want to keep it."

"Then hit it on the head with the net handle. Right between the eyes."

Tommy glances at his uncle, who is regarding him with an interested, carefully neutral expression. He reaches down into the net to untangle the struggling creature. When he grasps it in his hand the trout goes still, as if bracing itself. Gingerly, he brings it up to his lips as he's seen his uncle do. Then he holds it down on the aluminum seat with one hand and uses the other to strike it with the net handle.

"Harder, Tommy."

Tommy hits it again, but the fish is still alive. He hits it a third time, feeling sick because one of the eyes is bulging out and the blood is dripping from its gills into the muddy rivulet in the rowboat's hull. He wishes he had let this one go, too.

"Once more, Tommy. *Hard*."

He bludgeons it as hard as he can, and this time he feels a vibration down the length of the fish's body, an electric shiver like that of the released trout but more pronounced. More final.

The man leans forward, holding open a canvas creel, watching the boy closely. There is something in his eyes: empathy perhaps, a glimmer of buried pain. Tommy feels a wave of guilty relief as he deposits the trout in the wide, rubberized mouth of the creel, and the lifeless creature slides away into the green darkness.

On shore at midday, Tommy's uncle shows him how to clean a trout: make an incision at the vent and slice up through the belly to the pectoral fins; cut a tab under the lower jaw; insert two fingers and pull back forcefully to extract the neat package of gills, pectorals, and rose-gray bowels; submerge the fish in the lake and run a thumbnail down the spine inside the empty cavity to clean out the vein of purple blood. It seems miraculous that a wild animal can harbor such a ready-made solution, like a Ziploc bag or a Jiffy Pop.

There are several more fish now, a hearty lunch for three. Jack comes to watch the gutting. He squints unhappily in the bright noonday sun, rifle slung professionally over his shoulder, blue bandana tied in a folded strip around the blond crew cut.

"Why don't you build a fire, Jack," the man suggests, "while I show Tommy the proper way to dress these?"

Jack frowns sullenly but does as he's told, while his father demonstrates the technique of shaking the trout in a plastic bag with flour and lemon pepper. The fish come out of the bag like dusted mummies; Jack's father embalms them with wedges of lemon and tabs of butter.

Once the fire is going he fries them in a skillet while the boys skip flat stones over the lake. The smell of cooking trout piques their appetites, and they return to the fire and wait hungrily while the man serves the fish on paper plates. He shows them how the fillets come neatly off the spine if you slowly raise the tail. He tells them to eat the cheeks first, as a small ritual of thanksgiving to the warrior spirit of the trout.

"Is that why we kiss them, too?" Tommy asks.

His uncle nods. "Thanking the quarry is a way to close the circle. That's what makes us human, Tommy—what keeps us in balance with all creation. It doesn't matter what the rituals are, as long as you have them."

"Dad, do you really believe that crap?" Jack asks from across the fire. His mouth is twisted in a derisive thirteen-year-old's smirk.

"I'm still waiting to hear what *you* believe, son." The man's voice is patient, with an undertone of mild irritation—with a hint, perhaps, that the patience won't always be there. Jack shakes his head and glances pointedly off into the spruce glades, as if alluding to his morning of target practice. The wind has begun to gust off the lake, sending up plumes of sparks from the fire, the blown smoke stinging their eyes. Tommy yawns, then gets up and crawls into the boys' tent for a nap.

He can't sleep. He tells himself that he should feel a sense of accomplishment for learning how to fly-fish, but something has made him anxious. The tent zipper splits and Jack's grim, freckled face peers in. He's still wearing the blue bandana, and Tommy has a sudden image of his cousin as an Indian-hunter: General Custer come to scalp him in his sleep.

"Let's go shoot," Jack says. "You're not sleeping anyway."

Tommy sighs and gets up. He follows Jack out of the tent and over to the edge of the meadow, where a weathered log is already set up with a shooting-gallery row of beer cans.

"Where's your Dad?"

"I don't know, probably off hunting squirrels. He kills them with his bare hands by twisting their necks, then he hangs them on the pine trees like Christmas ornaments."

Tommy looks up sharply, stunned by the news.

"Just kidding," Jack murmurs, squinting down the barrel of the air gun. "He's taking a stroll around the lake."

Tommy flushes, embarrassed by his own gullibility, but in truth, it's mostly relief he feels. He watches while Jack shoots the cans off the log, one after the other. Jack is a good shot. When all the cans are lying on the spruce litter, he hands the rifle to Tommy and goes over to set them back up. Tommy's shooting is less accurate, but when the shots do connect, it's satisfying: *Plink. Plink.*

A camp robber lands on the top of a spruce behind the shooting gallery, and Jack reaches over to jerk the gun out of Tommy's hands.

"Hey! What are you doing?"

The older boy aims the gun at the jay, which sways back and forth on its perch atop the spruce.

"You're not going to shoot it, Jack, are you? *Don't* shoot it."

The blond boy looks up at his cousin with a grave, wide-eyed expression, then presses his cheek to the polished oak gunstock to aim at the bird again. For a moment everything is peaceful: the breeze wrinkling the surface of lake; the mountain summits; the faint sound of the creek bubbling in the background; the wise-looking, gray bird regarding them from its swaying perch. Then the airgun's mechanism lets out a gassy exhalation and the camp robber jerks, reels, and plummets in a drunken spiral into the shadows at the base of the tree.

"Aw, *man*!" Tommy exclaims. "Why'd you have to do that?"

Jack looks up with a forced grin. "It was a good shot, Tommy. You have to admit, it was a good shot."

Tommy shakes his head and looks away, not wanting to meet his cousin's eyes. The two boys walk over to the tree, and Jack uses the gun barrel to poke around in the shadows. The jay jerks weirdly on the spruce litter, wings akimbo.

A twig snaps some way off and the boys look up to see Jack's father striding toward them from the other side of the meadow. Tommy feels his cheeks and temples burning with shame. Jack's thin face has gone white.

"There you are, boys," the man calls cheerfully. "What's going on?" As he approaches, Jack points with the gun at the mortally stricken bird. His father squats down to get a closer look. "What happened, son?"

Jack opens his mouth to say something, but no words come out. He just shakes his head, looking away angrily. The man glances at Tommy, who shrugs helplessly, feeling a spasm of panic down in his crotch as if he's the one in trouble.

His father takes the air gun from Jack's hands, and uses the stock to sweep the jay out from the tree base and onto the dry meadow grass. He raises the gun, barrel up, and prepares to bring it down on the twitching creature's head. But then he hesitates, gazing at Jack with a look of strange intensity. It isn't mere anger Tommy sees clouding his uncle's face—or scorn, or disgust. It is a series of more frightening reactions: recognition, dread, and—worst of all—self-doubt.

The man shakes his head as if to rid himself of an unpleasant daydream, and brings the butt down hard on the jay's skull. There is a faint, dry pop, like the crack of a hard-boiled egg on a kneecap, and the bird is still.

Tower Eight

I haven't been back in years, but I have no doubt the Fitzwilliam Quarry still exists. To get there you have to hike a mile or so through a yellow-birch and hemlock forest and negotiate a field of massive splintered blocks, talus left over from the extraction of the New Hampshire granite that built the cities of the Eastern Seaboard. The quarry is impossible to miss, a yawning cavity cut in stepped gradations, like benches in a steep amphitheater down to a pool of pure black water. If it is a sunny day the surface of the pool glints like obsidian until something disturbs it, at which point faceted reflections leap like ghosts across the high granite walls.

For much of the summer of 1982, Kimball Jones and I had the place to ourselves. We would arrive, take a cold plunge, climb to our favorite ledge—smooth and comfortable, with a birch sapling growing out of a mossy crack where the shelf met the cliff—and doze like zoo animals on the sun-warmed granite. Scrawled in peeling red paint on the opposite wall was this proverb:

THERE IS NO GRAVITY
THE EARTH SUCKS

One day in July, as we sat on the ledge with our legs dangling, I asked Kimball what he thought the words meant. My voice was louder than I'd expected it to be, a high-pitched echo ringing out through the deserted amphitheater.

"Who knows?" Kimball replied. He cupped his hands around his mouth to get a better echo. "Maybe whoever put it there never took *physics*."

"Or maybe he was just *depressed*," I answered, following Kimball's example and shouting the last word.

"Or maybe he thought you could *fly*, if you could just—" Kimball rose to his feet and took a deep breath, the word *fly* volleying back and forth across the granite walls. "If you could just break free of—"

He threw himself off the ledge, disappearing with a white flash into the pool below. He stayed under a long time, until the surface of the water was unbroken by a single ripple. For a moment I considered the idea that he'd never existed at all—that he was just a creature of my lonely imagination—but eventually he came up, laughing, and frog-stroked to the edge of the pool.

Back on the ledge he shivered happily. Water dripped from the frays of his jean cut-offs onto his pale, hairless legs. He was a strange-looking boy, with a big, beak-like nose, a weak, almost nonexistent chin, and eyes that were abnormally wide-set and often appeared to be gazing in two different directions. His light blond hair was crew-cut, and from certain angles he looked like an enormous baby bird. Because of his bizarre appearance, no one at school wanted anything to do with him. I myself had befriended him with great reluctance, mainly from a lack of other options, although by now his ugliness didn't trouble me unless there were other people around to make fun of us.

"Hey, check this out." He knelt to extract something from his daypack and then sat beside me on the ledge, holding out a sheet of stiff paper the size of a cocktail napkin. The sheet was divided into dozens of tiny squares, each square stamped with the image of a cartoon character: Mickey Mouse, Wile E. Coyote, Daffy Duck, three or four others in a repeating pattern like wallpaper.

"Cool," I said. "What's it supposed to be?"

"It's LSD. I got it from Temple."

I took the sheet and held it to my nose. It smelled like normal paper, maybe a hint of peppermint. "Temple sold you this?"

"No, dude, he *gave* it to me. I saw him at the record store. He said I should share it with you."

"Cool," I repeated uncertainly.

Kimball took the sheet back and tore off one of the squares, a Tweetie Bird. He held it out to me on his outstretched palm, with a smoldering, chinless smile.

"No thanks," I said. "I read somewhere that taking LSD can make you certifiably insane."

"Don't be ridiculous," he replied. "Certifiably? Do you think they give out little certificates? Come on, Jeff."

"Not *interested*, dude."

"Snatch this pebble from my hand, Grasshopper," he ordered. "Then you will understand." He took my wrist and pressed the Tweetie Bird into my palm. He ripped off another square for himself, a Roadrunner, and stuck it on his outstretched tongue.

With a powerful sense of foreboding, I swallowed the Tweetie Bird.

The Fitzwilliam Quarry was not the place to hang out that summer. The place to hang out was Hobie's, a river-fed swimming hole with a series of pools and waterfalls running through a stand of old hemlocks. There was a long, smooth rock exposed to the sun that served as a kind of beach, with well-trodden pathways leading upstream and downstream to jumping ledges of different heights and difficulties. Kimball and I had gone there once or twice, but it was not our scene. We told ourselves there was too much broken glass and too much noise—the dueling boom-boxes playing Lynyrd Skynyrd and Van Halen; the outbursts of shouting and laughter from the soccer players and their grinning sycophants—but the truth was, we didn't feel welcome there. We, or at least I, got the sense that we were on probation; that at any moment, if we loosened up or did something construable as less-than-cool, the entire clique would close ranks around us like a pack of blood-thirsty hyenas.

We liked it better at the quarry. It was a hike to get there, so we had it all to ourselves except on weekends, when the rednecks came. Fortunately, most of them had to work during the week.

Kimball and I did not work. It wasn't that our parents were rich. His mother was an occupational therapist who'd returned to her native state of New Hampshire after his father had been killed in a skydiving accident in Utah. My father was an underpaid college professor; my mother, a social worker. The reason we didn't work was that we didn't want to: we lacked motivation. We'd discovered this common truth about ourselves the previous November, when we'd both gone out for the ski team. We were good at the sport, having skied with our families from an early age, but the pre-season workouts were too grueling, and there was another problem as well. The ski team was a winter occupation for many of the same popular soccer players who frequented Hobie's during the summer. Kimball was far too much of an oddball to be acceptable to that crowd, and I was one of those slow-maturing boys for whom the hormonal starting gun had yet to be fired.

To make a long story short, Kimball and I quit the ski team before the first snowfall. We started hanging out on weekday afternoons, smoking pot and playing Ping-Pong in Kimball's windowless basement suite. On weekends, newly licensed to drive, I borrowed my father's beat-up old Volkswagen Beetle and we drove up to Mount Cratchett, our local ski area. By spring our friendship was ingrained. When summer came we staked out the quarry, and by that day in July when we dropped our first hits of acid, we'd come to feel as if we owned the place.

The drug kicked in as a bee-like humming in the back of my throat. Then I was plummeting toward the water; then I was piercing the cold black depths in a protective capsule of silver bubbles. When my breath ran out I kicked my feet and ascended in a perfect spiral to the surface, where I gulped the air and imagined the blood delivering fizzy oxygen molecules to every cell in my body. I followed Kimball up to our ledge and jumped off again. This time I let myself sink deeper and stay under longer, fascinated by the bubbles that shimmered all around me like beads of buoyant mercury, rising steadily to the surface. I came up for air and saw Kimball scaling the granite wall, his movements quick and jerky, like a film character on fast forward.

I made a halfhearted effort to follow, but I was drawn back to the silent underwater world, so I dove off the ledge I was standing on. Who knows how much time had gone by when I spotted him perched atop the Podium, the quarry's highest viable jumping point. I'd never actually seen anyone go off it, but apparently people did. It was breathtakingly high, a jutting rectangle of granite framed by twin hemlocks. The Podium stuck out into the air like the aborted beginning of a bridge; even so, it was set far enough back from the water that a running start would be required to clear the lower ledges. Kimball stood with his toes on the lip, swaying slightly. From where I was treading water in the middle of the pool, he looked tiny and impossibly far away.

"Are you sure?" I asked.

He peered down from the heights, head cocked to one side like a curious bird. "What, dude?"

"Now may not be the best time to do that," I shouted. The echo of my voice returned to me sounding thin and scared.

"Come check this place out," he called down.

I swam over to the edge of the pool and scaled the wall as quickly as I could. Near the top, the granite angled out in a slight overhang, and I found myself without a toehold. I repressed a detailed vision of my braincase shattering like crockery as it hit the lower ledges. My unoccupied foot probed frantically, finding nothing but sheer granite. The ankle of my weight-bearing foot began to spasm, working up and down as if it were pedaling an antique sewing machine. I couldn't bring myself to look either up or down, so I concentrated on a patch of orange lichen in front of my face, struggling to regain my composure. But the lichen began to squirm and bubble, and fearing that it was about to splatter out and burn my eyes I shrank away from the wall, nearly losing my grip. A chill went down my spine as I realized how close I'd come to simply letting go.

"Danger, Will Robinson." Kimball's calm voice sounded close. I risked an upward glance and saw his pink, overbit face only inches from mine, a curious glint in the one eye trained down at me. He extended his hand. I reached up and took it, and in one effortless movement he hoisted me onto the flat top of the Podium. I staggered to my feet and backed away from the edge, blood roaring in my ears like whitewater.

"Dude!" he exclaimed, tilting his head with an expression of kindly puzzlement. "What were you so *afraid* of?"

I struggled for breath. "Did you see what was happening to that orange lichen? I almost had to let go."

He nodded solemnly. "Well, it's probably good that

you didn't. But check this out. I've got a theory." He drifted back into the trees, muttering to himself under his breath. I thought he was going to take a piss, but then there was a rush of air as he shot past me. His gangly body seemed to hang in midair for a moment, arms windmilling, before he plummeted out of sight.

I cursed and got down on all fours to peer over the edge. The pool was a long way down, and the water was eerily still. The seconds stretched on. I scanned the lower shelves for blood; dungaree shorts; a pale, twisted corpse. There was a payphone in the town of Fitzwilliam. I pictured myself scrambling over the talus, sprinting along the trail through the shady forest. I imagined the announcement coming over the loudspeaker at school, and then I felt ashamed to be having such thoughts.

Finally his head broke the surface. "I knew it!" he sputtered.

"What?" I shouted, feeling both irritation and relief.

"There is no gravity! Just like the graffiti says!"

"Dude! Then how come you fell when you jumped?"

"I didn't fall!" He was treading water, his head a small pink cork in the middle of a circular ripple at the center of the blackwater pool. "Going down was my *choice*! There's no gravity!"

"Okay. Okay." I nodded, swallowing. The acid was hitting with a new wave of intensity, tightening my throat muscles and causing everything in my field of vision to dance in sync with my pulse. The granite around the edges of the pool had melted and was floating on the surface like sea-scum. Kimball's foreshortened legs scissored underwater, feet webbed like tiny duck feet. Vertigo was a physical suction pulling me over the edge. I lay flat on the granite with my arms spread wide as if to embrace it, gazing down at my distant friend.

"Come on!" he shouted. "Don't be afraid!"

I shook my head. Speech was beyond my power at that point.

"*Think* about it, Jeff," he urged. "Let the concept seep into your mind. There is . . . no . . . *gravity*!"

Seconds passed, maybe minutes. A parade of clear paisley amoebas floated down across my field of vision. When I blinked, the parade would start again from the top, sliding over my eyeballs like ice melting on a windshield. It was strangely soothing.

I took a deep breath, picturing the blood cells carrying their happy little messengers. I blinked away the amoebas one last time and everything snapped into focus: the perfect circle of the sun reflected on the water; the exact geometric angles of the cliffs and ledges; the birch and hemlock saplings outlined sharply, as in an architect's draft. I sketched a trajectory from the lip of the Podium in a steep arc straightening to a downward vector, ending at the exact point where my toes would cleave the meniscus of the pool. And of course, Kimball was right. There was no gravity.

So I jumped.

The rest of that season plays out in my memory like a sunny cartoon, with Kimball as the daring hero, myself as the sidekick, and a badly recorded Grateful Dead bootleg as the soundtrack. Sometimes I wish I could rewind the cartoon and watch it from start to finish. I wonder if I would be able to stop laughing long enough to spot the heat blister in the corner of the frame, the small but unmistakable harbinger of the coming meltdown. Of course, time doesn't have a rewind function, and there's no slow motion either.

Summer flew off the reel and fall was upon us, the fleeting swirl of red and yellow leaving the hillsides bare and battened down for winter. Kimball and I may have lacked motivation, but we were not wholly without discipline. Limiting ourselves to one dose per week, we were able to make the cartoon sheet last until mid-October. Around that time Kimball offered our services to help Temple after school in the wood shop. Temple was the assistant shop teacher and the high school's unofficial handyman; the Nordic coach had asked him to build an indoor ski jump for pre-season training. We were paid hourly wages. We did need the money, but our underlying goal in taking the job was to get our hands on more acid. Another attractive aspect was that it was short-term employment: Temple estimated it would take two weeks of afternoons to finish the jump.

Temple did all the actual carpentry. Kimball and I hauled lumber into the gym and held the boards in place while he cut them with a table saw, drilled pilot holes, and fastened it all together with a screw gun. We didn't mention the cartoon sheet. Temple was a quiet man, not given to small talk, and he had a way of clenching his jaw when he worked that made you worry that he would lash out if you said the wrong thing. Not that he ever lost his cool with us—even when Kimball dropped a two-by-six on his foot—but you knew the potential was there. He was in his forties, a biker-type with a salt-and-pepper ponytail and a pockmarked face from what must have been a bad case of acne in his youth. There were rumors that he'd been a Hells Angel in the '60s, that he'd been at the Altamont Speedway, that he'd done time in prison. He'd always taken a special interest in Kimball and me. As a long-term outsider, he probably saw something of himself in us.

The jump took shape as a long, slanted ramp held up by what looked like a railroad trestle, with a rolling platform mounted on skateboard wheels. A ladder led up twenty feet to a starting box with handrails for the jumper to push off. The jumper would stand on the platform and assume the inrun position: knees and ankles bent, chest flat to thighs. When the platform reached the end of the ramp he would spring up and out, launching himself as far as he could onto two consecutive high-jumping mats. Kimball and I spray-painted white lines on the mats to mark distance: twelve feet equaled thirty meters, fifteen equaled forty, and so on. The afternoon we finished the project, Temple let us take half a dozen runs. It was fun clattering down the ramp and blasting off into the air, almost—but not quite—enough to get us to go out for the ski team again.

Afterwards the three of us stood back to admire the jump. Temple looked happy. He wasn't smiling or anything, but you could tell he was pleased with the way his invention had turned out by the fondness in his eye.

"Phenomenal,," Kimball said, shaking his head with a toothy, fawning smile. "Pure genius."

"Yeah, it's really something else," I said.

Temple grunted distractedly. Then his face clouded over and he turned to Kimball. "What are you trying to do? Kiss my ass?"

Kimball flushed pink. "No, no, no. Not at all. I was just pointing out how well it turned out. It works super, doesn't it, Jeff?"

I nodded vigorously.

"The ski team is going to get a kick out of this," Kimball blabbered on. "I wouldn't be surprised if this season—"

"Shut your goddamn *trap*," Temple ordered, his face having gone a deep red under the pockmarks. "Stop trying to kiss my ass. It's disgusting."

Kimball swallowed. "We weren't trying to—"

"I know very well what you were trying to do," the older man said. "Let me guess. You want more acid, right?"

Kimball glanced at me. I gave him a tiny, noncommittal nod.

"So, you liked the cartoon sheet, did you, boys? I thought you would." Temple grinned like a pirate. "Well, well. Any bad trips?"

We shook our heads in unison. "We can handle it," Kimball said.

"What about you, Jeffrey?" Temple asked. "Can *you* handle it?"

"Sure," I replied. "Why not?"

We followed Temple out to his car, a brown Mustang. When he opened the door a vodka bottle fell out and rolled a few feet on the pavement before spinning to a stop. Kimball picked it up and Temple took it from him and tossed it into the back of the car as he sat sideways in the passenger seat. He sprung the glove compartment and produced a zip-lock baggie full of what looked like sugar cubes. He counted out twenty of the cubes and dropped them into a second baggie, which he handed to Kimball.

"This'll cost you eighty bucks. You can pay me later if you don't have the money on hand."

"Right on," Kimball said happily.

"Thanks a lot, man," I said, glancing nervously around the parking lot. Temple stood up and closed the door of the Mustang.

"We'll help you clean up," Kimball offered.

"No need," the older man replied magnanimously. "You boys go and have some fun. One thing, though. Sugar cubes can be stronger than cartoon tabs, so for Pete's sake take it easy. This stuff can make you feel like God on a Harley, but you're not God, and even a Harley can run out of gas in the middle of the desert. You got that?"

"Got it," Kimball said confidently. I nodded and gave Temple an insider's smile, although I wasn't really sure that I *did* get it.

Meanwhile, socially speaking, things were looking up for me. Mike LaRochelle, the captain of the soccer team, was in my Geometry class. This was his second time taking the class, and although I was in a lower grade, I'd always had a knack for academics, especially math, so I was helping him out, and for this crucial service I was now recognized in the halls and cafeteria. Two of the prettiest senior girls had even come giggling up to my locker to tell me they thought I looked like a younger version of Gilligan from Gilligan's Island.

Well, it was *something*.

One Saturday afternoon, LaRochelle and his buddy Steve Mann threw a keg party at the Shrubs. It was billed as a big event; the halls of the school buzzed with excitement for weeks in advance. Invitations were never mailed out, though: you either knew you were invited or were not. Due to recent events I was pretty sure I was invited, but Kimball was not. So I felt anxious when he suggested that we crash the party together.

"They don't *own* the Shrubs, dude," he said, as we sat on the floor of his basement hunched over a game of Risk. He'd grown sideburns and a wispy white-blond goatee. It did nothing to improve his outlandish appearance, but at least he was beginning to look older. I was still shaving once a week, if that, so in that sense I envied him.

"I just don't feel like it," I repeated.

"Is there something you want to tell me, dude?" he asked coolly. "Do you have a date or something?"

I shook my head. "Of course not."

"Good. Then why don't you pick me up around three? We'll have a little fun at their expense."

The Shrubs was a vast thicket of sumac and hardwood saplings in a field beside the railroad tracks at the south end of town. Viewed from outside, the thicket looked dense and impregnable—even with the leaves gone it was a visual barrier shutting out parents and town police—but there was a narrow trail leading into the middle of it, to a broad clearing of bare dirt and fire rings overflowing with charred beer cans and broken glass. I drove my father's Beetle, an embarrassing forest-green car with rust ulcers on the fenders and floor, and a rear hatch plastered with the nonconformist aphorisms of the era: "Bread not Bombs," "Think Globally/Act Locally," "One Nuclear Bomb Can Ruin Your Whole Day." I parked it next to the Buick town cars and Ford pickups beside the railroad tracks and, heart pounding in the slanting afternoon light, followed Kimball on the narrow path into the thicket. We could hear the hum of conversation, laughter, Led Zeppelin played low on a boom box.

When we stepped into the clearing the chatter stopped, as if someone had thrown a switch. Mike LaRochelle and Steve Mann and four or five others stood by the keg, while the rest of the party clustered in a loose group around the clearing. No one looked at us; all eyes were fixed upon the hosts to see what their reaction would be. Mann leaned to LaRochelle and murmured something under his breath; LaRochelle nodded and smiled thinly. I saw that it had been a mistake to come.

Gradually the hum of conversation resumed, lower-pitched and less carefree than before. Having succeeded technically in his goal of crashing the party, Kimball seemed to feel no need to attempt the keg; the two of us hovered awkwardly at the edge of the clearing for a few minutes and then slunk away. I heard a contemptuous voice utter the word "freaks"—it was plural—and there was no mistaking the derisiveness of the laughter that reached our ears as we emerged from the thicket. I could hear some of the girls laughing too. That hit me hard, like a blow to the solar plexus.

Back at the Beetle I sat in the driver's seat and fumbled around with the key. My hands were shaking. I stole a look at Kimball in the passenger seat; as usual, he seemed unfazed.

"Don't worry, dude," he said, lighting a match on his tooth and holding it up to the twist at the end of a joint. "We don't need those people. They think they're some kind of elite, but really, they're just leading these little . . . tiny . . . lives!" He exhaled a cloud of bitter smoke and passed the joint to me. "We, on the other hand, dude, know what it means to live *large*. Right?" He gave me a buck-toothed grin, one crazy eye dancing, the other staring kindly into mine.

I took a drag from the joint and turned the key in the ignition. The VW chugged laboriously and then started up with a cheerful cough. Kimball had a way of putting things in perspective. Who needed *their* reality?

The snow came early that year. It snowed so much that by the second week in December we had to post-hole uphill through thigh-deep drifts to get to Indian Head, a sheltered granite outcropping on the forested hillside above the high school. It looked nothing like an Indian's head, and there was not much to recommend the place, other than a clear view of the school and the brick-and-shingle mill town beyond. But for various reasons our houses were by this time off-limits, so we frequently put on snowmobile boots and ski parkas and used the place to hang out, smoke dope, and, sometimes, drop acid.

One Friday afternoon in early January, an hour or so after we'd each swallowed a sugar cube, we found ourselves standing beneath a horseshoe-shaped cliff hung with icicles: thick, fluted stalactites that gleamed like a row of giant teeth. A leeching mineral in the granite had stained the icicles with ugly yellow streaks, and Kimball got us started on the idea that we were toothbrush mercenaries, just like in the TV commercial, on a mission to rid the teeth of the deadly scourge of plaque. He broke off an icicle toothbrush and started waving it around, screaming at the top of his lungs in a garbled British accent. I broke off my own weapon and stepped into the fray.

Eventually, things got weird. The teeth began to fight back. On the first swing of my fourth replacement icicle a molar the size of an anvil broke off and slammed into my skull, driving me to my knees in the deep snow and shattering my equilibrium in a psychedelic explosion of glittering shards. Kimball, a red-faced Viking going berserk on the teeth, hadn't noticed my distress. I tried to call out his name, but no sound issued from my throat. I felt as though there weren't enough oxygen in the air, as though my lungs were flooding. I closed my eyes and tried to suppress my rising panic.

When I opened them he was standing above me, shaking his head wordlessly.

"How bad is it?" I managed to whisper.

"It doesn't look good, dude."

The panic swept me up like water from a burst dam. My skull ached where the icicle had hit, and it felt cracked open, as if part of my brain were exposed to the air.

"Here." He handed me a crumpled red bandana. I wiped my eyes with it and hallucinated that his cheeks were pulled back and rippling with g-forces, like an astronaut in a rocket. He started giving me instructions, but his voice was weirdly slow and deep, like a tape player with low batteries, and my hearing kept cutting in and out like a distant radio signal: ". . . bandana to stop the bleeding . . . from doctors for now . . . to your house. And you . . . stay out of sight of your parents, okay, dude?"

Staying out of sight of my parents was not a problem, luckily, as they were away for the weekend. But I had other hazards to avoid in the empty house. The most terrifying of these was the bathroom mirror, where I went to check the extent of the damage to my head. A vivid picture had formed in my mind of what the wound would look like: slivers of white skull-bone poking through the flesh; a strip of gray brain matter visible through the pulsating gash in my scalp. When I worked up the courage to peel away the bandana in front of the mirror, it turned out to be no big deal, just an egg-shaped welt and an insignificant scab of coagulated blood sticking to the hair follicles. I was so relieved

I nearly cried, but then I made the mistake of staring at myself in the mirror. My face was perfectly normal: boyish, hairless, an underdeveloped face for a teenager to be sure, but normal. That is, until it started to morph.

I stared in growing horror, unable to tear my eyes away, as my occipital crest bulged, receded, and bulged again. The tips of my chin and nose blurred, and there was a throbbing in my jaw and mandible as the lower half of my face fused together in a kind of blunt, atavistic snout. I let out an inhuman groan and held my head, staggering out of the bathroom. I slammed violently against one wall after another as I ricocheted down the hall to my bedroom. I sought refuge in a tiny closet, where I spent the rest of that horrible day and night in darkness, vowing that if God allowed me to wake up the next day as a normal human being, I would never do LSD again.

It took me several weeks to recover. Kimball tried to get me to laugh it off, but the two visions of myself—first as mortally wounded, and then as a beast-like mutant—lingered in my mind. The knowledge that Kimball had been unable to protect me from these terrors was unsettling. From the beginning, his confidence had been a given; only now do I realize the extent to which I'd come to depend on it. I'd taken it for granted that nothing bad could happen as long as he was there, and when something bad *did* happen I felt like a tight-rope walker who completes his act only to discover that the circus grunts never bothered to string up the safety net. A part of me bore a grudge against him, I must admit, while another part was worried for both of us—justifiably so, as it turned out.

Once a month the school offered a free Winter Sports Day. Some people went to the skating rink to play hockey, a few dedicated souls went to the country club to cross-country ski, and the rest of us took buses up to Mount Cratchett for a day on the slopes. Kimball and I boarded the second bus—the same vehicle, unfortunately, that carried most of the soccer clique. It was a noisy, unpleasant journey. By now we were complete pariahs, a painful state of affairs for me, but one that I was able to ignore as long as we were left alone. Today, however, we had no such luck. The sting of the first spitball on the back of my neck caused me to flinch visibly, and this set off a round of snickering. I knew better than to turn my head. The next one hit Kimball, who reddened and gritted his teeth, staring at his hands in his lap. The goatee had come in nicely, but contrary to his intentions for growing it, it hadn't added any mass to his chin. We shrank down in the seat so our heads no longer offered targets from behind. This provoked a round of call-and-response derision:

"Aw, isn't that sweet. Kimby and Jeffy making out on the bus."

"Hey, lay off, guys, they need a little freak-to-freak time."

"Did we scare you? Why don't you stand up for yourselves, losers?"

Kimball's face was very red, and his whole body shook. I'd never seen him so angry. "Sometimes I wish I had an AK-47," he said. "I'd love to just blow their brains out."

For a moment the idea made me smile—*rat-tat-tat-tat*, blood and brains sprayed all over the windows at the back of the bus—and then I started to worry. "You don't really *mean* that, dude—do you? We're *better* than them, right? I mean, our life is better."

His face was right next to mine, and the emotions I saw flickering there were far more terrifying than anything the soccer players could say or do. But slowly, the old smile came back, and the crazy eyes took on their familiar merry glint. "Don't worry, Jeff. I was just kidding about the AK-47." He fished around in the pocket of his ski parka. "But I'm *not* kidding about this." He shook his fist as if he were rolling dice, and opened it to reveal four sugar cubes: little white bricks looking cheerful and frosty on the pink skin of his palm.

"Four?" I asked.

"Two each."

"Dude," I whispered. "I'm not even sure I want to *take* acid again, much less increase my dose. Remember what happened last time? I'm not really that into it any more."

"Jeff." The goofy, bucktoothed smile was disarming, irresistible. The back of the bus was noisy again: Led Zeppelin on the boom box, the hoarse voices of our tormentors singing along. Ourselves comfortably forgotten again, at least for the moment.

"I'll take *half* a cube," I conceded, feeling a strange sense of removal, as if I were watching the two of us from a seat across the aisle.

"Take a whole one, Grasshopper. I'll take three and we'll call it even."

I stared at him. "Okay," I said finally. "I'll take a whole cube, but only if *you* stick to one as well." The idea of either of us trying to ski on two cubes scared the crap out of me.

"Deal." He handed me a cube, quickly popping another into his mouth. He made a show of putting the remaining ones back in his coat pocket, but his fist stayed closed when he took it out and I think he must have taken the extras, too. In the end, it probably didn't matter.

We liked to ride the lift as singles, propping our skis and boots up to stretch comfortably across the chairs. In the chair ahead of me Kimball lounged in his dirt-stained down parka, a sky-blue Gerry coat held together with duct tape. He wore a headband with the Rossignol rooster logo, and his light blond hair had grown out so that a good four inches of it curled up and forward above the headband like the crest of a woodpecker. He was as bizarre-looking as ever, but he didn't seem out of place on the slopes. The fact was that we were both lifelong skiers, as comfortable as could be in the lift-served environment.

The sugar cubes had begun to kick in. Kimball kept peering back at me over his shoulder, nostrils bubbling with snot, cheeks red in the frosty air, chin with its white-blond goatee all but lost in the folds of his neck as he snorted and cackled with glee. He'd been laughing like that ever since we'd boarded the lift: giggles building to crescendos of crow-like cawing, punctuated by episodes of descending hoots and hiccups. Whenever his eyes met mine I would crack up, too, and just when I would start to get a grip on myself, he would crane around and make another face—eyes rolling divergently under that ridiculous blond woodpecker crest—and the red-white-and-blue rooster on his headband would detach itself from the wool and do a little jig in the air in front of his forehead. The lift cable rollers squeaked noisily in the background, like a pack of excitedly fleeing rats.

My stomach cramped up. The laughter had begun to feel ominous, as if it were coming not from me but from some alien force in possession of my body. I started to worry that I would get trapped in laughing mode, like that urban legend about how if you play with your eyelids they'll get stuck permanently inside-out. I strained to keep my mouth clamped shut, having convinced myself that if I opened it, my tongue would freeze solid and crack off in the snow.

The lift deposited us on the hoar-frosted mountaintop. The scenery cut to slanting planes of bright white, the DayGlo blur of other skiers, the frigid wind licking our faces as we plummeted down a broad slope called Arrow. We were good skiers, but the drug made us even better. No hesitation, no false moves: all the vectors were at our disposal; our skis were flexing extensions of our feet. We soared downhill with delicate precision, gloriously, like hawks on the wind.

At the bottom of the slope we glided into the lift line, a harrowing arena brimming with potential danger: strangers' eyes lingering just a moment too long, or worse than strangers—the familiar faces of teachers and schoolmates, faces that must be ignored at all costs. Hazards were everywhere, even in something as apparently harmless as the lift-shack window, if one were inadvertently to catch a glimpse of one's own reflection.

There was too much of a line now for us to ride as singles, so we boarded the chair together, shaken and introverted, desperate to get back to the thoughtless freedom of ski-borne travel. I began to ponder the physics of skiing: the actual movements of hips and knees and ankles that translated into long arcing turns on the snow. I should have known that was a mistake. If you think too hard about anything, even something you're very good at, it's easy to convince yourself that you don't really know how to do it.

Approaching the off-ramp Kimball raised the safety bar. I stared straight ahead, trying unsuccessfully to visualize the body stance of a competent skier.

"Hey, dude?" I said in alarm. "I think I forgot how to ski."

He gave me a sidelong glance. "Bullcrap. You've been skiing like a banshee all morning. You're hell on skis, dude."

"Okay. Okay." I nodded, desperately trying to believe him.

The chair shuddered as the cable fed through the rollers on the last tower. When my skis touched the snow, I rose stiffly. At the end of the ramp I fell over backwards. Kimball skated back and gazed down at me, leaning on his poles, with an amused look on his face. He seemed to have the drug more or less under control.

"What the *fuck*, dude? Do you seriously believe that you forgot how to ski?"

I sighed despairingly, and let my head rest on the frozen ground. The sun hung low in the January sky, contracting and expanding to the rhythm of my pulse, but seeming to give off no heat. It was hard to believe that this weak and trembling orb was the same sun that had once warmed the granite ledges of the Fitzwilliam Quarry.

Kimball clicked out of his bindings and knelt beside me in the snow. In the background, the flywheel groaned like a grief-stricken monster.

"Skiing is a memorized skill of your body," he said. He kept trying to hold my gaze, but his eyes wouldn't cooperate. As he focused one, the other would drift; he would tilt his head to rein that one in, and the other would wander off. "You learned how to do it when you were three years old, Jeff, and you still know how to do it. Okay?"

He offered me my poles, grips forward. I accepted them, used them to push myself upright, and glided down the knoll to the billboard that held the trail map. He skied by and gave me the thumbs-up sign, but his head flash-morphed into that of an enormous bird of prey—a hawk or a vulture—and I yelped and fell over backwards again.

I lay on the snow, heart pounding against my rib cage. It was time to face the truth, I thought. I was not some kind of god; in fact, I barely deserved to call myself human. The LSD had wasted my body down to something weak and despicable, bringing genetic tendencies to the fore that had been masked by thousands of years of evolution. I was an underdeveloped Neanderthal with arms too long for my body, and a neck too skinny for my massive, tottering head. And what of Kimball? A bird, was he? The soccer players and their sycophants were correct to ridicule us. We were freaks, both of us: debased, ravaged, mutated beyond recognition, and beyond repair.

He skated back to where I lay. He looked more rattled now; his head twitched a little as he tilted it from side to side trying to maintain a steady downward gaze.

"Okay, Jeff. Forget what I just said, and think about this." He placed the tip of a ski pole squarely in the middle of my chest. "We are not bound by the normal rules of physics, do you understand? Suck up your heels and strike a mind-body fusion within your energy field. And remember:" He lowered his voice and pressed the pole-tip firmly into my sternum. "There is. No. Gravity."

"That may be true for you, dude," I said, unable to summon the will even to sit up. "But I *believe* in gravity."

"No, Jeff, dammit! That's not what I'm saying. *Don't* believe in it! You don't *have* to! It's a personal choice! Just get the fuck up and let your energy field carry you down the mountain, dude!"

Slowly, reluctantly, I got to my feet and started sliding downhill, past the billboard and the trail signs and all the clustered skiers watching us out of the corners of their eyes. Something Kimball had said about sucking up my heels had lodged in my mind, and I found myself striking a new equilibrium, hurtling downhill in a state of controlled acceleration, held securely in a double-vortex with its axis at the very spot in the center of my sternum where he'd pressed the tip of his ski pole. The physical world was rushing by at a very high rate of speed, but within my energy field, all was calm and still. I could tell from the rhythmic *whoosh-whoosh-whoosh* off to my right that Kimball was also in a groove. Temperatures must have been in the teens, but the sun on my face felt warm again as the two of us raced cackling and hollering down the steep mogul field under the Wildcat lift, cresting and dipping through the Volkswagen-sized bumps. Someone cheered from a chair above.

Then the moment came. In my peripheral vision, I saw Kimball veering upward. He might have taken the opportunity to catch air, or perhaps he lost control and was launched accidentally skyward by an inconveniently placed mogul. By the time I skidded to a halt, he was well along in his flight. I watched him arc across the sky—arms windmilling, body backlit by the sun—and the sight filled me with exhilaration. It must have been even better from his perspective, twenty or thirty feet above the snow, wind whistling around his ears, his shadow tracking across the dimpled slope like the shadow of a soaring bird, or an alter ego, or the final glimpse of a departing soul.

And I'm sure he saw the lift tower. He may even have had the chance, as I did, to dwell for a moment on the meaning of the number painted on the tower cylinder he was about to hit, the design of it, how if you let your eyes follow the curves it formed a continuous loop, number eight in fresh white paint on a field of dully glinting black. Just a painted number, true, but also a symbol of something as real as it was impossible to comprehend.

In my mind I can still see him clearly, red-faced with laughter on the chair ahead of me, or at the quarry, cockeyed and grinning, always ready to show me how easy it is to keep going and going and going.

"Holy shit," I said. "Holy *shit*," and I felt my weight settle on the rounded hump of the nearest mogul. For an instant the feathers from his Gerry coat swirled all around me, like snowflakes from a clear blue sky.

My memory of what happened next isn't exactly clear, but I do recall that they stopped the lift, and that a deep, cruel silence came over the mountain. A crowd began to gather at the base of the tower, and I withdrew to a safe distance. People began to shoot covert glances my way, and eventually an old patrolman in a red jacket, with a white cross on his back and a crackling radio strapped to his chest, traversed the slope to ask what I was doing, standing there all by myself. I didn't know what to say.

The Afternoon Client

POINT OF PRIDE: I always clean the boat between clients. Before anything else. Before gassing up or using the john or going to get a Coke and a sandwich and my daily dose of heartbreak from the college girls who work in the marina. So as soon as my morning client drives off in his Jeep—ninety percent of my clients drive Jeep Wranglers rented from the same island agency—I lower a bucket on a halyard for seawater. I splash it over the deck and sluice the blood out through the scupper holes. I rinse the rods with the freshwater hose from the dock, inspect the leaders for tooth frays, and stow the tackle box in the stainless steel cabinet beneath the windscreen.

A man drives up in a shiny black Land Rover. He rolls down the window and a few notes of Hotel California spill out before he turns off the stereo and calls out across the dock: "You Zimmerman?"

I nod. "What can I do for you?"

He parks the Rover and gets out. He's wearing expensive shoes and a yellow polo shirt. His black hair is slicked back with product and he has a lantern-jawed face some might consider handsome. "I'm Jay Clawson, your afternoon client."

"You're more than an hour early," I observe. "I have to get lunch and put gas in the boat."

He looks at his watch, a stainless steel TAG Heuer on a sleek, hairy wrist. "I called the marina. They told me you were in, and I was hoping we could go early. I'm supposed to tee off at four."

I stare at him. His voice is smooth but edgy, like someone used to giving orders over the phone. Mechanical trouble with the boat, I could say. Unlikely to catch fish anyway, sunny weather like this.

"Totally appreciate it," he says, opening the hatch of the Rover and taking out a red gym bag. He steps onto the dock and stands beside the boat.

"All right," I say gloomily, reaching up to take the gym bag. He comes aboard. I start the engine, untie the bowline, and motor around the dock to the gas tank.

"What are we after today?" he calls out over the noise of the engine. He's donned a pair of aviator glasses and stands next to me, too close, behind the windscreen.

"This time of year we're looking at bluefish, mostly. Maybe a rogue striper or two if we get lucky."

He raises his eyebrows behind the glasses. Perhaps he was thinking bonito, or marlin, or, who knows, a great white shark? I can tell it's going to be a long afternoon. My stomach is empty, and I feel a bit lightheaded.

The blues are running. I can smell them in the air, and long wavering slicks of fish oil reflect the sun on the water beyond the red and green buoys marking the entrance to the harbor. This morning we anchored over a slick and caught two dozen of the big carnivores, razor teeth snapping as I held them down on the blood-spattered deck with my bare feet and whacked them with a truncheon to extinguish their primitive little lights. Not that he deserves it, but this guy is probably in for a superb afternoon of fishing.

It takes about twenty minutes to get to the spot I have in mind, a submerged bar that boils up a small, productive rip. I cut the engine and lower the anchor slowly to avoid frightening away any stripers. I hand the client a blunt rod with a chartreuse bomber attached. It's the same lure my morning client used to excellent effect, a four-inch plastic teardrop scored by the teeth of countless marauding blues. I prefer fly fishing myself, and stripers to blues, but a man's got to make a living.

Clawson holds up the rod and squints doubtfully at the bomber. "It's pretty scratched up. Can't you give me a new one?"

"Those tooth marks are from this morning," I explain. "It means the fish find this particular lure desirable."

He hands back the rod. "I'd prefer a new one. Call me superstitious."

I hold my tongue, unclipping a rod with an unused lure and passing it to him. "If the fish are here, we're sitting right on top of them. You shouldn't have to cast far."

"From the platform?"

"From anywhere you like."

The client climbs up to the platform. He doesn't have sea legs; his rebalancings are jerky and awkward. He looks to be in decent physical shape, but it's artificial, a city-bred fitness gained from the weight room and the treadmill. I feel sorry for him, because it's pretty clear that he'll never truly appreciate the ocean the way one should, in all its fierce, changeable beauty—its awesome, biding power. On the other hand, I can tell he's fished before. He knows the basics of casting a spinning rod, though he puts more muscle into it than he needs to.

"Reel it faster," I suggest.

"Pardon?" Clawson stops casting and stares down from his perch on the platform. It's as if I've said something surprising.

"Just letting you know, you need to reel in a little faster for bluefish. They won't notice the lure as much if it's not splashing around on the surface."

He casts again, and doesn't adjust his retrieval speed. Suit yourself, I think, glancing at my watch.

After a few more casts Clawson comes down from the platform and hands me the rod. "I need to piss."

"Aim it off the stern," I suggest. "And hold onto the rail—it's getting rougher out here, and I wouldn't want you to fall in."

He starts aft, ignoring my advice to hold the rail. The tide is at full ebb and the rip is a compact, standing torrent of whitecaps tugging on the anchor. A gusty southwest wind has picked up, and the water around the rip is choppy, unsettled.

The client stumbles and catches himself on the rail. I can't suppress a derisive snort. He hears it or senses it above the wind and the roar of the rip, and shoots me a look over his shoulder. I smile innocently and give him an encouraging nod. He stands at the stern without touching the rail. With his feet spread wide for balance, he makes an adjustment and starts pissing across the wind.

"How long you been doing this?" he asks on his way back to the platform.

"Pretty long while," I reply.

"What'd you do before?"

"This and that. Wasting time, mostly." He holds out his hand for the rod and I give it to him.

"I would have guessed you were new to it," he says.

A surge of anger clamps my throat. "What makes you say so?"

"You don't seem entirely comfortable. With people, I mean."

I feel my ears redden and for a moment I can't think of anything to say. I watch him climb the ladder to the platform. It's an unsteady place to stand, especially without a life preserver. These are dangerous waters. A sudden tilt of the boat in the choppy swells; an abrupt shift in the wind; or, if I were to rev the engine suddenly, causing the bow to jerk on the anchor chain. These currents are trickier than they look. If you're not a strong swimmer, a rip like this one can suck you under before you know it.

There isn't much conversation after that, which suits me. The client keeps casting, but he's still reeling it in too slowly to attract any attention from the blues. After a while, out of boredom, I cast the rod with the chewed-up bomber. Seconds after I start skipping the plug along the choppy surface, a big tail splash erupts behind it. I pull up to set the hook; the rod bends and the reel drag whines as the fish runs for deeper water.

The client stops casting and watches glumly from the platform. From the way it's fighting—intermittent and forceful, like a Rottweiler tugging on a stick—I can tell it's not a bluefish, but a big striper instead. This is unexpected. Stripers don't often follow lures on the surface, especially with so many blues in the water.

Striped bass are my favorite fish. They correspond to bluefish approximately as an eagle does to a buzzard. Their intelligence and selectivity make them difficult to catch at the best of times, but especially in midsummer. They're prized by restaurant chefs up and down the East Coast for their firm, buttery flesh, which is perfect for grilling, but I prefer to release them. An old girlfriend once accused me of loving stripers more than people. She was joking, but the funny thing is that as the years have gone by, I've come to realize she wasn't too far off the mark. Sometimes when I have no clients I drive to a certain sheltered beach I know of, and I wade out to a sandbar and cast a nine-weight fly rod. Each time I bring in one of these dignified predators, I feel a visceral link to the wild essence of the sea. Their life force flows like an electrical current into my hands, and it fills me with an enduring sense of peace. It gives me solace to imagine them cruising beneath the troubled surface, patrolling their realm in groups of three or four, fast, green shadows flying over the eel grass.

Once I've fought the fish into the boat I cradle it gently in the clear water of the holding tank. It's a big one, probably forty-two or forty-three inches from nose to tail. It rests under the water with its gills flaring, luminous, tranquil, like a platinum missile with five black stripes running along its muscular fuselage.

"I hope you're not thinking of letting that go," the client says from the platform.

"Actually, I am."

"Look. I've been fishing all afternoon, and I haven't had a nibble. Seems like it would be nice to bring something back to show for my trouble. Would you mind if I kept it?"

I let out my breath and stare down at the striper. "If you would reel in your line just a bit faster, like I told you, I can pretty much guarantee you'd bring in a bluefish."

"Who's paying for this trip, anyway? I forget. You or me?"

I look up. Some time in the last hour he's put on a long-billed fishing cap, like the one Hemingway used to wear, and his eyes are hidden behind the aviators. But the corners of his mouth are compressed in a sour little smile that reminds me of my second grade teacher, Mrs. Bergeron.

"You're paying," I say calmly. "But I'm pretty sure you didn't catch this fish."

"No, that's correct," he conceded. "But you did. And your time is costing me a lot of money, isn't it?"

The fish awaits its destiny, fins and tail fluttering patiently to and fro as I grip it lightly in the cold seawater. The customer's always right. That's the first thing you learn when you try to make a living in the service business.

I lift the noble creature out of its native medium and set it dripping on the deck. It senses the end and panics, flopping vigorously and throwing itself around until I manage to wrestle it under control and press my knee onto the cool scales of its side to keep it down. I pick up the truncheon, hesitate for a second, then bring it down hard on the golden skull. Its body quivers along its entire length. The broad, slightly forked tail comes up and slaps the deck three times. Clenching my teeth, I whack the beautiful fish twice more to be sure it's dead. Then I pick it up and drop it in the holding tank. Blood fumes from its gills, staining the brine a shameful pink.

I wipe my hands with a rag and walk back to the pilot's chair. I've killed hundreds of fish, maybe thousands, but habit doesn't necessarily make it easier. And I don't like to kill stripers. Especially when it's against my better judgment, and for the purposes of impressing the golf buddies of a man like Jay Clawson.

Just then something strikes me hard on the forehead. Through a blinding red haze of pain it dawns on me that I've been hit by the client's bomber. He's on the platform with his back to me, calmly reeling in his line.

"Be more careful, chief," I say, rubbing my forehead. There's already a good-sized egg rising where the lead-core plug hit.

He doesn't hear me, or pretends not to. When the bomber is a foot from the end of the rod he whips it back and flings it out. This time it sails true and lands just short of the rip. I try again, raising my voice over the roar and slap of the ocean so there can be no question about whether or not he hears me. "Hey, Clawson. You hit me with your plug on that last cast. Watch what the hell you're doing, okay?"

He stops mid-reel. His shoulders rise and fall, a long sigh. Then he puts the rod down on the platform and turns to face me.

"Pick up that rod and finish reeling it in," I say. "Don't leave it there unless you want to replace it when it falls off."

He glances down at the rod and then back at me. "I'm docking half your fee."

"You're *what*?"

"On your website you claim to be an experienced guide. I haven't caught a single fish, and you've made *no* effort to help me. It's ridiculous. Now you're resorting to verbal abuse. I'll pay you *half* the stated fee, and if you have a problem with that, you can call my lawyer."

I let out my breath. Just then the line catches and my four hundred dollar spinning rig rolls off the platform and disappears into the sea with a gentle splash. The rest of the world recedes. It's just the two of us on my rocking boat, with the island a low, green haze in the distance across the dancing shimmer of water. I can hear the roar of the rip but it seems far away, nearly drowned out by the ringing in my ears.

Like me, the Coast Guard officers and sheriff's deputies live out here year-round. They know very well that terrible and unexpected things can happen at sea. The ocean is a hungry and capricious mistress; there's no use spending too much time or effort questioning her appetites. And of course, no one will ever suspect foul play. Because what motive could there possibly be?

I radio for a cutter and a helicopter, but none of us can find Clawson. We search until the tide slackens, and after that there's really no point. If he ever does come to the surface, it's likely to be pretty far from where he went under. By the time I point the boat back to the marina, it's nearly dusk. The rip has subsided to a gentle riffle, like a country trout stream in the middle of the green Atlantic.

Mouth of the Tropics

Puerto Ayacucho is a port more than a thousand miles from any ocean. Stranded like flotsam on the muddy banks of the Orinoco, it is the Venezuelan embarkation point for the network of rivers that are the only highways through the vast jungles of the northern Amazon basin. It is a frontier town, and it has the raw, lawless edge you would expect of such a place, but its violence lies mainly under the surface, stifled by the fevers and the heat, waiting to bubble up and attach itself to you in unexpected and permanent ways. The town is hot as the surrounding rainforest never is; the heat rises up from the pavement and presses down from the unshaded sun. After rain it can be oppressively humid, even early in the morning, as it was on the morning after Meech arrived. He'd showered at the hotel but already he could feel his linen shirt clinging to his back and armpits as he strode through barrios of corrugated tin shacks to the market center. The air was dank with the smell of raw sewage—a familiar smell, though he knew it would take him a few days to get accustomed to it. With each step his sandals sucked the asphalt and he couldn't avoid splashing through puddles of stagnant water, imagining as he did so microscopic waterborne larvae burrowing unnoticed into the flesh of his feet, only to emerge, months later, as thick, hairy flies.

At the entrance to the open-air market a group of *mestizo* teenagers wearing heavy metal T-shirts watched him with lazy menace from the stoop of an open storefront. Meech strode past them into the crowd, feeling the uncomfortable contact of sweaty flesh on his chest and back. A large black woman shoved past balancing a melon saddled in cloth on her head. He followed in her wake as she barged through the murmuring crowd until he spotted the vendor he was looking for, a tall old man standing beside a cart of fried *arepas*. Meech veered and held his ground against the shifting press of humanity, leaning his thighs against the cart as he waved to get the man's attention. The smell of frying *masa* dough brought back pleasant memories, and he reflected that, as job-related travel went, he had it pretty good.

He held up three fingers. The old man put three steaming *arepas* in a brown paper bag and Meech mouthed the word for coffee. The man smiled in a friendly, gap-toothed way, filled a styrofoam cup, and handed it across the cart. Meech raised the cup in a silent toast to his old friend, the *arepa* man. Both hands occupied, he used his chest and shoulders to open a channel through the shifting mob of tanktops and *guayaberas* until the crowd began to thin out, and he was back at the entrance to the market. He stood on the curb under the stares of the idle teenagers, chewing the *arepas* and gulping the sweet coffee.

Dr. Juan Sánchez pulled up in a beige Land Cruiser with the university insignia painted on the door. He leaned over to roll down the passenger-side window, trademark aviator sunglasses perched on his forehead, raven hair tied back in a ponytail. Meech felt the cold rush of air conditioning as he chased the final *arepa* with the last of the coffee and climbed into the Cruiser. Sánchez put the truck in gear and steered them through the crowded streets to the outskirts of town. The Cruiser was clean and hermetic, like a space capsule or a diving bell; Meech sighed and leaned back against the cool leather seat. It was the first time he'd been able to relax since he'd boarded the plane at Logan Airport twenty-four hours ago. He needed something big from this trip, a result he could build the rest of his career on. The department chair had been making that clear enough recently in his mild, oblique way; one more research trip to South America with no original findings and Meech doubted another grant would be forthcoming. It was entirely possible that the rest of his tenure would be spent teaching undergraduate biology, or perhaps, if he was lucky, cataloging pollution-related mutations among the amphibians of the Charles River watershed.

Sánchez was his best hope to escape that fate. They'd met six years earlier at a biodiversity conference in San Diego. A University of Caracas ethnobotanist specializing in Amazonia, he maintained a large and useful network of contacts among the indigenous villages. He and Meech had traveled together on several previous research trips, and they were frequently in touch by e-mail.

It didn't take long for them to reach the edge of the rainforest, where the road sliced into the looming wall of vegetation like a machete-wound. Meech could hear the cicadas even with the windows up. The whole forest throbbed with the sound. Even the road seemed to vibrate under the wheels of the Land Cruiser.

He turned to the Venezuelan. "So where're we going?"

"I think we should try Esmeralda."

"That's a Ye'kwana village, right?"

Sánchez nodded. "It's about six hours upriver, near the junction with the Rio Negro."

"They haven't captured a specimen by any chance, have they?"

The Venezuelan grinned. "You know they don't think of it that way, Meech. And no, they haven't caught any. Bright-red creatures are considered bad medicine. The Indians keep their distance."

"But they've reported seeing the *rana roja* recently?"

"Reports. Nothing substantiated."

Meech nodded, drumming his fingertips on the dashboard. The *rana roja* was the reason for his trip. He'd never seen one, but there was a history of sightings along the upper Orinoco and its tributaries. Most of the reports were ambiguous, secondhand, shrouded in layers of myth and superstition, but what had captured his interest—and what had proved decisive in getting the travel grant—was that the hearsay was consistent: a bright-red tree frog with a pattern of black, diamond-shaped markings on its back. Such dorsal markings were definitive and unique. If the *rana roja* existed, in other words, it was a nondescript species—unknown to science. Meech intended to collect the first specimen.

He awoke to something wet and unpleasantly sticky lapping his face. "*Off!*" he growled, waving his arm to brush away whatever it was. Then he opened his eyes and experienced a moment of panicky disorientation. It took him a moment to get his bearings. He'd been asleep in the prow of Sanchez's hardwood dugout, motoring up the Orinoco River toward Esmeralda. He put his hand to his cheek and picked off one of the mango peels Sánchez had been tossing to wake him up. The Venezuelan was at the rudder, grinning and pointing with his free hand at something upriver. The engine was running at a low purr.

Meech turned in the prow and saw the smooth ocher trunk of an overhanging *indio desnudo* tree. He turned back to Sánchez with a shrug and the Venezuelan nodded and put his finger to his mouth. Meech looked again and this time he saw the constrictor, a yellow-gray snake with geometric dorsal saddles coiled in the shade on the trunk like a stack of tires. At the top of the stack, a cinnamon tuft of fur was just visible, and as they approached Meech made out the scalp and forehead of a red howler monkey, *Alouatta seniculus*, black eyes peering in dull disbelief over the rim of the coil. The dugout passed beneath the tree and the scientists gazed back at the spectacle until a bend in the river obscured it.

Sánchez sighed happily. He had the proud, eager-to-please temperament of a good host.

"Maybe it's a positive omen," Meech said.

"I wouldn't have guessed you'd be one to believe in omens."

"I don't. I was being facetious." Meech yawned and started to let one of his hands trail in the lukewarm water, then thought better of it and rested it on the edge of the dugout. "So do you think this frog is the real thing, *amigo*? Think we can capture one in Esmeralda?"

"I don't know, we'll have to see. I have no doubt that it *could* exist. There's one thing I haven't told you, though. My Ye'kwana contacts say it has a stinger." Sánchez tossed the rest of the mango overboard.

"You mean it has poisonous glands in its skin?"

"No, they say *stinger*—like a wasp or a scorpion."

"And you believe them?"

"Why not? The Ye'kwana have no reason to lie to me."

Meech chuckled. "Amphibians don't have stingers, Juan. It's physiologically impossible. Certain tree frogs have glands in their skin that excrete poison. Even so, to get enough venom to cause more than a mild rash in humans, you have to boil the skin. But you know all this."

"Maybe it's *not* physiological. Maybe it's a *spiritual* stinger, or a supernatural one. But if the Ye'kwana say it's real, then believe me—one way or another, it's real."

Meech shrugged and leaned back against the ribbed slope of the prow. Juan Sánchez was a trained biologist with a Ph.D. from Ohio State, but his empirical rigor was often undermined by a childlike credulity that Meech found touching. His worldview was expansive, encompassing the belief that anything was possible in Amazonia—from cancer cures to lost tribes—and Meech was inclined to hold his tongue rather than shatter such lovely illusions. Among his colleagues in the competitive world of academic biology, the Venezuelan was the closest thing he had to a friend.

The motor was propelling them upstream at a good clip, and the wind on his face was cool and dense, almost liquid-feeling. He inhaled deeply, imagining the extra oxygen coming off the massed vegetation all around. The cicadas were stirring up a loud metallic chorus from the tangled lianas and poor man's umbrellas walling the banks of the river, and he concentrated on trying to internalize the sound, as he had on previous trips, so that it would fade to a mere background hum: a cyclical soundtrack driving him forward to the completion of his task.

He drifted slowly into sleep and dreamed of the *rana roja*. It was a gigantic specimen, scarlet and translucent as it gripped the side of the canoe with its suctioned toe-pads and peered at him with one huge eye. It hoisted itself up and slid silently into the boat facing him, dripping mucous water into the vee of the hull, the black, diamond-shaped markings on its back heaving rhythmically as it breathed. It adopted the expression of a solicitous physician and pulled a surgeon's mask over its wide, amphibian mouth. Meech felt strangely calm.

The frog furrowed its brow and leaned over him with a large syringe.

"What's that for, Doc?" he asked, in the dream.

As they motored past the stilted shacks marking the edge of the Esmeralda *colonia,* Meech climbed into the waist of the dugout to assemble his equipment: stacked tupperware containers with mesh airholes on the lids; vials of isopropyl alcohol, formaldehyde, and a special solution for preserving genomic samples; a field dissection kit; and a fishing net with a threaded handle he screwed onto a telescoping aluminum pole. He hoped the stopover would be brief. The land upriver was technically Ye'kwana territory—though he knew that most people ignored such legal designations in the wilds of Amazonia—and Sánchez had insisted they stop out of respect for the tribal elders.

The village occupied a blackwater lake fed by a side canal lined with tall Mauritius palms. A half-dozen mocha-skinned children dove into the canal—the water let off the familiar, mild, raw-sewage smell—and swam a little way out toward the dugout as it motored past, through the clustered shanties to the *Asociación,* a stilted shack slightly larger than the others and distinguished by a roof of corrugated tin rather than thatch. Meech seized the bowline, leapt onto the dock, and tied the dugout to one of the stilts. A Ye'kwana with bowl-cut hair and a deeply pockmarked face shook the travelers' hands but avoided eye contact. Sánchez introduced himself in Spanish, and the Ye'kwana led them into the shack to meet the tribal council, which had been alerted to their visit by sentries posted downriver.

Inside, eight tribal elders clad in mustard-colored loincloths sat with their backs to the walls on a horseshoe of rough-hewn benches. There was no obvious place to sit, so Meech and Sánchez remained standing in the middle of the room. The shack had no electric lighting, but sunlight filtered in through gaps in the hardwood planking, illuminating the entire convocation in bright horizontal stripes. Sánchez spoke with his head bowed in a quiet, formal Spanish that struck Meech as unnecessarily submissive—it wasn't as if they were asking for all that much. He understood enough to get the gist of the conversation: Sánchez respectfully asking permission to continue upriver; a white-haired elder who Meech assumed was the *presidente* nodding serenely; Sánchez gesturing toward Meech, calling him an eminent scientist from the United States, and inquiring about any recent sightings of the *rana roja*; Sánchez breaking the ensuing silence with a reminder of their good intentions; an angry exchange between the three elders and the toothless *presidente*, conducted in Ye'kwana so that Meech had no hope of understanding it; the *presidente* addressing Sánchez with an emphatic chopping gesture; and, finally, more silence.

Sánchez was quiet as he steered the dugout down the canal through the shanties back to the main artery of the river. Meech was puzzled.

"What happened at the end there?"

Sánchez shook his head, sighing. "They denied us permission. They say it's for our own good."

"Well, at least we asked."

"You're right. Back in Puerto we can inquire about other locations."

Meech nodded distractedly for a moment and then looked up suddenly. "You're not saying we have to go back *now*, are you?"

Sánchez lifted the aviator sunglasses off his eyes and perched them on his forehead. "Well, yes. I'm afraid we do."

Meech was incredulous. "But this is a scientific inquiry," he said. "It's not as if we're drilling for oil, or mining gold. We have no intention of disturbing sacred ground. So how can they—"

Sánchez was shaking his head, and Meech knew him well enough to see that he'd made up his mind. "Look," he said, trying to keep his voice calm. "You're an academic, too, so you know how pressurized the environment can get. I don't have time to scout another location."

The Venezuelan looked at him with compassion. "I'm sorry, Meech," he said softly. "But without permission we can't proceed upriver. It's a bad idea."

The dugout reached the main river and Sánchez aimed it downstream. With the extra impetus of the current, they'd be back in four or five hours. The wind on Meech's face felt moist and intrusive, like hot breath. A reservoir inside him broke, and desperation flooded his veins, filling him with tight-chested resolve.

"Look. Turn the boat around and go back to the village. You can wait for me there. Tell the elders the gringo needs a specimen and is willing to pay the *Asociación* if he finds one."

Sánchez's coffee-colored cheeks darkened a shade. The engine sputtered out and they were drifting downstream on the slow current. "You're making a mistake, Meech. Just because you're a scientist doesn't mean you don't have to respect the rules. The Ye'kwana belong to the forest, which means that their rules are *nature's* rules. Take my word for it, you don't want to mess with this stuff. It's bad medicine."

Meech smiled grimly, his heart pounding. "Do you really believe that? Because you're a scientist, too, Juan—or did that slip your mind?"

Sánchez shook his head and spat in the water. He shrugged and restarted the engine, turning the boat back upstream toward the village. At the *Asociación* he climbed up onto the dock while Meech held the bowline; he watched with an expression of deep foreboding as the North American oversteered the dugout through the shanties and throttled toward the open river.

Meech motored along slowly, jaw clenched and shoulders drawn up in acute concentration, keeping the dugout close to the riotous greenery along the river's right bank. This was it, he knew. His last chance, or at least his best one, to escape the straitjacket of mediocrity that was drawing ever tighter around him. His solitary routine was a suffocating bore, and the frightening thing was that it was becoming comfortable: the frozen dinners in a small apartment overlooking the Charles; the daily bicycle route to his office and the lab; the increasingly rote lectures he delivered, in the same order, every semester. No. There had to be more.

A flash of scarlet in a leafy weave of lianas overhanging the river caught his attention, and in his excitement he stood and nearly fell out of the dugout. He circled back a few times, but it was no good; he couldn't relocate whatever it was he'd seen. So he continued upstream, shivering a little though the air was thick and warm around him.

It was nearly dusk by the time he gave up the search. As he turned the boat downstream, it dawned on him that there was no way he could make it back to Esmeralda before dark. Indeed, night was falling already in its abrupt, tropical way, with velvety black shadows concealing the broken stumps and driftwood jams and other hazards of the waterway. Gingerly, he edged the dugout up to the bank and grabbed a handful of vegetation, looping the bowline around the branches supporting it into what he hoped was a secure knot. The dugout swung downstream until the line held steady. Hunched in the prow, he tried to sleep. He was more discouraged than fearful, though in his wakefulness the occasional unrecognizable grunt from the forest or gurgle from the black river shallows caused him to stiffen, heart pounding, before he could ease back into a semblance of the relaxed mindlessness that was a prerequisite for sleep.

Eventually, he did fall into a dreamless slumber, and when he awoke it was already light. There was a burlap bag full of mangoes in the bottom of the dugout. He ate one, slicing the pulp off the big seed in wedges with his pocketknife, and nervously dipped his hands in the river water to wash off the stickiness. A crashing noise very close by on the bank gave him a start, but he couldn't see anything through the dense vegetation. He motored slowly up the bank, hoping to spot a frog on an overhanging branch. If it were raining his chances would be better, he reflected.

The sun rose high enough that its glare turned the river into a wide, eddying mirror. He decided to head back to Esmeralda, where he assumed his Venezuelan colleague was still waiting. If he saw the need to apologize, he would. He wasn't ruling it out, anyway.

Back in the village, the pockmarked Ye'kwana at the *Asociación* gave him a cool, appraising look before telling him that Sánchez had caught a ride downriver with a dugout of artisans bound for the Puerto Ayacucho craft market. It was logical that the Venezuelan hadn't waited overnight. On previous trips, he'd been a proud and gracious host, even a little over-protective as he shepherded Meech through the backwaters of his home bioregion. But Meech understood that he'd crossed a line this time. That his angry insistence on pressing forward, in addition to proving futile, had been an affront to his friend's innate generosity.

Not that Meech needed a guide. There was an extra tank of gasoline in the stern and he'd be traveling with the current all the way back to Puerto Ayacucho. But the fact that Sánchez hadn't waited confirmed his suspicion that his impulsiveness had been ill-advised. He hoped their friendship would survive it.

The children watched him from the porches of their

stilt houses as he steered the dugout awkwardly back to the river. Their faces were grave and unyielding, and he became uncomfortably self-conscious; it was as if they were sitting in judgment, or knew something about himself that he did not. He was glad when he'd traveled downstream far enough to put a wall of vegetation between himself and the village.

He awoke sweating and disoriented in his Puerto Ayacucho hotel room. The ceiling fan hung immobile above his head in the half-dark, and the air in the room was as torpid as a sauna. He'd left the dugout tied among the barges at the town docks. It had been too late to buy a water bottle for his bedside, and his mouth and throat were so dry that he could barely swallow. He got up and slid open the slatted screen covering the narrow window. It was just before dawn. The logging trucks with their precious cargoes of rainforest hardwoods were already beginning to clank and rumble through town to the northern highway. The close tropical night was only half-diffused, a black diesel haze squatting like the underbelly of some enormous stinking beast over the corrugated roofs of the town.

He knew that he had to do something about dehydration, but it was still too early to go out and buy bottled water, so reluctantly he decided to drink from the tap. It was a risk, but he figured that since he was leaving later that day he could take care of any ill effects with antibiotics back in the States. In the bathroom he turned on the tap and let it run for a few minutes, wondering if he could still count Sánchez as a friend. He leaned over the sink to sip, and then reflexively guzzled the lukewarm water. It had a slightly metallic taste from the pipes, but other than that it didn't seem too bad. Nothing obvious, anyway.

His plane left at noon, so he had more than five hours to kill. He took a shower in the same tepid water and then unpacked and reorganized his equipment case. He sat on the bed for a while, replaying the last conversation he'd had with Sánchez before he'd dropped him off at the *Asociación*. Was it too late to make amends? It was only a little after eight by his watch. Still plenty of time.

Outside the hotel, he flagged a rusting Plymouth Valiant with a taxi sign affixed to its roof and gave the driver Sánchez's address, scrawled in the Venezuelan's block-letter handwriting on the back of a tattered Universidad de Caracas business card Meech had kept in his wallet since his first field expedition seven years before. They'd taken a dugout three days up the Rio Negro. There had been an extraordinary range of wildlife: pink river dolphins, claw-winged hoatzins, harpy eagles, even a school of piranhas boiling the surface all around the carcass of a sloth that had been killed by a jaguar. Meech hadn't accomplished much in terms of herpetological research, but they'd had a wonderful time—sleeping in hammocks strung up between tree branches over the water, passing the long hours of river travel teaching each other jokes in Spanish and English. Since then, he'd grown accustomed to thinking of Sánchez as one of his closest friends, but it was odd:

he knew little about the Venezuelan's personal life, and had never visited his home. The driver agreed to wait a few minutes while Meech went to the door.

The earthen yard was decorated with a smattering of recently planted date palms and Meech had to walk around a puddle of rust-colored water to get to the front of the house, a low bungalow built of whitewashed cinderblock with a polished ocher floor continuing out onto the porch. He knocked, and after a moment, a little girl opened the door and peered out at him from the gloom. She was shirtless and dark-skinned, probably five or six, with shiny, black, shoulder-length hair. Something about her head seemed slightly out of proportion, but he couldn't figure out what it was. She folded her arms across her chest and he realized he was staring.

"*Profesor Sánchez está en casa? Tu padre*?"

The little girl was solemn-faced. She turned her head to call to someone inside and Meech saw what was wrong with her hair: there was a big shank of it missing, a shiny patch of scar tissue the size of a sand dollar on her scalp. Meech remembered the story of a Harvard entomologist who'd been bitten by a botfly in Panama. He'd returned home knowing full well that he was incubating a larval worm under the skin of his scalp, and a few months later he'd captured the emerging fly in his baseball cap at a Red Sox game. The anecdote troubled him more now than it had when he'd first heard it.

Sánchez, shirtless, his long hair loose and sleep-tousled, came to the door. He folded his arms over his chest and Meech noticed the family resemblance to the little girl. "I'm glad to see you made it back, *amigo*," he said, making a special effort to project warmth in his smile. "I left the dugout tied at the town dock. Stowed the engine, covered everything with the tarp, and so on."

Sánchez nodded distractedly, but did not invite him in. His eyes searched Meech's face. "Did you get your specimen?"

"No, unfortunately." Meech felt dizzy.

Sánchez stared at him for a moment more and then shook his head. "You don't look well, my friend."

"I'm just a little tired. Anyway, I wanted to tell you that I'm grateful for all your help over the years, and I apologize if I . . . if I caused you any . . ." He trailed off, overcome by a momentary spell of lightheadedness. He reached out to support himself on the doorframe. "I just wanted to make sure there were no hard feelings before I leave the country."

Sánchez gazed sharply into his eyes. "No hard feelings, Meech. I only wish you'd have listened to me back in Esmeralda. I'm afraid—"

"No," Meech interrupted, shaking his head. "You were just standing up for what you believe. But I had to go on." He was struggling to hold a linear train of thought. Sánchez shook his hand and patted him on the shoulder, and Meech walked across the yard feeling dizzy and confused. Halfway to the taxi he turned and called out, "By the way, what happened to your daughter's scalp?"

"Nothing serious. She's fine. Get some rest, Meech."

As he climbed into the taxi, he experienced a wave of nausea that he thought might be owing to an empty stomach. It was nearly two hours before he had to be at the airport, so he told the driver to drop him at the market for coffee and *arepas*. That was a mistake. The crowd was too dense, the air too rank, and the sensation of all the hot moist flesh pressing in on him drove him into the putrid shadows behind a fruit stall where he retched until his gut was dry. Walking back to the hotel he began to notice things, maladies, misfortunes: a man with a baseball-sized lump on his neck; a small child with smooth blank skin where an eye should have been. He thought anxiously of Boston, where it was already getting cold, where people would be doing their Christmas shopping. Where once a year winter swept in like a frigid housemaid to make sure the air was sterile and clean.

The plane to Caracas was a light Cessna, only seven passengers. As they taxied down the runway Meech felt a rush of excitement, a familiar sense of unburdening and narrow escape. Although he was returning empty-handed again, he was newly confident that he could make something happen with his career. After all, who else in the department could claim his expertise on Amazonia? Somehow he would get another grant, and next time—well, there was always a chance.

The takeoff was rough. They were flying into a northern headwind and the small plane got tossed around a bit. There was some uncomfortable sideways slipping as they climbed, then an air pocket caused a sudden plunge in altitude. The other passengers gasped in unison, and

Meech noticed that his palms were cramped from gripping the hand rests. He did not feel well.

Soon the plane rose above the turbulence and stopped bucking. Meech exhaled and looked out the window at the shadow of the Cessna, crossing the Orinoco as it meandered out of the steaming rainforest and onto the dull green expanse of the savanna. An intense wave of foreboding blurred his vision, and he blinked to bring things back into focus, heart pounding in his chest. Something about the way Sánchez had looked at him back at the house had been most disturbing. It was the kind of look you would give a condemned man: fearful, resigned, pitying.

Beneath the plane, the river continued north, looping in lazy curves like a fat worm over the floodplains to the coast, where it disgorged in a vast delta of brackish mud. The delta was no longer much guarded by the ancient mangrove swamps, most of which had been taken out for shrimp farms, salt mines, oil refineries. He couldn't shake this feeling of dread. Borders were being blurred, filters removed, forces unleashed. He was part of it—a cause, a catalyst. The mouth of the tropics was open to the world.

A Winter Break in Rome

I WAS dealing out a deck of cards when the compartment door flew open, letting in a blast of frigid December air and a girl so classically beautiful—lively hazel eyes, cheeks glowing, a cascade of loose blond curls—that she might have walked straight out of a Botticelli painting. She was American, college-aged, wearing faded Levi's and an expensively cut Italian-leather jacket. She leaned down to kiss Silvio on both cheeks and then sat beside him on the upholstered seat facing me. Outside the window the Umbrian countryside flew by, a blur of fields and hillsides in desolate shades of brown.

"You're Justin, right? Kate Higgins. Art History 101. Don't you remember me?"

"Of *course* I remember you," I lied. I didn't, which was surprising, but it didn't matter, because from that moment on I was under her spell.

The three of us chatted all the way to Rome. An Italian major, Kate had spent the previous semester in Florence. Every so often her gaze would come to rest on mine in a way that made me feel singled out, understood, appreciated. As we pulled into the Roma Termini station she scribbled the address of her *pensione* and handed it to Silvio. She pressed the button to open the compartment door and smiled at me as the clatter and whine of the braking train flooded in behind her. "Justin. I know you don't remember me."

"Of course I do."

"You're lying."

"No, I'm not."

"Yes, you are. But I do remember *you*. You said some intelligent things in that class."

"I did?" I was annoyed to find myself blushing.

The door slid shut behind her, and Silvio punched me on the shoulder. "There you go, dude. I told you Rome was gonna be fun."

Silvio was an actual baron, with a title-laden name that took more than a minute to recite, which he sometimes did as a party trick. He'd grown up mostly in Scarsdale, so he was fluent in the idioms of the American upper-middle class, and he was quite charming; people generally thought highly of him until they saw him drunk. Like me, surprisingly, he was a financial aid student. His parents had divorced when he was young, and they'd burned through their respective inheritances. In the end his father had been forced to work as a taxi driver in New York City, which was not something that Silvio was eager to talk about.

And although he really was a baron, his Roman cousins one-upped him: they were dukes. Filippo was a ruggedly handsome university student around our age; Tomasso, an army officer in his mid-twenties. They lived in an old palace with their widowed mother, the *duchessa*, who never smiled and rarely spoke. There were marble statues in shadowy niches, time-blackened portraits on every wall, and a set of antique halberds on hooks above the hearth in the great room. The mantelpiece was a marble bas relief of Hercules and the Nemean lion. The palace was more like a neglected museum than a home, and I was fascinated by it, though it was dim and chilly and I couldn't stop shivering the whole time I was there. At certain moments I felt homesick, a little guilt-stricken for neglecting my family over the Christmas break. On a side table in my guest suite I discovered a stand-up frame containing a black-and-white photograph of Benito Mussolini; I recognized the military uniform and the ugly little smile from a twentieth-century history course. Picking it up to get a closer look, I experienced a moment of vertigo.

On our first morning in Rome, Silvio and I borrowed Filippo's battered Fiat, which rattled and stuttered as Silvio drove it up out of the dukes' underground garage. On the way to Kate's *pensione*, I mentioned the Mussolini portrait.

"My great uncle was part of his inner circle," he explained.

"So your great uncle was a fascist?"

"Sure. A lot of people were fascists back then."

"And now?"

"My great uncle died a long time ago, Justin."

"Of course." I'd been thinking more about the cousins than the great uncle, but it didn't matter. It was history now, water under the bridge.

The *pensione* was in a neighborhood near the Villa Borghese, on a steeply tilted street edged with small stores and cafés. Silvio parked the car and set the emergency brake. "Why don't you wait here while I go in and get her."

"What for?" I asked.

"Someone needs to stay with the car."

"Okay."

As the minutes stretched on, I became increasingly annoyed. Silvio had lied. No one needed to watch his cousin's banged-up Fiat; there were much nicer cars unattended all up and down the block. The truth was that he wanted time alone with Kate. In Madrid he'd strung together an enviable record of success with American college women, but I sensed that Kate wouldn't be such an easy mark. She was too self-assured for that, too confident in her own persona. On the train, I believed I'd felt an authentic jolt of electricity between Kate and myself, though perhaps I'd only imagined it. Even so, she didn't strike me as the type to be taken in by Silvio's brittle charisma.

A gang of teenagers streamed by on the sidewalk. One boy rapped his knuckles on the Fiat's trunk and glared in through the windshield as he strode by, as if daring me to come out. Rome puzzled me. It still does. There seems to be something ugly in the air, a whiff of ancient savagery seeping up through the flagstones.

Kate wore an ivory fisherman's sweater, and her golden curls were gathered back in a ponytail. She gave me a bright smile as she and Silvio strolled arm in arm down to the Fiat. Her radiance cut through the Roman winter like May sunshine, and for the rest of the day, we were a companionable threesome. Silvio drove, pointing out the monuments as we passed. Kate rode shotgun, enthusiastically taking it all in. I sat in back, trying not to say anything stupid.

We wandered through the Vatican museums and climbed the long spiral staircase to St. Peter's dome. Out in the freezing wind we looked across the *piazza* to the Castel Sant'Angelo. As we waited in line to descend the staircase Kate turned and flashed me an intimate smile. My heart leapt, but in the very next moment I succumbed to an attack of defeatism. If only circumstances were different. If only I'd been born to a different family. If only I had money, looks, a pedigree.

On our way out through the basilica we stopped to admire the Pietà. I remembered the sculpture from that art history class. The professor had dedicated an entire lecture to showing slides of its finer details from various angles. He'd lingered on the tenderness of the Virgin's mournful expression, the great artistry of her fingers, the loving way she cradled the corpse of her son, the fallen god. "Now I see what all the fuss was about," I remarked.

"Mm." Kate stood beside me, our shoulders nearly touching as we peered in through the glass at the beautifully sculpted marble.

On an impulse, I took her hand in mine and held it up. "Michelangelo would have loved these fingers." Even as I said it I wished I could take it back, but she was smiling, and I saw that everything was okay.

At the church of Santa Maria in Cosmedin, we took turns kneeling before the massive stone disk known as the Bocca della Verità. Believed to have been a manhole cover in the ancient city, the Bocca is carved in the bearded likeness of a pagan river god. If you stick your hand in its maw and dare to tell a lie, the legend goes, you will lose the hand. Silvio went first. I asked if Filippo and Tomasso were fascists. He denied it, pretending to be amused. I went next. Silvio asked if I'd voted for Reagan. I said no, which was the truth, but not the whole truth, which was that I'd neglected to vote at all. When Kate's turn came, Silvio asked her if she had a boyfriend. I watched carefully as she stared into the idol's vacant eyes. "We haven't seen each other in months."

"The Bocca requires a yes or no answer," Silvio said sternly.

Kate smiled. "Okay. If you insist, the answer is no. As of this moment, I do *not* have a boyfriend." She glanced up at me as she said it, and the adrenaline shot through my limbs.

That night I lay awake under a heavy woolen blanket in my chilly suite in the palace with a feeling of almost physical pain, an exquisite ache centered below my sternum and radiating outward. My mood fluctuated between ecstasy and despair. A few months earlier I'd been chasing grocery carts at my local Safeway, scrimping and saving to get to Europe. Now I was in Rome, the ancient capital of Western civilization, in a ducal palace, deeply infatuated with the prettiest girl I'd ever known. Thinking about it now it seems vaguely preposterous, like a scene out of some overwrought nineteenth-century novel. But in the moment, my feelings were as real as any I'd ever known.

The next day was New Year's Eve. Kate was meeting some other friends, and Silvio and Filippo and I took the Fiat down to Ostia Antica. I could think of nothing but Kate. I recognized the slant of her nose in a third-century mosaic; I heard the timbre of her voice in a crowd on the steps of the ancient amphitheater. The toga-draped hips and waistline of a headless statue filled me with longing, and my mind seethed with vividly remembered images. The way her eyes crinkled at the edges. That quick meaningful smile at the Bocca della Verità. How she'd tucked a few of her luminous golden curls behind her ear when they'd escaped her ponytail. The day was bittersweet torment. The only way to ease the pain was to repeat her name over and over to myself, like a mantra.

We'd made a plan to meet that night at Filippo's favorite *trattoria*. We were nearly an hour late due to Silvio's dawdling, which I suspected—groundlessly, perhaps—was intentional, and by the time we arrived, I was unbearably agitated. Kate sat alone at our table for four, sipping a glass of red wine, looking fresh and elegant in a simple black dress with those glorious blond curls unbound and the stylish leather jacket draped over the chair. She stood for the ritual cheek-kissing. The brush of her lips was a precious gift, but it wasn't enough. I needed to possess her.

Over dinner, out of deference to Filippo, the conversation was conducted entirely in Italian. Every once in a while I would catch the drift of what was being said, and occasionally I would chime in myself, speaking Spanish in my best approximation of a Roman accent. Filippo stared sourly whenever I tried this—his close-cropped ringlets and prominent cheekbones bringing to mind busts I'd seen of the young Caesar Augustus—but Kate seemed to find it amusing, so I kept it up. At one point I went to use the *stanza da bagno*. Silvio strode in behind me. "She likes you," he said, taking the next urinal.

"You think so?"

"Yeah, dude. Too bad she's so fickle. Did you notice how fast she dumped her boyfriend yesterday?"

I zipped up and walked over to the sink. Silvio joined me at the mirror, frowning at my reflection. His eyes were bulging a little, which I recognized as a sign that he was about to be drunk. "Be careful, Justin. That's all I'm saying."

I dried my hands on the cloth towel. The silence between us was heavy, toxic, broken only by the buzzing of the fluorescent bulbs and the muffled background clink of dishes from the restaurant kitchen. "Leave it alone, Silvio. Okay?"

"Sorry, dude," he said, giving me an offended look in the mirror. "Just trying to help."

Back on campus, Silvio had gained a reputation as an out-of-control boozer. We would be at a keg party and he would climb up on a table and start belting out an old Italian mountaineering song, or he would pick a fight with every single person in a crowded bar, or he would break a bottle and threaten the bartender with the jagged neck until the bouncers muscled him out into the frigid New England night. I'm not sure why I stuck by him, except that he had been my freshman-year roommate, and I felt a certain loyalty. And he was never dull.

It must have been two o'clock in the morning on that first day of 1986 as I sat in the back seat of the rattling Fiat, staring out at the blur of sooty architecture and flashing traffic lights. Filippo was driving, Silvio riding shotgun. The Fiat was moving too fast, though I have to admit that part of me was thrilled by the danger, even as I feared it. My palms ached from gripping the back of the driver's seat as Filippo sped through the roundabout below the Campidoglio, past the Arch of Titus and the crumbling Colosseum. Silvio was in top form, slurring his words as he rolled down the window to hurl insults at late-night pedestrians, mostly street sweepers and prostitutes. I could feel Kate sitting tensely beside me, although out of shyness or possibly embarrassment for Silvio and his reckless cousin, we'd mostly avoided looking at each other.

Silvio had a gram of hash in his pocket and suddenly he decided he wanted to smoke it. None of us had tobacco or rolling papers, so Filippo pulled into a small *piazza* lit by a single streetlight. Half a dozen young Romans loitered there, leaning against their Vespas and smoking hand-rolled cigarettes. Silvio rolled down his window and asked for one. His tone struck me as dangerous, because it was both arrogant and patronizing. This was not a group of schoolboys. These young men were muscular and thuggish, with blunt faces that seemed at once bored by life and animated by a kind of dull, slow-burning anger. None of them responded to Silvio's request, and in the next moment he spat out a well-known Italian insult.

As one, the Romans arose from their Vespas. Beside me, Kate drew in her breath. Silvio's door flew open and he sprang to his feet. He broke a half-empty Barolo bottle against the lamppost and waved the broken neck at the Vespa gang as if it were a conductor's baton. Filippo got out of the driver's side. I started to open my door too, but Kate grabbed my arm. "Justin. Don't."

"I'm not going to fight," I said. "This won't be the first time I've had to rescue Silvio from one of his idiotic suicide missions. I'll just get him back in the car. Why don't you take the wheel?"

Kate clambered up into the driver's seat and I opened the door and stood. My plan was to run at Silvio and knock the bottle out of his hand. I would put him in a headlock and wrestle him into the back seat. Hopefully Filippo would see how things were and jump in on the passenger side.

The night air was bitter with exhaust fumes. Somewhere a vent exhaled the breath of ancient sewers. Before I could execute my plan, a heavy object—it might have been a truncheon, or possibly brass knuckles—hit me hard on the side of the head, and I crumpled to the ground. I held up my hands to protect my skull from the Vespa gang's sharp-toed kicks, but it did little good. The last thing I remember before losing consciousness was that in the weak yellow glare of the streetlight, my blood spattering on the flagstones didn't look red, but as black as the shadowy corners of a Caravaggio painting.

I gained consciousness in the Fiat with my head in Kate's lap. One of her hands rested on my chest and the other, cool and soothing, was stroking my hair as she gazed tenderly down at me. The whole left side of my face throbbed. I felt ashamed about the bloody drool seeping from my mouth onto her dress.

She seemed to be waiting for something, and then I realized that she'd just asked me a question. No, I couldn't remember my birthday. How about my name? No, I couldn't remember that either. Nor where I lived, nor her name, nor how I'd come to be driving around in the middle of the night in this half-familiar, soot-stained European city. Exploring my mouth with my tongue I discovered an emptiness that gave me a shock. Kate must have noticed me sucking my lips. "Open your mouth," she said. I did. "Silvio, you fucking bastard. Look what you've done. Jesus, he's missing half his teeth."

To me, she murmured soothingly: "It's going to be okay, sweetie. We'll get you home and you can go to bed."

"Did you swallow them, Justin?" Silvio's voice was thick-tongued from the alcohol. "Did you swallow the teeth, or did you spit them out?"

"What the hell does it matter?" Kate retorted. "They're not in his *mouth* anymore. You can't just put them *back*."

"Actually, yes, you can," Silvio said, sounding wounded. "If you keep them in milk you can put them back in, as long as not too much time has gone by."

My memory had begun to come back. I knew my birthday, and I could sense the past filling in like a Polaroid. I was sad about the teeth, but it was amazing to be lying in Kate's lap. "Maybe they took them," I said, lisping cartoonishly. "Ath thome kind of trophieth or thomething."

"Hush," Kate said, rubbing my chest. "Don't try to talk, Justin. We're almost home."

The next morning my face was so swollen that I couldn't open my left eye. My tongue kept finding its way back to the sockets of the missing teeth. I couldn't get the mindset of my attackers out of my head. What had they been thinking? It was incomprehensible to me that anyone would wish to inflict such violent damage upon another human being. I didn't yet understand the true nature of chaos. That if you insist on cultivating it, on being entertained by it, you have no right to be outraged when it reaches out of the frame to engulf you.

The ducal palace was dim and cold. It seemed less grand than before, and shabbier. The upholstering was threadbare, and the walls were in need of a paint job. At breakfast the *duchessa* shook her head and gave my face a long, disapproving look with no hint of warmth in it. I drank coffee and picked at my fruit plate. Silvio and the dukes chewed their bread in silence, stone-faced and furious. It turned out that Tomasso was an avid connoisseur of antique weaponry. The three cousins spent all morning loading up his jeep with sabers, crossbows, World War I–era Mauser C96 pistols. They dressed themselves up like commandos in black turtlenecks and balaclavas, shook my hand with firm grips and steely eyes, piled into the jeep, and set off to restore their tainted family honor.

While they were gone, I went upstairs to ice my face and think about Kate. I kept replaying the car ride home. The sweet tenderness with which she'd gazed into my face. The way she'd held me in her arms, as if we were already lovers, and the ferocity of her reprimands for the drunken Silvio. My parents would adore her, I thought. They would have to pinch themselves—heck, so would I—to believe that in anything other than our wildest dreams a son of theirs could bring home a young woman so genteel, so spirited and elegant and kind.

Much to my relief, and the *duchessa's*, too, I think, the aristocratic Delta Force returned after several hours without having fulfilled their mission of revenge. Unable to locate the Vespa gang, they'd settled for an empty lot and some crossbow practice. I'd called Kate, and we'd made a plan to meet that afternoon. Silvio, no doubt feeling guilty for what had happened to me, was uncharacteristically considerate. In order for Kate and I to be alone, he called a taxi instead of volunteering to drive.

When Kate saw my face, she winced. "Oh, Justin. I am *so* sorry." I attempted a devil-may-care grin. Excruciating little needles of pain attacked the nerves deep in my jaw, and I held my breath until it passed. Kate was as luminous as ever, though slightly blurred in the watery view of my one functioning eye. We found a corner table at the café near her *pensione* and ordered coffee. The waiter had trouble looking at me and kept his eyes on Kate as he took the order. The January sun slanted in through the windows, adding to my lacerating headache. Kate reached across the table and squeezed my hand. "Are you in a lot of pain?"

"Not really. Some."

"How many teeth did you lose?"

"Three." The waiter brought out our coffees. I blew on mine, then took a sip. It was too sweet, the sugar blending with the iron-ore taste of the blood still seeping from my gums. "Listen," I said. "I'm thinking of heading down to Greece for the rest of winter break. I've got a Eurail pass that will cover the ferry from Brindisi to Patras, and then I'll catch a train to Athens, maybe take another ferry down to Crete. Want to come?"

The waiter appeared with a plate of pastries. Kate spoke to him in Italian and he responded, glancing in my direction without really looking.

"The pastries are on the house," she said when the waiter was gone. "He says the whole staff wishes you a speedy recovery."

"That's nice. I'll be fine. The biggest wound was to my pride."

She nodded. "Orthodontists are so good these days. Your smile will be as handsome as ever."

"I know." We sat in silence for a moment, staring down into our coffees. "Did you hear what I said about Greece?"

"Crete should be beautiful this time of year. Also Mykonos. You should definitely go there."

I nodded.

"Are you okay, Justin? You look pale. Do you need to lie down?"

"No. I'm fine."

Soon, we ran out of things to say. Kate told the waiter to call me a cab, and offered to go down to the train station to arrange my ticket for Brindisi. I told her thanks, but I could take care of it myself. Out on the street we said goodbye. She leaned in for the double kiss, thought better of it, and gave me a hug instead.

The Dragon of Conchagua

THE BUS CREAKED to a stop in the central square of the mountain village. John sat for a moment gazing out the window at the scenery, which was exactly as he remembered it: cinderblock houses, yellow dirt streets, deforested hillsides drained of color by the equatorial sun. When the bus was empty, he took a deep breath, hoisted his pack, and emerged into the achingly bright Andean afternoon. On the way up to the *guardaparque*'s house he encountered a pair of elderly women walking arm in arm. One greeted him with a nod of recognition and a shy smile. The other, looking perturbed, muttered something under her breath and steered her friend to the far side of the street. John took this reaction in stride. The village was remote and insular, its inhabitants superstitious. He understood how his return might be viewed as alarming.

He stood below the *guardaparque*'s steps and announced himself. After a moment the man appeared in the doorway, a lean mestizo with an honest symmetrical face marred only when he opened his mouth by several missing teeth. Apart from a few streaks of gray hair, he'd changed little in the intervening years. "I'm here to climb the volcano," John said in Spanish. "Do you still manage the papers?"

The *guardaparque* nodded, scrutinizing John's face. "Where are the others in your party?"

"Just one other. He arrived separately. I'll be meeting him up at the *refugio*, and we will come down together."

After a few moments the *guardaparque* returned with a clipboard. John filled out the form in triplicate, and the man tore off the front copy and handed it back. He peered into John's eyes. "Are you sure you want to do this? We do not recommend climbing alone."

"I understand," John said. "And I thank you for your concern. But you don't have to worry."

An hour later he was swaying uphill under a green tarp in the bed of an aging Toyota pickup. It was a strange view of the town—a tunnel-vision microcosm of human civilization receding as the Toyota labored up the access road, a deep groove of yellow earth cut between high banks that bristled with yucca and prickly pear. A tied goat watched the truck pass and bleated pitifully in its wake like an abandoned child.

At a certain point, they crossed an invisible climatological line into what South Americans call the *páramo*, a high-altitude plain carpeted with bright green moss and yellowish grass. The air cooled noticeably, and fast-moving tongues of fog swept over the hillsides as if preparing to devour them. At the gate marking the edge of the national park, the Toyota shuddered to a halt, and John leapt out. Resting his pack against the barbed wire, he paid the driver and watched the truck for a few moments as it began its grinding descent into town. Then he let himself through the gate and continued on foot. Ahead, shrouded by fog but an unmistakable presence nonetheless, loomed the massive broken cone of the Conchagua volcano.

The trail was quickly swallowed up by the moss, which grew like emerald-green coral, one layer atop the last, making the ground mounded and spongy, like a moonwalk. He was definitely feeling the altitude. He reminded himself of the advice once given to him by his brother Gabe, an accomplished mountaineer: take small steps and lock your knees between strides so that your skeleton bears the weight, and your muscles can rest. After an hour or more of trudging, he sat on a grass hummock to rest. The volcano was still covered, but every once in a while he glimpsed a black spur sloping violently upward, and higher still, the occasional bluish gleam of snow. He would soon run out of daylight. If the fog continued to descend it would complicate things. Not being able to see the sky made him surprisingly skittish.

Hoisting the pack, he continued uphill toward the *refugio*. The ground ahead was dotted with white orbs. It was odd to see mushrooms on the *páramo*, but when he got close enough to examine one, he discovered with a jolt that it wasn't a mushroom at all. It was a skull, the bleached braincase of a goat or a sheep. The horns had broken off, but the upper jaw was intact, a leer of rotten teeth. "Christ," he exclaimed, stepping back. The skull's empty sockets seemed to stare up at him in a shockingly personal way, as if it had been placed deliberately in his path.

Heart pounding, he walked on. The entire ground was littered with bones: goats, cows, horses, another large animal that he could not identify. Skulls and vertebrae, limbs and pelvises bleached white, or more recently dead and still oily with fat. There were rib cages half-sunken like shipwrecks in the hungry pillow moss. There were teeth loosely retained in their jawbones, or scattered like dice over the bright-green mounds. He felt a strong desire not to be alone—and in the next moment, as if in answer to his wish, he heard the distant notes of a nimbly picked guitar. It was an old Grateful Dead tune, "Eyes of the World," one of the songs in his brother's repertoire. Relieved, he hurried on through the swirling fog.

Another hundred yards and he could make out the *refugio*, a squat, whitewashed cinderblock structure that looked as familiar as if he'd left it only days before. Taking a deep breath, he pushed open the metal door and stepped inside. Gabe was sitting on a camp chair with his guitar on his lap. A fire crackled in the hearth, though it didn't seem to be throwing off much heat. The air inside the dreary building felt just as cold as the windswept páramo.

Gabe stopped playing and glanced up from the guitar with an air of good-natured annoyance. "Took you long enough."

"Sorry about that. I had some things I needed to do."

"I was debating whether or not I should give up on you." Gabe looked good, lean and tanned, flushed from the mountain air. He wore a retro-pile Patagonia fleece, off-white with a black chest pocket, eighties vintage, a garment so familiar that the sight of it caused John's throat to ache.

He went into the kitchen and laid his pack on the candlewax-spattered picnic table. Though he hadn't eaten all day, instead of hunger he felt only a mild nausea, attributable, no doubt, to the effects of the altitude. His hands shook as he lit the propane burner and used the lever to pump water from the tap into the blackened kettle. He dug around in the side pocket of the pack for an envelope of freeze-dried tomato soup. "I assume you haven't had dinner?" he called out. There was no answer from the other room.

When the water was ready, he mixed the contents of the envelope into two of the *refugio*'s chipped blue-enamel coffee cups and took them out to the lounge. He placed one beside Gabe's chair and sat on the floor with his back to the fire, shivering. He couldn't seem to get warm. "Do you remember what it was like up on the summit last time?" he asked, holding the hot mug with both hands to blow on the soup.

Gabe smiled fleetingly, setting down the guitar but ignoring his mug.

"It was such a clear day," John went on. "You could see forever, remember? It was like we were literally standing on top of the world."

Gabe nodded, his eyes shining in the firelight. "Sure, John. I remember."

Later, unable to stop shivering, John made his way to the bunkroom. He shook out his mummy bag and climbed inside it. It was ridiculous to carry on a conversation with a person like Gabe. Still, he was determined to try.

The following morning John got out his map, and they traced out an acclimation hike. Their destination was a minor summit that showed up as a dark convergence of lines on the map perhaps an hour's walk from the *refugio*. Several times as they crossed the *páramo*, John thought he glimpsed something overhead, a little roll or flourish in the corner of his eye, a serrated flutter in the distance like a blowing oak leaf. But when he looked up, there was never anything to see.

The minor summit turned out to be a granite pinnacle like something out of Dr. Seuss, a lopsided tower of lava festooned with knots of *páramo* grass. Partway up, John started to feel exposed. The fog had lowered again, and he didn't like not being able to see the sky. There was nothing but empty air around the spire, nothing visible above or below but swirling fog. The black rock was veined with a harder, whitish stone, loops and spirals telling the story of an ancient eruption suddenly congealed. Tussocks of grass clung to a meager existence in cracks in the stone; he grabbed hold of them for support as if they were hanks of strong yellow hair. His lungs burned from the altitude, and his knees felt weak, but he forced himself to keep moving. He tried to keep

Gabe's scuffed mountaineering boots in sight as they faded into the fog above his head.

"Take a drink of water," Gabe's voice called down. John leaned into the steeply slanting rock and reached for his water bottle. He didn't feel thirsty, but he unscrewed the cap and took a few swallows.

Later, pulling himself up over the edge of the summit, he collapsed on a mound of pillow moss. Gabe stood with his hands clasped behind his back, gazing out at their first clear view of the snow-capped massif. In peripheral vision, John caught a glimpse of a flickering shadow circling overhead, enormous and bat-like. Groaning softly, he massaged his eyelids with his fingertips.

"What's the matter?" Gabe asked.

"Nothing."

"Come on. Tell me."

John let out his breath. "Okay. Well, yesterday, on the way up from town, I came across a bunch of skulls scattered all over the moss. Skulls and skeletons, actually, quite a few of them. It looked like some kind of slaughtering ground."

"That sounds farfetched."

"It's what I saw."

"There's no dragon, John. I don't know why you keep bringing it up."

John shook his head, puzzled. "I never mentioned anything about a dragon."

"But you were thinking it. If you think it, you don't have to say it."

"Okay. I'll try not to think it."

"Good boy. Now drink some more of your water."

On the meandering walk back to the *refugio*, John stumbled upon the wreck of a vintage Cessna. The wings were gone, and, like everything else that had been resting on the *páramo* for a certain amount of time, the fuselage was half-consumed by pillow moss. A section of the cockpit was exposed—the glass of the windscreen long since shattered—leaving a rectangular black hole set in a background of rusting metal and emerald-green moss. Kneeling to peer into the cockpit, he sensed a fast-moving object overhead and glanced up reflexively, fear gripping his gut like a fist. But apart from blue sky and a few lingering wisps of fog, there was nothing to see. Taking a deep breath, he squinted down into the cockpit. Once again, there was nothing to see but darkness.

When they were young boys, perhaps eight and ten, he and Gabe had taken an unsupervised canoe trip on a tiny drainage canal near their home in southern New Hampshire. It had been early spring—a year of plentiful snowmelt—and the water in the canal, normally just a trickle, had been deep enough to float the canoe. The canal led downstream from their house to a culvert that passed under a frontage road. The current was fast, and coming around a curve in the stream, they saw that the brown water was being sucked powerfully into the culvert, with a gap of only about six inches between the rushing V of water and the top of the tunnel. They'd tried to back-paddle, but the water was moving too fast. Somehow they got turned sideways to the culvert. The canoe jammed up against it, the dirty water flooding into the boat, and they capsized. John was swept under and down into the culvert. He fought his way to the surface, struggling to keep his mouth above water as the current hurried him along under the gap at the top of the tunnel. It was pitch-black and freezing cold. He experienced the terror of knowing that he was going to die.

Somehow he made it through to daylight. Gabe had managed to reach the bank without getting sucked down into the culvert, and he was waiting on the other side of the frontage road to pull John to safety. John lay on the sodden bank, gasping ineffectually like a landed fish, the panic having constricted his lungs to the point that he was simply unable to process the air. "Breathe," Gabe ordered in a calm authoritative voice, and John clung to the word as if it were a buoy. His lungs relaxed, and he started swallowing the air in great life-giving gulps. It was only then that he understood he was not going to die.

The alarm went off. John shook himself from his stupor, leaving the sleeping bag on the bunk. By the light of a headlamp, he took everything out of the pack except his crampons, an ice axe, a few extra layers, water, and a light lunch of trail mix and beef jerky.

Out in the pre-dawn chill, the rhythm of his stride worked to numb his mind, and the hours passed quickly. By the time the sky was showing the first signs of dawn, he'd arrived at the wall of dirty ice marking the lower edge of the snowcap. His hands shook as he fumbled with the crampons. He was concerned that he would lose contact with Gabe, who—with his usual invincibility—had continued on toward the summit.

As day broke on the snowfield, John ascended through a spectrum of unearthly colors, from moon-blue to milky gold to an intense, foggy whiteness that hurt his eyes. He was struggling for breath, his muscles feeble and shaky in the altitude. The truth was, he hadn't spent enough time acclimating. Every step jarred his skeleton, worsening a pulsing headache that was like the tolling of a cracked bell.

When the fog lifted, he finally remembered to put on his sunglasses. The mountain was a geometrical abstraction: a steep angle of bright white against a pure background of electric blue. John, exhausted, had no choice but to rest. He used the axe to hack a shelf in the nearly vertical snow slope that he could use as a kind of bench. He unscrewed a water bottle and took a little swallow, and as he screwed the cap back on, he was nearly overcome by nausea. Determined to press on, he made himself stand and shrugged on the pack without losing his balance. But the effort left him depleted. He stood in place for a long moment, swaying dangerously and gritting his teeth against the dizziness, before he was ready to move.

He resumed the climb, step by step, using the axe and the teeth of the crampons to keep from sliding to his death. In the corner of his eye he kept glimpsing shadows—dark flickers and rolling flourishes. A knot of dread lodged like a swallowed pinecone in his esophagus, and it took all his concentration to keep himself from vomiting.

At the summit, he stood on the edge of the corniced crater. The day was clear enough, though not as crystalline as that previous day. A few of the neighboring volcanoes were visible to the north and south, perfect snow-covered cones rising from the yellowish haze. To the east, beyond the crater, lay the jungle lowlands of the Amazon Basin, an endless dark-green carpet stretching out to the horizon. Overcome with emotion, he sank to his knees, then sat on the snow. Everything was fine. He'd done it.

The bus sped along a narrow highway hugging the sides of the Andean foothills that cradled the chaotic ugliness of the outer barrios of Quito. From his seat in the front of the bus, John took in the grim scenery: the garbage-choked ravines, the rivers brown with silt and sewage, the squalid shacks of rusted tin and unpainted cinderblock clinging to gray hillsides long since stripped of trees and clawed by unchecked erosion into deep, barren gullies. To his right the land fell away abruptly. In places the shoulder of the road had collapsed, leaving huge bite marks of missing asphalt the driver had to swerve to avoid.

The driver was reckless, whistling to himself as he took the curves at maximum speed. John glanced across the aisle to Gabe, who was gazing out the window with his usual calm. "What do you think of this driver?" he asked.

Gabe turned his head slowly. His face had an alarmingly vague appearance: a strange, blurred lack of definition, like a photograph taken with a waterlogged lens. John swallowed. "Never mind."

Gabe shrugged and turned back to the window. It was another clear day. To the west they had a good view of some of the volcanoes—not Conchagua, but the broken, crevasse-wrinkled snowcap of Antisana, and to the north and south, the distant white cones of Cayambe and Cotopaxi. For Gabe, mountains had always trumped cities. Unspoiled wilderness was his creed, providing a deeper and more encouraging reality than the garbage-strewn human mess sliding by outside the bus window. Gabe's worldview was immensely appealing to John, even if—in his own mind—he'd never quite been able to make it stick.

The driver hawked and spat into a soda can. A bus from the same transportation company passed going the other way, and the driver took his hand off the wheel to wave—which might be a problem, John thought, with a sudden surge of adrenaline, because they were coming up to a sharp left curve and the ravine to their right fell away so abruptly that there was nothing beneath them but empty air. He gripped the metal bar in front of the seat, pressing his foot to the floor in search of the nonexistent brakes. He called out a warning in Spanish as they barreled into the curve. The driver recovered himself just in time. The real brakes squealed and the bus rocked sickeningly from side to side before recovering.

John let out his breath. The driver gave him a madcap grin in the rearview, and John shook his head. Gabe, too, was holding on to the metal bar in front of his seat, but he didn't seem concerned. His attention was still bent on the distant peaks, the snowcaps like piles of pure confectioner's sugar beneath an electric-blue sky. John stared at them for a moment, trying to fix their profiles indelibly in his mind. It was a relief to have made the climb, and to have come away with Gabe at his side, despite all the omens and dire premonitions.

Suddenly Gabe leaned forward in his seat, as if to look more closely at something outside the window. Then John spotted it: a small, airborne figure approaching from the direction of the volcanoes. It looked like a hawk or a vulture, except that it moved with a strange flickering wing-beat. John watched in horror as the figure grew larger and larger, the great flapping wings webbed and charred-looking, and then the long black head. The creature was not at all what he'd been expecting—less like a lizard, more like a kind of demented, predatory horse.

It swooped down and hovered over the bus, close enough to block out the sun, and cast a pulsating cloak of shadow over the road. John called out to Gabe. Gabe turned to look at him, only it wasn't Gabe at all. It was only a city-bound *campesino*, with mocha skin and wind-chapped cheekbones, and black uncomprehending eyes beneath a battered pork-pie hat.

Steal Your Face

My brother Josh rolls into town on his way to a Dead show in Portland, Maine. He's three years older than I, a modern gypsy with a tie-dyed scarf wrapped around his skull and a gold hoop earring that glints red in the light of a highway sunset or a concert stage. He's been following the Dead for the better part of two years from his moveable home, a sky-blue Volkswagen camper-bus with a Steal Your Face painted on the front panel, the VW symbol replacing the lightning bolt in the skull's oversized forehead.

He's packing a sheet of cartoon acid and offers to take me along for the ride. Before I know it I'm tripping my brains out in the middle of a dancing crowd, the bassline shaking the floor and Jerry Garcia's carnival-messiah voice filling the air of the Portland Coliseum. Josh has melted into the crowd, but it doesn't matter because we're all one here, everybody moving to the music in perfect synchrony like a school of tie-dyed fish.

"Terrapin Station" into "Franklin's Tower" into "Big Railroad Blues." This is my third Dead show, my second time on acid. Now I'm channeling some kind of historic trip, a vein of nostalgic imagery from a lost America. "Wharf Rat" into "Cumberland Blues," "Sugaree" into "Brown-Eyed Woman." I see broken-down gold mills, bootleg whiskey stills, hoboes sitting around a fire inside a rusty boxcar. The images are clear but fleeting, except for one that keeps cycling back: a riverbank at the edge of a pine forest that rises up in a series of steep ridges to a range of snow-covered mountains. At the edge of the forest, a clothesline is hung with colorful dresses that snap in the wind. I can smell pinewood burning; I can hear distant female laughter and singing. The scene shimmers around the edges of my consciousness, bittersweet, luminous, maddeningly hard to pin down. Everything about it seems so familiar—so charged with emotion—that I think I must be remembering a real place, a campground or a music festival I might have visited as a child. But I've never been out of New England, and there are no mountains or forests like that around here. So I figure it must be the memory of a dream, or maybe a fleeting prophecy of something yet to come.

A week of rain at the end of May turns the lawns green, and the buds on the beeches and maples burst overnight in leaves so perfectly formed they seem altogether too good to be true. High school is grinding to an end, and the future stretches out like an empty highway. For my girlfriend Otter, the future means

Dartmouth, and after that—she hopes—medical school. For me, things are up in the air. I've gone to three more Dead concerts since Portland. At each of them, I've had the same vision. It's 1983, and the band is at the top of their form. You can travel from place to place on the money you make selling T-shirts, trail mix, or jugs of Tang.

The weekend after graduation, Kevin Rodgers's parents go away and he has a keg party at his house. He's captain of the baseball team, normally not my crowd, but Otter wants to go and I hate to let her go alone. She lives in the same neighborhood as Kevin—the rich, Republican neighborhood—so we agree to meet at the party. It's a new house built to resemble something older: hardwood floors and a big, open kitchen with pots and pans dangling from hooks on the ceiling. The nucleus of activity is the spacious living room, spilling out onto the redwood deck where the keg is. I scan the crowd for Otter, already wracking my brain for an excuse to get us both out of there, but when I see her my stomach drops. She's sitting on the couch with Rick Morgan, the baseball coach.

Morgan is from Florida. He has an overgrown, swashbuckling moustache, like General Custer. He's blond, tanned, young for a coach, and highly charismatic; all the baseball players are trying to grow those moustaches. He and Otter are deep in conversation, gazing into each other's eyes with rapt expressions. It chills me to the bone.

You see, Otter's special. She's completely unconcerned with standard high school issues like popularity and good looks. She's smart and funny, and she has a generous turn of mind. Her instinct is to give people the benefit of the doubt, which is probably the only reason she's ended up as the girlfriend of an oddball like me. If you saw her in a picture you might think her jaw was a little too prominent, and her eyes a little too close together, but in person she just has this aura. And she has a great body. One day she came to visit me at the IGA, where I was working as a stock boy. My boss, Mr. Mayo, was impressed. "Jesus, kid," he remarked after she'd gone. "Are you man enough for that?"

At the time it didn't bother me, because Mr. Mayo had a big square head and brushy hair coming out of his nostrils and kept five or six pens in his front pocket. Rick Morgan, though, is a different story.

When Otter sees me, she gets up and makes her way through the crowd. Morgan watches her ass the whole time, eyes shining and lips pursed appraisingly beneath the Custer moustache. Then he looks up at me and gives me the most evil smile I've ever seen.

"Fuck you," I mouth, but he's already turned his attention to someone else.

Otter takes my hand, and I follow her outside. We fill our beers and stand at the railing of the deck, gazing out over the Rodgers' expansive lawn, which rolls down in graded berms to a mist-shrouded hedge of brambles along a small brook that runs through the property.

"What the heck were you *doing* in there?" I ask.

"Oh, just chatting. Why?"

"Just chatting, Otter? Didn't you see his *face*? If it were up to him he would have fucked you right there in the middle of the party."

"Good thing it wasn't *up* to him then, isn't it?" She smiles, but when I fail to smile back she turns serious. "I'm sorry, Jeff. It was harmless."

"He's thirty years old."

"I said I was sorry. Do you have a list of people you don't want me talking to, or are you issuing a blanket injunction?"

Down by the brook, a red-tailed hawk lands on the crown of a young hemlock, glancing sidelong at the humans on the deck. It leaps free, flapping its wings twice before presenting them to the wind. Otter laces her fingers into mine and pulls me closer. I take a deep breath, beginning to feel more at ease.

"What would you think if I hit the road with Josh next year, instead of college?"

"Is that what you want?"

"Maybe. I've been thinking a year off before college might do me some good."

"If it's what you want, Jeff, then that's what you should do."

"Would you miss me?"

"Of course. But we're going to be in different places anyway. If following Jerry Garcia around the country is what you really want to do, then you should do it. Listen to your heart."

We leave the party looking for a place to have sex. Her parents' car isn't in their driveway, so we're in luck. We go inside, close the door to her bedroom, and take off our clothes.

Afterwards, I feel better. I feel reassured that Otter's love for me is unconditional; that I can stop worrying about the likes of Rick Morgan; that she will wait patiently as I follow my dreams.

The next day Josh and I take the Magic Bus down to a show in Hartford. I'm tripping nicely, an internal strobe light flashing split-second frames of white nothingness to the percussion beats coming from the speakers. Between beats I try to bring back the vision. For a while there's nothing, just a flashing white void, and I start to worry that I've lost touch with it, but then it comes, flickering weakly at first and then materializing in rhythmic bursts like a slide show in my head: riverbank; pine forest; snowy mountains. Three calico summer dresses pinned to a clothesline, flapping and dancing in the wind. The mountains look familiar, although I'm sure I've never seen them in real life.

The band goes into a holding pattern, a long, rolling drum jam. Then there's a disturbance in the crowd. In front of me on the floor of the stadium people are separating as though choosing sides in a universal, unspoken argument. An aisle forms, and I'm standing in the middle of it. Everyone's looking at me. It's as if the aisle has been created for my benefit.

The next thing I know, a figure comes dancing down the aisle toward me. He's about my age and height, but slimmer, with a blond ponytail, and the surprising thing is that he's buck naked. He seems lost to the world, crouching and spinning like a demented shaman, his penis bobbing up and down in a blond bush of pubic hair. People are pushing back against each other to give him room, grinning as they follow his progress. Some raise fists in the air to cheer him on, mocking him in a way that strikes me as unnecessarily cruel. The boy's face is flushed, and his expression is rapturous: a fierce, sanctified smile. A rivulet of drool glistens on his chin. I want to turn away, but my feet are rooted in place. People are laughing openly at the guy now, giving him playful little shoves as he dances past.

When he's ten feet away he stops. He looks up at the jeering crowd, confused, and suddenly he seems to awake from whatever dream he was having. He glances down at his naked body. Then he looks straight at me. His face changes—his expression that of a small child about to burst out crying—and he runs up and throws his arms around my neck, locking in a tight embrace and mumbling nonsensically into my shirt.

"Get *off!*" I shout, putting my hands on his shoulders to try to pry him loose. He chokes out a sob and clings even tighter, and I can hear the jeers and laughter from the people around us. The boy's sweat is acrid with fear, and his wiry limbs seem to possess supernatural strength. I have no idea what to do. It's like a nightmare. I look around for Josh, but he's nowhere to be seen.

Eventually, a phalanx of security guards comes pushing through the crowd to rescue me. Twisting the naked boy's arms behind his back, they lead him away.

My trip is irretrievable, all jagged edges and dissonant noises and harsh flashes of light from the stage. The jam crystallizes into "Black Peter," one of my favorite tunes, and the stadium erupts, but I can't get back in the groove. I can't shake his memory, the way he danced down the aisle, crouching and spinning like some kind of reincarnated medicine man. And the way his face dropped when he awoke from his dream into the nightmare. The way his face changed when he saw me, as if he recognized a kindred spirit, and imagined that I was the one who could save him.

After the show, I tell Josh to go by the police station. I want to find out what's happened to the guy, and help him if I can. I think maybe, if I see him again in a more rational state, I'll be able to purge the disturbing memory that seems to be stuck in my mind: how desperately he clung to me, as if he would drag me down with him into his own private Hell. The desperate terror in his face as the security guards hauled him off toward the exit.

At the station, a policeman brings the boy out. He's wrapped in a coarse woolen blanket. His cheeks look slack and slightly bloated, like a week-old balloon, and the vacant look in his eyes is as frightening as anything I've ever seen. I feel the panic flooding in. It's worse than I expected. It's as if whatever personality he had before has been erased, crushed into a fine dust which has leaked out through his nostrils.

Josh fills out a form for the police, and we take the guy out to the VW, supporting him with our shoulders. Josh gives him an old army-surplus jacket that hangs off his skinny body unnaturally, like drapery on a post. I manage to get an address out of him; he lives in Brattleboro, Vermont, not far out of our way. As we get on the highway headed north, he climbs into the back and collapses among Josh's assembled worldly possessions.

"Bad trip," Josh remarks under his breath.

"I know," I reply. "Have you seen this kind of thing before?"

"Sure. Happens all the time at shows. You have to be careful not to overdo it. 'Know thyself,' as the Greeks would have it."

Soon after we cross the border into Massachusetts, the engine starts making a grinding noise, low scraping clicks like sporadic Morse code. There's a faint, chemical smell of something burning.

"Pull over," I say.

We step out into the ink-black night. I follow Josh around to the rear of the bus, and he points at the ventilation grill on the engine hatch. A narrow tongue of flame licks out of the grill and halfway up the rear window, receding into the bowels of the engine only to flare up again, and recede. There are peepers nearby—an urgent, high-pitched chorus.

Josh pounds on the rear window. "Out of the bus, kid! Come on!" I run around and fling open the sliding door.

"Get out, dude!" I yell. There's no answer, so Josh and I climb in and lift the boy out. We drag him to the edge of a field by the side of the highway, where he sinks into the grass as if his skeleton can no longer sustain its own weight. Josh and I go back to look at the ventilation grill. The engine's making ominous sounds now, metallic pops and twangs. It's like one of those dreams where you see what's coming but there's nothing you can do about it, so you just stand there, open-mouthed and paralyzed.

The bus rocks a little, and we realize to our horror that the boy's climbed back inside. We sprint around to the open door and try to drag him out, but it's impossible. He's holding on to something inside the bus with nearly superhuman strength. Finally he lets go, and the three of us tumble out onto the pavement.

"Get up, *idiot*," Josh says. "It's going to explode any minute now. *Fire! Explosion! Boom!*" We yank him to his feet and lead him away, but he's sleek and boneless, like a seal. He slips out of our hands, runs back to the bus, and dives in. He's driven by some irresistible natural force—like a moth to flame, or a pilot whale beaching itself. We wrestle him out into the field again, and Josh holds him in a headlock while I kneel on his chest to keep him still. In the distance I hear a siren.

By this time the flames are roaring out of the grill. Then the gas tank blows, sending shards of blackened metal clattering over the asphalt and sizzling in the grass. The flames subside briefly, as if partially satiated, rippling around the body of the bus in a teasing, polychromatic dance. Then the whole bus is consumed in a firestorm that sends a plume of red sparks high into the New England night.

A policeman gives us all a ride home, stopping first to drop the naked boy off at his address in Brattleboro, a slump-porched Victorian just off the highway. Josh and I watch as he staggers up the steps and disappears into the house. An upstairs light goes on. Who knows what his parents think, but for me it's a tremendous relief to be rid of him. I can't get the vacant look in his eyes out of my mind. It haunts me.

Josh is philosophical about having lost his only form of transport, which had doubled as his sleeping quarters and contained all his valuables—sleeping bags, rock-climbing gear, and his prized collection of Dead bootlegs. But he borrows money from my parents for another VW bus, a white one this time with brown patches of fiberglass where the body has rusted away. He convinces me to drive out west with him. A series of shows is planned for the famous Red Rocks Amphitheatre, and he knows some people we can stay with in Boulder.

The vision from the concerts is foremost in my mind. I'm deeply concerned about losing touch with it and never being able to revisit it. It's taken on great significance for me, and I feel that my happiness depends on following it wherever it leads. I'm convinced that I need to go to more concerts to find it, and that I need to take more acid. What if that pine forest and those mountains are somewhere in Colorado?

I tell Otter about the bus explosion, but I never tell her about the naked boy. I describe my vision to her, leaving out the part about the calico dresses and the female voices. I try to explain the bittersweet feeling of destiny I get whenever I think about it. She says she wants to understand, and I think she sincerely does.

It's hard to leave her. Although she says she loves me, I have trouble believing it when we're not together, and it occurs to me that I'm taking a risk by going. As we're loading up the new bus I almost tell Josh I've changed my mind, but in the end I climb in, and the drive begins.

The Red Rocks shows will be over in two short weeks. I'll have Otter to myself for the whole month of August before the day comes for her to move into her dorm at Dartmouth.

Vermont, New York, Pennsylvania, Ohio. The Rust Belt, Chicago, the endless cornfields of Iowa and Nebraska. As we cross the Colorado line, I turn down the music and tell Josh about my vision. "Do you think it might correspond to an actual place?" I ask.

He shakes his head, smiling. "I doubt it. More likely, it corresponds to Jeff on acid at a Dead show, seeing what he wants to see."

"So there's no camp on a riverbank in the mountains somewhere?"

"I'm sure there *could* be. Who knows?"

"But where's the *center*?" I press. "I mean, where do all the Deadheads go when the band's not on tour?"

He looks at me. "The center's wherever you *want* it to be, Jeff. Wherever you are at the time. That's the beauty of this whole scene."

I turn the volume back up, wondering if there's something about the Deadhead milieu that I've caught a glimpse of, something that maybe Josh has not. There *must* be a center, I think, a *real* center, if you're just persistent enough and follow your inner vision. And even if it's not the exact smoke-scented pine forest at the base of the snowy mountains that vision has shown me, it must be something equivalent, something equally mysterious and meaningful and sweet.

Outside the bus it's dusk. The land is brown and oppressively flat. It doesn't look like any Colorado I've ever heard of. But then I suppose that the best is yet to come.

❧

We arrive late and drive around Boulder looking for Josh's friends' place. At length we find it, a low yellow-brick bungalow with no lights on. We let ourselves in. No one's up so we crash in the living room, Josh on the floor and I on the sofa, which smells like stale bong-water. Before I drift off to sleep I feel a pang of homesickness, missing Otter.

In the morning I'm awakened by a callused foot pressing down on my back. I squirm out from under it, groaning and rubbing my eyes. A troll-like hippie stands over me, holding a bong. Josh sits cross-legged and bleary-eyed on the carpet, with his back to a broad picture window coated with dust and grime.

"Welcome to Boulder, Josh's little brother." The troll holds out the bong and a lighter. I seal my mouth over the plastic cylinder and take a long hit, watching the thick white smoke stream through the tube and fill my lungs to the point where they feel like they're going to burst. I've never particularly liked bong hits.

"Wake and bake," the troll declares, dropping heavily onto the couch beside me. He's in his mid-twenties, heavy-boned, shirtless, with tie-dyed carpenter's overalls, long dreadlocks, and a curly red beard. His name is Jack Straw. That's how he introduces himself, anyway.

There are two days left before the first show at Red Rocks. Time passes slowly. Except for Jack Straw and his ever-present bong, none of the Deadheads living in the yellow brick house pays much attention to me. They're all at least three or four years older, and I suppose they're too busy screwing and getting high and listening to bootlegs to bother with a novice like me. Josh takes up with one of the housemates, Amber, a pretty girl from California with silky blond hair, unshaven legs and armpits, very fine breasts, and the disconcerting habit of walking around the house topless. I might as well not exist as far as she's concerned; even when I speak to her directly she looks right through me. I pass the hours in a stoned fog, mostly regretting the decision to come. Several times I walk down to the 7-Eleven to call Otter from the pay phone, but my timing is off. She never seems to be home when I call.

Red Rocks is one of the Dead's favorite venues. The setting is spectacular, like one of those ancient cultures transplanted to a distant galaxy on Star Trek. Two red-sandstone monoliths jut out of a rugged hillside, and a three-thousand-seat amphitheater fills the gap between the rocks, spilling down the slope to present a panoramic view of the sprawl of Denver and the vast, empty prairie beyond.

The red-dirt parking lots are full of cars with license plates from all over the country: Volvos and BMWs with Steal Your Face or Skull and Roses stickers on the rear windows; rusty old station wagons; dozens of creatively painted VW buses like Josh's incinerated one. As we drive in through the lots, my heart leaps because I catch the scent of burning pinewood. I crane my neck around, trying to detect its source. On the tailgate of a battered Toyota pickup, I spot a girl whose pretty oval face I recognize from the crowd at Portland. She's wearing an old-fashioned calico sundress like the ones in my vision, and she smiles at me as we pass. My heart pounds in my chest, but by the time I think to raise my hand in greeting, we've already left her behind.

At our parking spot, Jack Straw doles out tickets and tabs of cartoon acid. Transient Deadheads line the walkway up to the amphitheater, holding up fingers to signify the numbers of tickets they lack. From their wide-eyed, inward expressions, it's clear that acid is a good deal easier to get. There's no assigned seating inside the amphitheater. We stay together until we've established a base as close as we can possibly get to the stage. Amber spreads out blankets, and Josh passes around a jug of Tang. Taking a sip of the sugary drink, I feel the first kick of the acid, a tiny oscillation at the back of my throat.

And in the next moment I'm tripping. The murmur of the crowd vibrates in my body as a generalized hum, bringing with it an acute sense of precision and control. Josh raises his eyebrows questioningly, and I give him the thumbs-up sign. My perception goes into pause/play mode, and for a moment I seem to have gained control over the flow of time. I can stop it, make it go forward, or play it in slow motion. But then I start to worry that it will get stuck in fast-forward mode, so I knock it off. Jerry sings something about headlights shining through the cool Colorado rain, the crowd cheers like thunder, and I catch another whiff of the burning pine. The vision of the riverbank in the pine forest fills my mind, clearer and more detailed than ever. I can pick out individual cliffs and crevasses in the mountains. I can see the boughs of the forest swaying in the wind. I can hear the dull roar of the river. I walk toward the snapping calico dresses and the laughing female voices, but I can't quite reach them. At a certain point my feet seem to lose contact with the ground on the riverbank, and a column of pure white light beams me back to the concrete steps of the amphitheater, leaving me gasping in frustration.

The next morning I fend off Jack Straw's bong hits so I can walk down to the 7-Eleven and call Otter with a relatively clear mind. No one's home. I assume she and her family have gone to Silver Lake; they have a powerboat there and like to go water skiing. For the rest of the day, though, I can't stop thinking about her. I picture her in a black party dress, in jeans and a tank top, in nothing but a bra and underwear. I picture her naked, standing beside me in front of the bathroom mirror at her house; her breasts, with their large, dark nipples and inquisitive upward tilt. Her image is so vivid it makes my chest ache.

Later that day, I walk down to the 7-Eleven again, but no one answers the phone. In the VW on the way to the second show, I sit in the far back, watching the foothills of the Rocky Mountains roll by, long, yellow-green ridges draped with mist from the afternoon thundershowers. Maybe I've died without knowing it, I think. That would explain why I can't seem to get in touch with Otter.

I awake at dawn, with a racing pulse and a premonition of rapidly approaching doom. None of the housemates is up, so I don't bother with the 7-Eleven; I just dial direct from the phone in the kitchen. Otter's little sister Gwen answers. Once again, Otter isn't home.

I take a deep breath. "Where is she?" Silence. I can feel the twelve-year-old thinking on the other end. "It's not even noon there, Gwen. Is she working?"

"Don't worry, Bones." Gwen calls me Bones; I have no idea why. But I know she sincerely likes me, and I don't like what I'm hearing in her voice. She sounds like she's about to cry.

I slide off the stool and go into a fetal crouch on the kitchen floor. The roots of my teeth throb. I feel like I could loosen them with my tongue if I wanted to, and spit them out on the floor. "Who's she with, Gwen?"

"Oh, Bones. It's the baseball coach."

"Rick Morgan?"

"Oh, Bones, I'm so sorry. I know Otter's feeling terrible. She's been crying a lot . . ." Gwen trails off, but it doesn't matter. There's no mistaking the pity in her voice, and my situation is clear enough. I've been gone for a week. The only girl I've ever loved has traded me in for a thirty-year-old man with glittering eyes and a moustache like the reincarnation of George Armstrong Custer. I'm eighteen, an apprentice Deadhead and increasingly frequent drug abuser who looks like the young Ichabod Crane. Even a twelve-year-old can see the problem.

We've run out of real tickets; we resort to fakes. We spend the whole day making them: scissoring up manila folders and painting them with watercolors to just the right shade of lavender, using a pizza cutter to make the perforations, painting on a coat of nail polish for the glossy finish. The fakes look good. Everyone agrees.

In the parking lot before the show, Jack Straw gives me a tab of acid. I put it on my tongue and hold out my hand for another. Jack Straw glances at Josh, who raises his eyebrows and then nods his consent. On the way up the ramp, I try to clear my head to make way for the vision, but my imagination goes off on its own track: Otter sniffing and wiping her eyes as she motions to Gwen at the phone; Otter naked, on her knees, crying out as the leering baseball coach takes her from behind.

At the top of the ramp, we wait until there's a bottleneck, and insinuate ourselves into the line of concert-goers holding out tickets for the uniformed gatekeepers. Jack Straw and another hairy *amigo* get through on their fakes. Josh and Amber get through on theirs. But when my turn comes, the way is blocked by a hamlike forearm. With a surge of panic I find myself looking up into the ticket-taker's unkind face. He holds my forgery between his thumb and forefinger and shakes his clean-shaven head with a look of extreme distaste. "Jesus Christ, kid. Do you think we're stupid?" He grips my arm and signals his partner on the other side of the gate. "Counterfeiter. Call security."

Josh catches my eye from the other side of the gate. "Run," he mouths. I twist out of the ticket-taker's grasp and sprint down the ramp, pirouetting through the tie-dyed crowd. My heart pounds, not so much from fear as from exhilaration.

I find the key under the driver's seat, start the bus, and drive slowly out through the parking lots. The acid hums in my chest and throat, and I feel the familiar sense of godlike clearheadedness. We have a contingency plan. It involves parking at the end of a dirt road a few miles away, the surface of which turns out to be barely passable, pitted and deeply grooved by intermittent washouts. I drive relentlessly, the bus bobbing and rocking and sometimes bottoming out on ruts and exposed bedrock. The road ends at an abandoned mine, a ruined edifice of decaying timbers with a caved-in roof of rusting tin. I experience a strong feeling of déjà vu. There's no river nearby that I can see, and the pine forest begins a little farther up in the mountains, but suddenly I have the sense that I'm closer to the place the vision has shown me than I've ever been before.

I step out into the red evening, the bus sighing and clicking its disapproval at such rough treatment. Alert and purposeful, I begin climbing the hillside in the direction of the amphitheater, each step loosening a glassy chorus of scree.

When I gain the ridge top the back of the theater rears up gloriously before me, the twin monoliths pulsating to the rhythm of my heartbeat in the golden pre-dusk light. Linking the two rocks is a high brick wall, and beyond this wall is my goal. I can already hear the thumping of the bass.

I take off my shoes to scale the wall. My hands and feet cling to the brick surface like the suction toes of a gecko. There's a guard pacing the wall; I slither over the top just as he turns away and melt into the dancing audience, laughing aloud at my own bold skill. The band is playing "Shakedown Street." Jerry's guitar notes are like basketball-sized raindrops splattering on the concrete steps all around me. I make a little game of dodging them. In the distance, the lights of Denver wink conspiratorially.

Things start to go wrong when I see the policemen. There are two of them, shoving their way up through the crowded amphitheater. One keeps scanning the crowd, looking for someone, and of course I assume he's looking for me, so I duck down beneath the head-level of the bobbing dancers, take off my shirt, and tie a blue bandana around my head. "Shakedown Street" is reaching a crescendo; the crowd whirls in synchronous fury. I forget about the policemen, but the feeling of unease has entered my bloodstream like a virus. Worrying that one of Jerry's huge guitar-note raindrops is going to hit me, I drop into a crouch, covering my head with my arms and scuttling this way and that like a sand crab searching for a hole. Then I worry that my lungs are going to collapse. I turn to the person next to me for help, but his face is distorted: sickly green, reptilian, devoid of any warmth or sympathy.

Overcome by an inescapable sense of calamity, I shoulder my way through the crowd up to the back wall. I consider making a swan dive over the edge, to end my pitiful existence on the same sharp rocks I'd scrambled up a short time before. But then the music changes. The band is easing into a rendition of "Mississippi Half Step," another of my favorites.

I take a deep breath and turn away from the wall. The crowd is blotted out in a flash of white light, and suddenly I'm back in the vision, and I mean really *in* it. I'm standing on the bank of a murmuring tea-colored river. On the far side of the river the forest rears up steeply, a dark mantle of conifers giving way to a high mountain cirque, a forbidding wall of white bowls broken by cliff bands and jagged granite spires. The wind peels fresh snow off the summits, long white meteor-tails backed by a sky of the deepest blue imaginable. Under my bare feet, smooth cobbles grind gently against one another, and my nostrils burn with the scent of pine smoke. I see the clothesline, with the snapping of its three bright calico dresses clearly audible over the low roar of the river. Faintly, beneath the other noises, is the female laughter and singing. It's the most beautiful sound I've ever heard.

I walk along the riverbank toward the clothesline, which is strung up between two small pines at the edge of the forest. My heart pounds with anticipation, and it occurs to me—not for the first time—that with their sundresses flapping in the wind, the three women will surely be naked. Out of consideration for their modesty, I take off my own shorts and underwear. Meanwhile, the wind has picked up, howling around my naked body. I lean into it, focusing all my energy on putting one foot in front of the other.

Finally I get to the clothesline and duck under the snapping dresses. The singing stops, and there are no women. There's an old campfire in a circle of blackened river cobbles, but the flames have long ago been snuffed out, and the wind has scattered the dead ashes. I sit on the ground with my bare back up against a boulder beside the fire pit. The wind seems to have reached hurricane force. From across the river comes the sharp crack of splintering tree trunks.

The Money Pill

Suppose a beautiful woman catches your eye on the street. A complete stranger, you understand, but unbelievably attractive, like a starlet, or one of those women you glimpse maybe half a dozen times a year and you say "damn" under your breath, and for the rest of the day your heart just aches. When she has your attention she gives you this smile, a smile meant only for you, and so full of meaning that it stops you in your tracks.

Or maybe she touches you on the arm as you pass on the crowded sidewalk. A little guitar pluck, somewhere between a caress and a grab, and she purses her lips as she does it. So again you stop, and you turn to watch the elegant sway of her hips as she walks away into the crowd. But just before you lose sight of her she turns and gives you this mocking look over her shoulder that says, Well? Why aren't you following?

My first Cuban girlfriend was only nineteen, slender and pretty, a student of accounting at the

University of Santiago. She caught my eye across a mobbed cathedral terrace overlooking the annual Burning of the Devil in the main square. A few minutes later—magical coincidence—she appeared at my side. We gazed down on the crowd filling the plaza: bare chests and shoulders shaking to the conga, black umbrellas bobbing like voodoo talismans to the rhythm of whistles and drums and old hubcaps. We talked about America, the embargo, politics. She professed to be astonished by the fluency of my Spanish. Her fingers brushed my forearm, then came to rest there, as if we were already lovers.

Down in the plaza, they set fire to the effigy. Yellow flames licked delicately around the sides of the horned straw man, tasting it, then leapt explosively, consuming the Devil in a roaring conflagration that illuminated the walls of the square and the faces of the crowd in flickering, orange light.

I told the girl I had to go. Her pretty mouth formed a pout. "Truly? You're leaving me?"

I leaned in and raised my voice over the loud drumming that had resumed down in the plaza. "I have a tour group coming in tomorrow. I need to be at the airport first thing. Otherwise, I'd stay."

"I thought we were going to be friends." She appeared deeply crestfallen. I hesitated.

"We *can* be friends. Give me your number."

She didn't have a phone, but she wrote down her name and address on one of my business cards: Lisbet Romero Morales, Calle Alfred Zamora No. 51, entre 5 y 6, reparto Santa Bárbara. "Ask anyone where is Santa

Bárbara," she said, gazing deeply into my eyes. "And if you come, don't bring the tour group."

❧

I couldn't get Lisbet out of my thoughts. Why not pay her a visit? I asked myself. What harm could it do?

So two nights after the Burning of the Devil, once the exhausted retirees were tucked in at the hotel, I stuffed a roll of convertible pesos into my pocket and stepped out onto the teeming street. It didn't take me long to locate a car to commandeer as a taxi, a red and white '57 Buick. The driver was a hulking *criollo* with a brushy Joe Stalin moustache. I told him to take me to Santa Bárbara.

"I don't know the address," I lied. "Just take me to the neighborhood, and I'll walk."

The driver nodded, gazing at me in the rearview. The fact is, he made me feel uncomfortable from the beginning. He kept glancing at me in the mirror, his eyes full of some vaguely unpleasant emotion, sadness or envy or anger.

Through the rolled-down windows the street noise was as jarring as ever, loud salsa music and cracked mufflers and the rattling undercarriages of decrepit trucks and recycled Canadian school buses. Santiago was a hilly city, like a disintegrating San Francisco. French-style colonial townhouses and slumping hardwood bungalows from the city's heyday as a pirate capital in the 1700's mingled with teetering, post-1959 cinder-block monstrosities. An old man in a beret and an olive drab uniform, sweat-stained and threadbare from half a century of use, hawked newspapers for the equivalent of a penny. The stagnant air smelled of diesel and urine and cigar smoke.

The driver let me out on a quiet street. I asked him to wait two hours. He grunted in assent, watching me with resentful eyes.

There were no working streetlights in the neighborhood, and it had a menacing flavor at night. Man-shaped shadows prowled the alleyways, and there were no police or soldiers on patrol. I concentrated on making my stride purposeful, unassailable. Images of Lisbet kept appearing in my mind. Long, slim fingers. The taut arc of her thigh and buttock pressing against my thigh on the crowded cathedral terrace.

The address written in my daybook matched that of a small wooden bungalow—not, I was relieved to find, one of the crowded cinderblock buildings or subdivided mansions. The pale-blue light of a television seeped out through gaps in the ancient hardwood planking.

I climbed the steps to the porch. I hesitated a moment, then knocked.

Lisbet answered the door wearing purple Lycra shorts and a faded military tank top with no bra. Long-legged and barefoot, she appeared both surprised and pleased to see me. Three small children craned their heads around to peer up at me for a moment before returning their gaze to the television. The whole room was bathed in that ghostly blue light.

Lisbet took my hand and led me down the hall to a back room lit by a naked bulb. A younger girl, whom

I later came to know as her sister, was sprawled out on the bed reading a dog-eared novel. Lisbet got the sister up and shooed her out. As she was leaving, the younger girl paused in the doorway to favor me with a very lewd wink.

"Maybe this isn't the best idea," I said when the sister was gone.

Lisbet shook her head, smiling. "*Qué va.* I'm glad you came. I didn't know if you would." She placed her hands on my shoulders and pushed me down onto the foam-rubber mattress. The bed was a sheet of plywood propped up on cinderblocks. I attempted to keep my breath even to slow down my racing heart. You might not believe it, but this was the first time I'd done anything remotely like this.

She knelt on the floor and put a cassette in a paint-spattered boom box that must have been at least twenty years old. A lukewarm breeze came in through the window slats as we both undressed. The cassette was Joni Mitchell.

Don't get me wrong: I'd had girlfriends before. Nothing like this, though. Not a girl I'd met in the street and come to visit for the specific purpose of having sex. But then, I'm not the only foreigner who's behaved differently in Cuba than he would at home.

After it was over, Lisbet and I lounged on the bed in silence. The Joni Mitchell tape ended, and down the hall the muffled television blared. At risk of drifting off to sleep, I got up and started getting dressed. Lisbet rolled over to watch me, a teasing smile playing across her lips. "Don't dress. I'm not finished with you."

"I have to get back," I explained. "The tour group. You remember."

She stopped smiling and sat up, not bothering to cover her generous, inquisitive breasts. "Stay with me. You can get up early. I'll make you a good Cuban breakfast."

"No. I really have to go." I took a roll of twenty-peso bills out of my shorts pocket and saw from her dismayed expression that I'd made a mistake. But it was too late to change course. She watched in wide-eyed alarm as I pulled three crisp bills off the roll. I held them out for her to take and she glanced at them in distaste.

"I'm not a prostitute," she said, quietly indignant. "I'm a student of accounting."

I was embarrassed, but I tried to put the best face on things. "I *know* you're not a prostitute. But I also know you can use this money. Please, take it, as a gift. For your family."

She shook her head. Her eyes had filled with tears. I sat beside her on the mattress and put my arm over her naked shoulder. It felt awkward, so I took the arm back. "Look," I said. "I'm sorry. But you *do* need the money, don't you?"

After a moment she nodded, tears flowing, and held out her hand for the twenties.

If you went to Cuba before the opening, then you know that the island held a peculiar kind of magic for visitors. It was a gritty time capsule, a rustic, communist Never Never Land. Cubans were lean, handsome, well educated, and literally starving for cash. Doctors and engineers had to skip meals in order to stay afloat. The government issued ration coupons, but it wasn't enough to make ends meet. If you were a tourist—if your pockets were full of international currency—everybody wanted to know you. You possessed a special magnetism, unlike anything you'd ever experienced in your home country. It was like one of those amazing dreams where you discover a new superpower. It was as if you'd swallowed a pill that had transformed you into Johnny Depp or George Clooney. It was easier than you might think to lose touch with reality.

My second Cuban girlfriend was older than Lisbet, and somewhat less educated. The retirees had gone home, pleased with the sanitized experience of Cuba I'd provided for them, and I had a few independent days before the next group came. I rode out of the city in the same '57 Buick as before, the driver having been pleased enough with the tip I'd given him to set up operations outside the hotel as my personal chauffeur. We took the western highway, past rusting tankers, billboards with anti-imperialist slogans, and oil refineries chugging out their clouds of poison. I told the driver to stop at a small beach overlooking a shipwreck. A Cuban tour guide had pointed it out to me several weeks earlier, a Spanish ironclad from 1898 visible as two massive, rusted gun turrets jutting out at weird angles from the turquoise sea. In college I'd done a term paper on Teddy Roosevelt's Rough Riders, and it was my intention to snorkel out and explore the wreck.

Stepping down off the highway onto the pleasantly shaded beach, I nearly bumped into Yanita. Lovely Yanita, with bracelets on her wrists and a thick Pocahontas braid teased forward over one nut-brown shoulder. Sexy Yanita, her curvy body only minimally concealed by a threadbare yellow sundress. She sold me a polished conch shell for a peso and offered to watch my duffel bag while I snorkeled. Her availability for other services was clear from the beginning, but I'd come to explore the wreck. Grinning sheepishly, I took my roll of convertible pesos out of the duffel and stowed it in the pocket of my swim trunks. The undivided attention of a woman so fetching made me feel like an awkward teenager.

The water was clear, fading out in all directions to voids of opaque blue. Not far beyond the beach, the bottom dropped away, algae-covered rocks slanting down to a distant blue basin of featureless sand. I hate deep water. It makes me feel vulnerable to attack from below. The wreck was farther out than it had looked. Several times, I almost panicked and turned back. But the basin slanted up again, and I began to see fragments of the ironclad. Soon I was drifting slowly over the prow of the ship, its well-preserved outlines encrusted by coral. The hull had been split in half by American artillery, but otherwise it was surprisingly intact. Beneath the coral crust I could make out the steam drivers, the bunkrooms, the galley, and of course the bases of the two gun turrets, one of which I climbed in order to take a rest. Dripping and pleased with myself, I took off the mask and breathed in the rich tropical air. I gazed at the distant shoreline: the sea grapes and gently swaying palms. I could make out Yanita in her lemon-colored dress, waiting faithfully beside the green speck of my duffel. I waved to her. She waved back. I decided to head in.

She was waiting in the shade of an old sea grape, leaning against the smooth sweep of the trunk with the duffel on the white pebbles at her feet. She handed me my towel and watched intently as I dried off and put on my t-shirt. Her desire for me was exaggerated, almost slavish, but I believed (and still believe) that it wasn't entirely artificial. I sensed primal forces brewing within Yanita's alluring frame. Deep loneliness combined with a lust willed into being by actual gnawing hunger.

She took me by the hand and led me to a rough wooden shack hidden in the mangroves at the far end of the beach. The shack was empty and there was no electric light, but bright slats of sunlight streamed in through gaps in the weathered planks. I could make out the ashes of a small cooking fire, and a military-issue cot with rusting sidebars. Yanita gestured toward the cot and I sat down. She shrugged off the sundress.

There's no point in going into detail about what happened next, other than to note that her hands were callused from manual labor and that she was passionate, beautiful, and quite vocal. There was no formal transaction, though I left a few twenty peso notes tucked discretely under a skillet on the bare earth next to the fire pit. It pleased me to think that this was probably more money than she would make in an entire year. That she and her children—and I had no doubt there were children—would be well fed for at least a few months.

On the way back into the city in the '57 Buick, I sang aloud to an Eliades Ochoa tune I was listening to on my iPod:

Como no tengo dinero, tu cariño es falsedad.
Falsedad, falsedad, tu cariño es falsedad.

The driver turned to me with a look of disgust on his big, mustachioed face. "Why you sing that?" he asked in English.

"I don't know," I replied, momentarily caught off guard. "I just felt like singing, and this is the music I'm listening to."

He turned his gaze back to the road. "So you do everything you want?"

"Sure. As long as it's not hurting anybody."

He shook his head, and the conversation ended. My mood had soured, and I resented him for it. He seemed to believe that he had some insight into my character that I couldn't see for myself. I decided that it was time to find a new driver.

My next Cuban love interest was Marisleysis, a dancer. She was one of a half-dozen salsa instructors at a rooftop studio adjacent to the main plaza, where I'd arranged lessons for a museum group from Chicago. The way she moved her body attracted my attention. She wasn't beautiful per se, but she was striking, with ice-blue eyes and the light, freckled complexion Cubans usually associate with Galician ancestry. Her face had a solemn, serious cast that I found intriguing. When she danced, it was pure magic.

I kept trying to catch her eye, but she refused to participate. So I joined the line to learn the dance step myself. When my turn came up Marisleysis was polite and professionally courteous, but cool. I found her reserve intriguing. I determined to win her over.

The Chicagoans were enthusiastic. They wanted to keep going beyond the hour-long lesson, which would end up costing extra and eating into my profit, but I didn't care. My eyes kept returning to Marisleysis. I loved her self-contained grace as she moved through the salsa steps. When my turn came I reveled in the sensation of my hand resting on the curve of her dancer's waist.

After the lesson I paid the studio director and gave him a generous tip to distribute among the dancers. I waited by the stairs for Marisleysis. She'd changed into street clothes, jeans and a black t-shirt. She had a book bag slung over her shoulder and wore heavy horn-rimmed glasses, which gave her an irresistibly studious, schoolgirl look. "Can I talk to you for a moment?"

"Of course." She nodded, eyeing me coolly from behind the lenses.

"Thank you for the way you interacted with the group. It was impressive. Everyone enjoyed it thoroughly."

"It was nothing," she replied with a modest wave of her hand. "We collaborate. Each one plays a role. I am glad you are satisfied with the class." She glanced toward the stairwell. I felt myself reddening.

"I was wondering if you'd be willing to give me private lessons. I would pay you well. In dollars, if you wish."

She regarded me with a stony expression. "Private lessons for foreigners are against the law in Cuba."

"So are private taxis," I replied, "but they still operate." I glanced at the studio director, who was standing just out of earshot, pretending not to watch us. "Listen, we could keep it between ourselves. No one would have to know."

She turned toward the stairwell. "I am glad the class was successful."

"Think it over," I called out, as she vanished down the stairs.

I got her schedule from another dancer, one who was more pragmatic about the power of foreign currency. Three nights after the salsa lesson, with the museum group wrapped up and headed back to Chicago, I walked over to a small theater near the university to attend a performance of what my source had called a "*baile folklórico*."

It was *carnaval* in Santiago. The streets were filled with lean, sweat-soaked revelers drinking white rum out of plastic water bottles. The mood in the air was tense and watchful, a feeling of repressed violence just beneath the surface. The theater space offered some refuge from the sweating mob outside. A few other tourists had found their way in, possibly feeling equally discomfited by the atmosphere in the streets, sun-bleached Australians or Germans, from the look of them. Other than those few, the patrons were entirely Cuban.

The other tourists stood sheepishly against the back wall, but I wanted to get closer to the stage. Some of the other audience members turned to glare at me as I shouldered my way down the center aisle. Their expressions were aggressively contemptuous, reminding me of the look the taxi driver had given me when I started singing to Eliades Ochoa on my iPod. I began to wonder what exactly these people thought they saw in me, but I quickly shoved that thought into the back of my mind. Marisleysis was so beautiful. I had to see her.

The performance began with rattles and bells and a weird, low chanting in Yoruba, an African language. At first, it seemed predictable enough, with the dancers filing out one by one in costumes representing the Orishas, the deities of the Afro-Cuban religion of Santería. Marisleysis came out in a lacy, white wedding gown. There was a veil covering her face, but I recognized her immediately from the way she moved. When all the Orishas were out on stage, it became clear that each one was associated with an element, such as fire or water, and some other state of being, such as purity, anger, or crippling illness.

Two of the drummers brought out a large slab of rusted steel. It might have been a part from a giant truck or a tractor. It was shaped like a plow, and something about the sight of it caused the hairs on the back of my neck to prickle. The drummers struck it with pipes. It made a sound like a bell, only flatter and much less cheerful. It was a deathly sound, in fact, and it chilled me to the bone. I had to struggle not to get up and leave.

Meanwhile, the dancers launched into a frenzy. Their movements were rapid and mechanical. Their faces had gone blank with an almost sexual ecstasy. One muscular dancer who'd been hobbling across the stage on crutches pretending to be a cripple fell into what looked like an epileptic seizure, clenched and twitching and literally foaming at the mouth. Another, dressed in black, lit three torches and began to juggle. Suddenly the drumming stopped, and the lights in the theater went out. The crowd gasped. The dancer who'd been juggling guzzled a clear liquid from a plastic bottle and then spit out a long tongue of fire that leapt across the crowd, filling the room with a ghastly orange light. The people around me, delighted, touched their hair to see if it had been singed.

I was transfixed by dread. I couldn't escape the fact that the fire dancer's eyes, glinting like coal in the flickering light, were staring directly and accusingly into mine.

After the performance, I was a bit shaken up. But I was still determined to talk to Marisleysis, and I found myself following her as she left the theatre. The crowd parted in her wake. She seemed to possess some kind of innate authority that even the drunkest of the revelers instinctively honored. At the door to what I assumed was her apartment, I stepped out of the shadows to make myself known.

"You! What are you doing here?" She was surprised to see me, obviously, and not in a good way.

I held up my hands and gave her a reassuring smile. "Don't worry! I saw your performance, and I thought I'd take the opportunity to circle back with you about those private lessons."

"You followed me *home*?" She was staring at me as if I were a giant cockroach that had just crawled up from the gutter. She was even more beautiful than I remembered, dressed in the same jeans and black t-shirt as before, with those library-chic horn-rimmed glasses.

She took out a key and pushed open the door to her apartment. "Goodbye," she said, half-turning. "Please do not follow me again, or I will be forced to call the police."

"I only wanted to talk," I protested.

Inside now, she started to swing the door closed. Seeing that this was my last chance, I darted through the door before she could shut it, and there I was, inside her small apartment. She lunged for the phone. I grabbed her forearm, which was wiry, but not strong enough to escape my grip. "Look, all I ask is that you give me a chance. I could help you out, you know, in a number of ways."

Her face was deeply flushed. She looked angry, but not frightened. Above the phone there was a signed photograph of a young Fidel Castro, a tall, bearded youth in a forested landscape, with rumpled fatigues and a rifle in his hand. I'd never been able to understand his appeal for Cubans, but now, looking at this picture, I could see how someone like Marisleysis might find him heroic. "You are a pig," she spat. "You and your whole *yuma* country are pigs."

Suddenly ashamed, I let go of her arm. I quickly apologized and let myself out. As I shut the door behind me, she was reaching for the phone.

I spent the rest of that night lying awake in my hotel room, bracing for the knock at my door.

The knock never came, and in that respect I suppose I was lucky. The whole incident left me in a depressed, self-loathing mood. I found myself replaying in my mind the events of the previous weeks. I began to wonder what kind of person I'd become. The thing was, I'd always thought of myself as a decent guy, someone worthy of affection and respect. But the look in Marisleysis's eyes—like the taxi driver's, and the people's at the theatre—told a different story.

I found my thoughts returning to my first Cuban girlfriend, Lisbet. Her playful friendliness. How she'd asked me to stay for breakfast. How she'd cried when she took my money. Was I wrong to imagine that she'd actually *liked* me?

After a few days of indecision, I decided to pay her another visit. That night, as with many nights, there was a widespread blackout in Santiago, and there was no moon, so most of the city was drowned in deep, tropical darkness. I sat in the back seat of my new taxi, a blue '58 Oldsmobile, as the driver guided me through the inky night to the Santa Bárbara neighborhood. This time, not relishing the idea of walking alone in this blackness, I gave him the address.

As I stepped up onto the creaky porch my heart pounded with excitement. My intentions are pure, I told myself. I looked forward to seeing Lisbet again, getting to know her for real this time, and letting her get to know me. It almost felt like a homecoming.

The younger sister, Lisbet's lighter-skinned double, answered the door holding a candle. She wore a tank top that glowed yellow in the light of the single flame.

"*Buenas noches*," I said with a brotherly smile. "Is Lisbet at home?"

The girl shook her head. "She went to Havana." I couldn't help noticing that she wasn't wearing a bra. The outlines of her nipples were clearly visible under the thin cotton. Behind her, the house was dark and silent.

Before I could say anything else, she'd taken my hand and pulled me inside. There was candlelight coming from the back bedroom where I'd made love to Lisbet. The girl led me there, and I didn't protest. On the windowsill, two guttering candle stubs illuminated the louvered window and a hardcover novel lying spine-up on the bed. The girl had been burning incense as she read.

"I'll return later," I said. "When do you expect her back?"

She was already peeling off the tank top. Despite myself, I felt stirrings of arousal.

"What's your name?" I asked. The words came out in a hoarse whisper. The girl stood in her panties with her arms crossed self-consciously over her breasts, gazing at me in the flickering yellow light like some kind of beaming, attention-starved wood nymph.

"Hiawatha."

"Hiawatha? Really?" I smiled sadly. Picking up the hardcover, I closed it and squinted at the spine: *Pride and Prejudice*, a well-thumbed Spanish translation. I rested the book on the windowsill.

Slowly, she let her arms drop to her sides and then opened them slightly, as if offering herself for my delectation. She was long-legged and as lithe as a gazelle, with dark-nippled breasts high and budding in the candlelight. I felt dizzy. "How old are you, Hiawatha?"

"Seventeen."

"I don't believe you. How old really?"

She frowned and shrugged. "Fourteen."

"Fourteen?"

"Fourteen." She raised her eyes and took a step toward me. "What does it matter? As you can see, I'm a woman already. And you are a man, no? An American?"

I fled that house like you would flee in one of those nightmares where you've committed a crime, and you don't remember exactly what the crime was, but it doesn't matter because you know it was bad, and the consequences will be bad, and there's nothing you can do to make it better. On my way out I tossed a roll of twenties into a plastic bowl that was resting on the television. Whatever was in my pocket at the time, maybe a few hundred pesos.

Out on the porch, heart racing, I stopped short. Suddenly I could see myself clearly: the person the taxi driver saw, the person the people in the theater saw, the person Marisleysis saw. I thought about going back to get the money out of the bowl, but it was too late. There was no way to take it back.

Six Feet under the Prairie

Surely I can be forgiven for misjudging Billy Hurley. I was only nineteen that summer, so it's understandable that I didn't see him for more than he appeared at first glance: a thirtyish Okie pretending to be something he wasn't. He couldn't have been a real cowboy anyway, not in the middle of the 1980s, even if he did look the part: the cowhide ropers, the alternating duo of threadbare western-cut shirts, the greasy, Custer-length hair, the straw-colored handlebar moustache of which he was obviously so proud. The crew gave him plenty of guff for his low-budget cowpoke look, but he wasn't easily provoked; he would just shake his head and stare off into the distance, his undernourished face taking on an air of moonfaced sadness, like a saint in some old Spanish painting.

I'll never forget the day I called him out. I don't know exactly what drove me to it. I was the college boy, the summer help, still uneasy among the full-time journeymen electricians on the crew. I suppose I was eager to overcome my discomfort by joining in on the sarcastic workingmen's banter. And though it shames me to think of it today, I must have seen Billy as a safe target.

From afar, the scene would have looked like this: two forest-green utility trucks at rest on a rolling yellow prairie among scattered pine glades and cottonwood gullies; beyond that, a band of green foothills; and beyond them, on the western horizon, the massive, blue-dun profile of the Colorado Front Range. Zoom in some and you would smell the air, clean and peppery with sage. Zoom in some more and you would see five men in hard hats, sprawled out around the two trucks in attitudes of insolent relaxation: an electrical line crew on lunch break, and the college kid sitting in one of the trucks leaning out of the open window to vocalize an unthinking insult.

In a surprisingly fluid series of motions Billy whipped off his hard hat, tossed his sandwich into it as he got up, and wiped his hands on his dirty boot-cut Wranglers as he strode over to the truck. "What'd you call me?"

"A cowboy-wannabe?"

"Step on out here and call me that, you little fuck." His face was only a couple of feet away from mine, and though technically I was bigger, I couldn't help noticing that the tendons under the freckled skin on his neck stood out like leather cords. His eyes—usually vague and bewildered, as if he'd gone to sleep beside a campfire and woken up beside a six-lane highway—had become small and mean, like one of those black-and-white archive photographs of Appalachian dirt farmers. Beyond him, arrayed on the ground and the fenders of the cable truck, were the other journeymen: Bruce, a middle-aged, ex-Navy man; and Mike and Ignacio, two Mexican-American cousins in their early thirties. Next to me, in the driver's seat of the utility truck, was Buck Blackshere, the crew chief. I glanced at him for support, but he shrugged noncommittally, making it clear that I was on my own in this. I opened the door and slid down off the seat, letting my weight settle into the soles of my work boots on the hard-packed dirt. It was a cloudless summer day, and the sun was hot on my shoulders. I slammed the door of the truck. The sound rolled out over the prairie like a gunshot.

"High Noon," I quipped, my attempt at a smile failing because my throat was clenched up with nervousness and I kept needing to swallow. It was the first time I'd seen anyone's temper flare up on the crew, and it took me by surprise. I felt caught in the act, like a schoolboy who lobs a snowball at a passing car, and the brake lights go on, and the car fishtails to a stop, and both doors swing open.

Billy put his head down and came at me. I ducked, grabbed his arm, and leaned in—I grew up with an older brother, so my reflexes were good for that kind of thing— and he came flying over my shoulder and landed on his backside, his head bouncing against the front tire of the truck. I spun to face him, but he just sat there panting in the dust, as if that one lunge had used up all his energy. By now, the rest of the crew was having a good laugh at his expense.

My uncle was a vice president of the Public Service Company of Colorado. He arranged for me to work on a line construction crew that summer, but the idea was my own. I had two years of college behind me, and although this may sound like a cliché, I felt ready for a passage into manhood. Line crews have a reputation for toughness, and a summer of rugged manual labor struck me as exactly the kind of thing I needed, like boot camp without the crew cut or the long-term commitment.

I was assigned to Buck Blackshere's crew. Buck was probably in his mid-sixties that summer, short and athletically built, with a handsome, leathery face, his silver hair cropped and slicked back like a 1940s film star's. He was the kind of chief who inspired his men to hard work without ever raising his voice. I heard him tell jokes, and I heard him recite poetry from memory, but I never heard him bark out an order. If you studied his face, as I did, it was possible to detect a certain tiredness—as if he'd seen too much of life—but he kept up a jolly front. It was well known on the crew that in his youth he'd been the state bronc-riding champ for seven years running, and there was an aura of subdued grandeur about him. I could imagine him as the captain of a privateer, or the good-hearted ringleader of a gang of outlaws.

My first morning on the crew coincided with the first day of the crew's main job that summer, which was laying down the power grid for the Highlands Ranch project, a big subdivision south of Denver. It was an important job, the vanguard of the suburban development that was then pressing southward over the prairie like the invasion of a fast-growing geometrical fungus. Before we left the PSCo warehouse, Buck unrolled the blueprints to show us the power grid, a spiderweb of pencil lines depicting the network of cables linking the transformers that would distribute the electricity to each new street and cul-de-sac. When he'd finished going over the plans, he asked if there were any questions. The only one came from Billy Hurley, who inquired about what type of transformer we'd be installing. Buck read some numbers off the blueprints. Billy spat tobacco juice into a Coke can and asked about the diameter of the cable. Buck read off a few more numbers, and Billy nodded solemnly, as if it made a difference. I noticed the other men exchange glances. Apparently this was a scenario they'd seen play out before.

The second confrontation came a few days after the first. It was one of those mornings along the Front Range when the outlines of the mountains are so crisp they could be painted on canvas, a flat backdrop of stone-gray peaks and wide bowls under a pure blue sky. We'd been digging trench, and as we did every day at ten o'clock, we broke for coffee. Preparing the coffee was the grunt's job, so while everyone else relaxed around the utility trucks I hoisted myself up and lifted the industrial-grade orange-and-white thermos from its bracket and eased it down onto the open door of a side cabinet, which doubled as a worktable. I dropped to the ground, got out a sleeve of styrofoam coffee cups, and stood it on end beside the thermos.

"Coffee, your majesties." Every day I'd been trying out new ways of announcing it, using different accents and titles and such. Billy usually grimaced, as if the sound of my voice made his ears ring.

"Pour me a cup, pin-dick." He was reclining on a spent cable spool between the trucks and the newly dug trench. Everyone's eyes came to rest on me.

"Get it yourself."

"Nope, pin-dick. You get it for me."

I poured a cup, carefully added the non-dairy creamer and a packet of sugar, stirred, and took a sip, all the while staring coolly at Billy, whose lean, freckled face had gone a deep crimson.

"Last chance, college boy. Final warning."

"Ease off, men," Buck said mildly. He was studying a clipboard that he held on his thigh with his elbow, one foot up on the bumper of the truck.

Billy glanced at the crew chief and let out his breath in a long exhalation, the low-drooping sidebars of his moustache trembling like prairie grass. With a kind of full-body shrug he made to get up, but the spool tipped over, pitching him on his backside in the dirt. The big spindle rolled away, seeming to pause for effect at the edge of the trench before it rolled in. There was a moment of dead silence. Then the whole crew burst out hooting and snorting.

Billy sat with his legs splayed on the dirt. The sun was inching higher, and in the heat-shimmer, his scrawny body seemed to quiver and blur, as if it might evaporate or burst suddenly into flame.

I kept an eye on him in case he came at me again, but his expression was more sad than angry, and he wasn't looking at me. He was looking at Buck Blackshere, who was still studying the clipboard, his face hidden in shadow under the brim of his hard hat.

When I was a boy, my grandfather used to take me out to Highlands Ranch to see the West as it used to be. He knew Mr. Carlson, the old rancher whose family had settled the area along Cherry Creek that would later become Denver way back during the Gold Rush. On a good day out at the ranch, you could see deer, antelope, coyote, red-tailed hawks, two kinds of falcon, and the occasional golden eagle. There was a horse-path that started from the old stone mansion and wound along a sandy-bottomed gulch through glades of scrub oak and juniper into the open prairie. After a fall rain, the smell of sage was strong in the air, a sharp, immaculate wilderness scent that will always be linked in my imagination to Arapaho hunting parties and leather-skinned cowboys riding the unfenced plain.

One day—I was probably twelve or thirteen at the time—my grandfather and I came upon a dying calf in a meadow at the edge of a ponderosa glade. We heard it before we saw it; it was caught like the prey of some huge, malignant spider in a length of barbed wire, crying out in hoarse, panicked bleats as it slowly strangled itself, the wire looped around its neck in such a way that the more it struggled, the tighter the wire became.

"Hold it steady while I try to free it," my grandfather said. I still remember the fragrant warmth of its flanks and the labored heave of its rib cage as I leaned into it and hugged.

We got it loose, but it was bleeding badly from the neck. It tried to run away, but one of its legs was broken or dislocated, and it sank to its knees in the buffalo grass, wild-eyed and softly moaning. My grandfather walked over to his horse and unstrapped his .22 rifle from the saddle.

"Do we have to kill it?" I asked.

The old man pursed his lips. He'd been a large-animal veterinarian, and although he was already retired by then, if there was anyone who could do something to save the calf, it was him.

"But there must be *something* we can do," I pleaded.

He put his hand on my shoulder. "Sometimes death is the only kindness we can offer, Tommy."

He held the barrel to the animal's forehead. It stopped moaning and gazed up at us, its sad eyes seeming to comprehend what was in store. I averted my gaze, but the shot rang out and I heard the bullet puncture the animal's skull with a fleshy pop, like cutting into a pumpkin. I turned back in time to see a tremor pass through the calf's body. Then it lay still. We rode on in silence, in a light drizzle, with the perfume of sage in our nostrils.

After that, my grandfather and I came out to the ranch less often. We would talk about it all the time, but somehow it became harder and harder to arrange. Soon I was a teenager, with plenty of other things on my mind.

My grandfather became ill the summer I worked on the line crew. When I visited him in the hospital, he asked me what I'd been doing with myself, and when I told him I'd been working out at Highlands Ranch, the light came back into his face for a moment. But then he must have realized the nature of the work—falling beef prices and skyrocketing property taxes had forced the Carlsons to sell out several years earlier—and his eyes dimmed as he let his head sink back into the hospital pillow. I had a strange sensation, as though I was sitting on the edge of a precipice and he was tumbling slowly away from me into the dark void below.

When my mother told me he'd died, the nature of my grief surprised me. It wasn't sadness so much as an overpowering emptiness. And there was something else worrying the edges of that emptiness, a gnawing sense of guilt that I didn't fully recognize at the time, but that has since grown as familiar as the ache of an ill-fitting pair of boots.

The morning was overcast and gray, a rarity on the Front Range in summer. The peaks were hidden by a dull billow of clouds, and we could have been in Kansas for all the featurelessness of the landscape. Bruce and the Mexicans had gone back to the warehouse to load a new spool of cable, and Buck was pacing out the day's work. I was shoveling out the bottom of the trench while Billy used the backhoe to open the ground ahead. I couldn't see the main body of the machine or the man in the cockpit, just the rusted hydraulic arm with its toothed steel bucket as it dipped to scoop a fresh load of dirt, rose and disappeared in the slot of gray sky over the trench, and returned empty a few minutes later.

My job was to square the bottom of the trench so that the cable would lie flat. The dirt was brittle and hard, shot through with rocks ranging from pebbles to boulders the size of anvils; when I came upon one of these bigger rocks I had to use the blade of my shovel to pry it loose. I was concentrating on an especially stubborn slab when I felt the trench walls shudder. I jerked straight, alert to danger, and saw that Billy had let the bucket come to rest, teeth down, on the dirt-pile just above my head. There was a hissing in my ears, and I remember the cascading dirt giving off a rich, metallic odor, like blood.

Then my world went black.

Next thing I knew I was laid out beside the trench, with Billy's narrow face peering down into mine. His eyes were inscrutable slits, and the sidebars of his stringy moustache trembled with every breath. "Cripes, kid, I thought you was a goner."

My head throbbed. I seemed to have lost the power of speech.

"Rock slid off the pile and clobbered you on the head. I came down and brung you out." Pokerfaced, he spat a long stream of tobacco juice, then resumed staring at me. Perhaps it was my imagination, but his voice seemed remarkably unconcerned, and to my ears the words sounded artificial, as if he might have been rehearsing them while I was unconscious. I sat up and felt my head. My hair was sticky and full of grit, matted with blood and dirt. In the corner of my eye I saw Buck's compact, athletic frame striding briskly toward us with the rolled-up blueprints in one hand. I felt a hot bubble of rage welling up in my esophagus.

"You lads taking coffee break already?" the crew chief called out good-humoredly, but as he got close he must have sensed something wrong, because by the time he came up to us his expression was stern. "What happened here?"

I glanced up at him and shrugged. "Ask Billy."

The crew chief turned to the wiry journeyman squatting on the dirt pile beside me. Billy twitched nervously. "Rock slid off the pile and hit him in the head, Buck. And, well, he wasn't wearing his hard hat."

Bruce and the Mexicans drove up in the other truck. Buck helped me to my feet and led me by the elbow to his truck, where I sat in a kind of daze.

After they'd unloaded the new spool I watched Buck take Billy aside to reprimand him. From my vantage point inside the truck I couldn't tell what he was saying, but I could see by the way he was jabbing his finger in the air that he was giving the Oklahoman a good dressing down. Billy was shaking his head, and every once in a while he would try to stammer out some kind of defense, but Buck wasn't brooking interruptions. Eventually Billy stopped trying to argue, and his face took on the pale gray shade of poured cement before it sets. The crew chief made a final angry point, and Billy spun and strode over to the backhoe, kicking dirt as he went. He hoisted himself into the cockpit of the big yellow machine and slouched in the seat, pulling his hard hat down over his eyes as if he wanted to take a cowboy-style nap.

Buck insisted on driving me in to the medical department, though I insisted that the bump on my head was nothing serious. We took the high road, a dirt track along an elevated ridge with a view of the whole area. As I gazed out at that landscape, it dawned on me that our work was having quite an impact on the prairie. The Highlands Ranch my grandfather and I had known was barely recognizable beneath the maze-like ridges of dry clotted earth piled up beside the trenches and foundation holes. I wondered where all the wildlife had gone. South, probably, although before long it would run up against Colorado Springs, which was undergoing its own sprawl northward. To the east was farm and feedlot country, where the soil was mostly used up, eroded by wind and rain, or saturated with chemical fertilizers. All of it had been prairie once. I closed my eyes and imagined the rolling hills, the herds of buffalo, the tall grass nodding in the wind.

We hit pavement on County Line Road and took a right, then veered left at University, which led north through the suburbs to downtown Denver. Buck drove in silence, looking wise and weathered, like an Indian war chief or an old time mariner, with one sculpted, brown hand on the wheel and the other at rest on his dusty, denim-clad knee. I asked him what he'd said to Billy.

"I reminded him that it's his duty to supervise the summer help when the rest of us can't. I gave him a few additional tips as well." He glanced in the rearview and said mildly, as if to himself: "I may have been a little hard on the little bastard, honestly."

"Did he say how it happened?"

He darted me an angry look. "What are you getting at, kid?"

There was an awkward pause. "Tommy," he said after a while, "Billy may be a fool, and being of your generation, you'd most likely call him a loser. He's got a thin skin, and he lacks the skill with words to say his piece in such a way that the other men will shut up long enough to listen. But he ain't deliberately vicious. It was an accident, just like he said."

The truck came to a stop at a traffic light and Buck turned to me. "And by the way, don't *ever* let me hear about you working in a trench without a hard hat on. You got that?"

I felt my ears redden. "Yeah. Got it."

We drove on in silence. The sun peeked shyly through the clouds, illuminating a gleam of new snow on the mountains. Nearer at hand, on both sides of the avenue, we were driving through a garish panorama of billboards, condos, and townhouses, unnaturally green lawns with sprinklers going full blast, strips of identical mini-malls of Seven-Elevens and Taco Bells and Kinko's that seemed to have sprouted up throughout the metropolitan area like colonies of bright, self-cloning mushrooms. We drove into the old suburbs, decaying brick Victorians with drier, weedy lawns, and I reached up to feel my head again, the mat of dried blood. In my grandfather's day these neighborhoods would have marked the very outer limits of the city.

"It's a shame," I said, though I don't think I meant to say it aloud.

"What's that, Tommy?"

I hesitated, embarrassed. "It's a shame what we're doing to the prairie. Back at Highlands Ranch, I mean."

"I hear you, kid. But if we weren't doing it, someone else would."

I stared out the window, wondering. Was my uncle to blame because he was upper management? Or was it the fault of the greedy developers—or, for that matter, of the young, middle-class families pursuing their pre-fab version of the American dream? Who could blame them for wanting to watch Rocky Mountain sunsets from their highly affordable decks?

"I'm sorry about what I implied back there," I said. "About Billy, I mean. I do get the feeling he doesn't like me very much."

"And you don't like *him* very much either, do you?"

"I think it's a natural reaction to the fact that he doesn't like me."

Buck regarded me coolly. "It's not as if you've really given him a chance, Tommy. You insulted *him* the other day, remember? Not the other way around."

I nodded, ears burning once again. I knew Buck was right, and I had the feeling that the trouble between Billy and me was far from over.

The next morning Billy and I were given the job of squaring the trench-bottom together. I don't know if it was because of the incident of the day before, or because Buck wanted us to work together, or if he truly felt he needed Billy in the trench, but whatever the reason, the fact that he'd been taken off backhoe duty seemed to bother the Oklahoman quite a bit. It was a hot day, hotter in the trench, where we were exposed to direct sunlight and removed from the cooling breezes that came down off the mountains. Billy was using his shovel as a pick to knock off the rough edges left by the teeth of the backhoe, and I was following behind him, scooping the loose dirt and tossing it up and out of the trench.

He'd been absorbed in the work all morning, aggressively silent. Finally, he spoke over his shoulder, his voice thick with suppressed emotion. "Have a nice ride yesterday?"

"What, down to Medical?" Under my hard hat I felt the slight, almost pleasant ache of the little egg-shaped bump where the rock had hit me. The company doctor had tested for concussion, but there had been no cause for concern. "I *did* have a nice ride, thanks, Billy. Thanks to *you*, I mean." I couldn't resist the urge to spar with him, despite what Buck had said. A certain process had been set in motion within me, an automatic attack mechanism that seemed to have a life of its own.

"Old Buck tell you some of his rodeo stories, did he?"

I scooped another shovelful and tossed it up and out. "Why, Billy? You jealous?"

He didn't reply, occupying himself instead with a flurry of shovel blows at a rock sticking out of the trench wall. I knew that he idolized Buck; in retrospect I see that it was one of the things we had in common.

Several minutes passed. Then he spoke over his shoulder again. "Everything's easy for you, kid, ain't it?"

"What are you *talking* about, Billy?"

He stopped working and turned around, his face pinched with anger. "You told Buck I did it on purpose, didn't you, you little son of a bitch."

"No. Why? It *was* an accident, wasn't it?" Sweat glistened on my forearms, each little pore marked with a pinpoint of black dirt. I gripped the shovel handle and braced for a fight.

"Of course it were an *accident*. I just assumed you'd tell Buck it weren't."

"What's your problem, Billy?"

He was leaning on his shovel, gazing at me. "Problem? Ain't got no problems. *You're* my only problem, pindick." He seemed to have calmed down, but his eyes were unnaturally bright, and there was a weird smile playing at the corners of his lips beneath the drooping moustache. Staring into his face I felt a sensation of vertigo, as if his eyes were exerting some kind of gravitational pull. All of a sudden the walls of the trench seemed to lurch inward, and there was that fresh-dirt smell again, like blood.

I dropped my shovel and heaved myself out of the trench, gasping for air. Up on the open ground I felt a rush of relief, as if I'd just escaped a living burial. Down in the trench Billy shook his head, spat in the dirt, and turned back to the work at hand.

Before I knew it, July and half of August had gone by, and it was my final week on the crew. We'd dug twenty miles of trench and unspooled the equivalent length of cable, splicing dozens of army-green transformer boxes into the circuit as we went. The power grid was nearly done; the gas, water, telephone, and television crews had laid their pipes and cables; and the homebuilders were excavating and pouring eight to ten foundations a day. Highlands Ranch looked less and less like the old prairie and more and more like what it had become: the largest new housing project in the state of Colorado. My time as an agent of the destruction of that patch of wild grassland, the landscape of my childhood, was almost at an end. But I'd be lying if I said I was concerned about it. I was proud of my hardened muscles, basking in the minor triumph of having held my own on a crew of tough workingmen.

Billy Hurley and I had settled into a kind of détente. Once or twice I'd caught him watching me with a strange intensity, brow furrowed and eyes asquint as if he was trying to puzzle something out, but when I met his gaze he would invariably turn away, spitting a stream of tobacco juice in the dirt. He no longer challenged me directly. In fact, we rarely spoke at all unless the work required it.

There were lightning storms every afternoon, fast-moving thunderheads gathering over the Front Range and unburdening themselves on the prairie. Around lunchtime, they would form in the high country for their afternoon march downslope, gaining mass as they zigzagged over the foothills and onto the plains around greater Denver. With these storms it was hit-or-miss. Sometimes they sped away to the east— lightning flashes illuminating the purple clouds like flickering lanterns, and the trailing white blur of rain—but when they were on target, they hit with violence: rain in roaring sheets, thick multi-forked bolts of lightning, earth-rattling thunderclaps, and sometimes hail clattering down on the hoods and windshields of the utility trucks. But the storms' rages were short-lived. The rain broke the heat of the day and left the air fresh and redolent of sage and moist dirt.

On Tuesday, August 21st—I remember the date exactly—all other details having been attended to, we prepared to make the final splices and bulldoze dirt into the remaining sections of trench, thus completing the Highlands Ranch power grid and finishing the job. The sky was clear that morning except for a sparse flock of cotton-ball clouds hovering over the mountaintops, harbingers of the daily pileup and its afternoon assault upon the plains.

The first surprise was Billy's outfit: he showed up wearing an orange-and-blue Denver Broncos T-shirt instead of his usual western-cut. More strikingly, the stringy moustache and the Custer-length hair were gone, replaced by a clean shave and a barbershop crew cut. The change did not suit him well. Indeed, he looked very odd, his narrow face all out of proportion without the tusk-like whiskers, a white tan-line halfway up his forehead under the enormous, shorn scalp. You would have expected it to fuel a whole week of teasing on the crew, but no one said a word. Apparently none of us felt comfortable joking with him anymore.

Due to the regularity of the thunderstorms, the routine was to take care of any aboveground tasks in the morning and work in the trench in the afternoon. As Buck said, there was no safer place to be with lightning in the air than six feet under the prairie. I was not allowed in the trench, however, when the journeymen were splicing cable. So instead of donning the foam-rubber safety gloves—the elbow-length orange Day-Glos the men wore to protect themselves against unforeseen power surges—I would simply swing up into the truck to read or play solitaire on the wide vinyl seat.

An hour or so after lunch that day, the thunderheads slid down off the mountains and extinguished the sun, eating back the stunted mid-afternoon shadows and cloaking the dirt piles and trench lines in weak bluish light. Buck told me to drive the utility truck over to the sector transformer to check on Billy. "See if he needs anything," he said, reaching into his shirt pocket for a plug of tobacco. "You know which transformer I mean, kid?"

I nodded. It was about a quarter mile off, an army-green box the size of a tipped-over phone booth that held the circuits linking the sector to the rest of the power grid. Under no circumstances, Buck reminded me, was I to go down into the trench with Billy. I was just to see if he needed anything and hand him tools if he asked me to.

I started the truck and followed the ridges of dirt along the trench to the transformer in question. Surprisingly, Billy was not down in the trench but sitting on top of the box, his foam-rubber gloves laid out beside him like slightly flexed amputations, radiating a blurry orange light in the overcast gloom.

I stepped out of the truck. He sprang up off the box and held out his hand, beaming at me as if we were long-separated *compañeros*. I still couldn't get used to him without the whiskers and the western duds; he looked strangely mischievous, like a spindly, overgrown two-year-old. I took his hand, thinking that it would be a relief not to have to see him every day, now that I was headed back to school.

"That Buck is some kind of thoughtful, ain't he?" he said, keeping hold of my hand in his vise-like grip. "Sending my favorite college man to wait on me hand and foot? Cain't tell you how much I appreciate this. It's truly an honor. Truly."

"Knock it off, Billy." I jerked my hand out of his grasp and backed away a step. "Buck told me I was supposed to ask if you needed any help."

He seemed to consider for a moment and, beaming anew, said that there was one simple thing I could do, which would save him the trouble of climbing out of the trench. When the word came over the radio that it was safe to make the splice, he would give me a signal—he would stand up and wave—and I should open the transformer box and flip the power switch to "off."

"Got that, Tommy-boy? 'Off,' not 'on.' That's simple enough to remember, what with all that college behind you, right?" He attempted the posh British accent I'd used to announce the coffee: "Are we quite clear, my fine young lad?" He patted me on the shoulder. There was something off-kilter about his voice—the last words had seemed to lag behind the movement of his lips, as in a low-budget foreign movie—and his eyes had retreated inward as if drawn by some captivating, private image.

He shook his head and his eyes refocused. He flashed a winning smile, and gave me the thumbs-up signal, like a dashing fighter pilot. Then he walked over to the trench and dropped in. I thought about driving back to let Buck know that Billy was acting strangely, but if I'd done that I would have risked missing the signal, and it was never my intention to put him in any danger.

The storm broke without warning, a sudden darkening in the air and then the rain was pouring down in sheets. I ran for the truck. From the passenger-side window I had a good view of the spot where Billy had dropped into the trench, and I kept the window cracked open, despite the soaking the seat was getting, in case he called for me. I figured he was hunkered down, waiting out the worst of the storm.

Then I noticed a bright, orange blur on the transformer: Billy's safety gloves. Reluctantly, but duty-bound, I got out of the truck, ran over to the transformer to grab the gloves, and ran on to the trench, where Billy was whittling at the ends of the cables with his utility knife, oblivious to the storm raging above.

"Come sit in the truck," I shouted, "until the storm passes!"

"Fuck off," he growled, not looking up from the cables. At that point lightning bolts started hitting nearby—I'd been counting off the ever-shorter delays between the bright forks and the booming thunder-cracks—and I squatted to lower my profile, heart pounding in my chest.

"Well, at least put these *on*, for Christ's sake," I yelled, tossing the safety gloves down to him as I turned to sprint, doubled over, back to the truck. The rain fell in torrents, drumming the windshield and splattering in through the gap in the window. Every few seconds the lightning illuminated the transformer and the muddy dirt piles, and loud claps of thunder shook the truck and the ground it stood on. I thought about shutting the window and turning on the heat to dry myself off a bit, but I didn't do it, and I kept a close watch on the trench.

In one of the breaks between thunderclaps I might have heard a faint pop over the drum and sizzle of raindrops, but I can't be sure; there are a lot of noises in a storm, and it might have been my imagination. When the rain stopped and the lightning had moved off to a safe distance, I got out of the truck and walked over the slick dirt to the trench. The smell of prairie sage was strong, along with the mineral pungency of wet earth, but there was something funny mixed in, a sort of chemical tang.

With a sinking feeling in my stomach, I paused at the edge of the trench. The first thing I saw was the pair of safety gloves, lying on the trench-bottom exactly where I'd thrown them, palms up as if to catch the raindrops before they dissolved in the mud. Beyond them, Billy lay on his side in the fetal position, his pale, hairless face half-submerged in a mud puddle.

My uncle happened to be in the vicinity and heard the radio distress calls, so he got to us first, even before the ambulance. He took me aside and led me over to his car, a white Chrysler with maroon velvet trim, and I sat numbly in the passenger seat while he went to confer with Buck and the other men. They'd already pulled Billy out of the trench and laid him on the ground beside the cable truck. No one had been able to get his eyes to close, so they stayed open, with bits of mud sticking to them as though they were peeled hard-boiled eggs.

The ambulance arrived, and its flasher was a hypnotic red pulse inside the Chrysler. I felt numb as the technicians lifted the body onto a stretcher, covered it in a shroud, and loaded it in the ambulance. I could summon no feelings other than relief that my time on the crew was over. I was certain that I would never see any of them again.

My uncle came back and got in the car, and I sank into the comfortable seat as he turned the key in the ignition. But there was a tapping at my window, and I looked up to see Buck regarding me through the glass. I straightened in my seat and rolled down the window. His leathery face was close, and I could smell his chewing tobacco.

"The only thing I don't understand, Tommy," he said quietly, "is how the power came to be on when Billy was making the splice."

I felt a spasm of panic down in my crotch. It hadn't really occurred to me that I could be in trouble.

"Well, kid?"

"There was lightning hitting all around. I tried to get

him to come sit in the truck, but he wouldn't. I must have missed his signal."

"Signal, Tommy? What signal?"

"That's good enough, Buck," my uncle put in. "Tommy, you don't have to talk about this if you don't want to."

"It's okay." I swallowed, staring up at Buck. "He said he was going to stand up and wave when he was ready. I was supposed to flip the switch on the transformer to 'off.'"

"So he had the switch *on* to begin with?" I nodded. Buck shook his head slowly. Patchy gray stubble was beginning to show along his jawline; suddenly he looked his age. "And he wasn't wearing his safety gloves."

I was going to point out that I'd thrown the gloves down into the trench for him, but just then several police cruisers pulled in, blue lights flashing.

"Okay, Buck." My uncle leaned over to address the crew chief. "I'm going to take him home, now. You got it from here, right?"

Gazing at me, Buck gave an absent nod. There was something in his expression that I'd glimpsed before, a terrible weariness. He tapped the roof of the Chrysler and my uncle drove away. I watched Buck in the rear-view mirror: the way his shoulders slumped and the effort he made to straighten them; how he seemed to take possession of himself, striding briskly over to the officers and the men gathered by the utility truck.

We drove off the site, past the open trenches and the gaping foundation pits for row upon row of new Highlands Ranch homes. I looked west, hoping to find some kind of relief in the soaring peaks, but the Front

Range was obscured by clouds. I tried to put myself in Billy's shoes, down in the trench under the dying prairie, with the smell of mud and the bare wire of the cable ends, with the rain pouring in and the thunder cracking. Would the smell of sage have reached him down there?

Scrimshaw

THE CESSNA BANKED and began its descent, which felt steeper than usual to Kevin. He hated this part. Most mornings, there was a gusty wind blowing in from the open Atlantic, causing the small plane to jitter and bump. The worst was when the plane shimmied sideways, as if at any moment it could lose its equilibrium and get blown out of its flight path. Easy enough to imagine how this could happen: an unexpectedly powerful gust coming in at a critical angle; the Cessna spinning out like a boomerang and then plummeting, as in an old war movie, a spiral of black smoke billowing from the tail as it plunged into the sound. He closed his eyes and gripped the hand rests. It had been six months since he'd had a drink.

When he opened his eyes, the island was visible below, early-morning fog just lifting, an Aladdin's-lamp crescent of sand and yellow-green heath; a rich man's playground of weathered cedar cottages and summer mansions. Kevin had used a shovel on this ground, and he knew it was just as hard as anywhere else—just as fatal, too. But for some reason he breathed easier once the plane crossed over dry land. Looking down he could pick out half a dozen building sites, the recumbent skeletons of newly framed mansions-in-progress, each clamped like a parasite to its own scar of bare yellow earth. He could even see his ultimate destination, the Beekman estate, a sprawling three-building compound in various stages of construction on a private peninsula jutting out into the harbor. The sandy rectangle where the tennis court was about to go in. The long staircase down the bluff to the beach. Kevin had built that staircase himself.

The plane tipped and bucked before it touched down, then at last planted itself firmly on solid ground, taxiing along the runway to the small island terminal. Kevin was the first of the seven passengers to deplane, accepting the gym bag that held his lunch and an extra change of clothes from the wingman and walking the asphalt strip between parallel yellow lines into the terminal building. He'd been spared to live another day, but it was only decompression he felt, not full-blown relief. After all, he had to fly home that evening, and return the following morning, and keep making round-trip flights every workday for the foreseeable future. At least, that was, until he found an affordable place to live on the island or—not likely—a job somewhere else that paid better. The building boom had created a shortage of finish-carpenters, and he was earning twice as much as he could on the mainland.

Phil was waiting out front in his vintage blue Ford pickup. When he saw Kevin he nodded, poker-faced but genial. It was a typical Phil expression, one Kevin read this way: "Picking you up every day is a waste of my time, but on the other hand I don't really mind, because I'm on Beekman's clock and I have time to waste." He was a good foreman, Phil. He gave his employees the benefit of the doubt and never yelled, even when they screwed up. Kevin had worked for plenty of worse men, for sure.

He tossed the gym bag in the bed and got in. Phil put the truck in gear and drove slowly out of the airport lot. He was older than Kevin, in his late fifties probably, and had lived on the island since the 1960s. There was a rumor going around that he was a Wampanoag Indian descended from Squanto, and another that he'd once been the island's principal supplier of cocaine. Like most long-term islanders, he was a maddeningly slow driver. With his messy white hair and olive-skinned, preppy-boy good looks, he could have been an artist or a college professor, although he was laid back to a point just short of laziness—which explained why he was still toiling for an hourly wage. He and his wife Ursula lived in an old houseboat they kept moored in the harbor.

"How was your flight?" he asked.

Kevin exhaled. "Fine. Hit some rough air on the way in, as usual."

Phil gave him a sympathetic look. "Ursula and I always take the ferry. Although I guess that wouldn't be possible in your case."

"Not unless you're okay with me showing up at eleven every morning."

"Yeah. I don't think that would sit too well with Mr. Beekman."

"Then maybe he could find a place for me to stay over here." Kevin rolled down the window and spat.

"Not likely," Phil said. "But it doesn't make a whole lot of sense, does it? They can't afford to put you up on the island, but they *can* afford to fly you back and forth every day?"

"No shit." Kevin stared glumly out the window as they drove past the old brick whaling mansions into town, the pickup lurching over the cobblestones on Main Street. It was April—still the off-season—but it wasn't hard to imagine what summer would be like: tax attorneys and CEOs trying to look like locals with their long-billed fisherman's caps, teenagers joyriding in Land Rovers, and—of course—the women: leggy college girls with peachy complexions and high firm tits; young mothers perfect as magazine models; well-preserved older housewives with their taut, freckled faces and the pampered little rat-dogs they carried around like baby dolls.

Phil parked outside the pharmacy, and they went in to get coffee for the crew. Kevin helped him carry the trays out to the Ford, where they used a length of two-by-six and Kevin's gym bag to prop them up against the front of the bed so the styrofoam cups wouldn't tip over if Phil took any fast corners. Not that there was much danger of that. Phil steered the pickup gingerly out of town at an unvarying fifteen miles per hour, past the single farm and the cranberry bogs and all the tasteful gray-shingled mansions nestled among the low hills of the moorland, eventually turning left onto the unpaved access road to Massassoit point and the Beekman compound. The property displayed the jumbled order of a typical construction site: stacks of particleboard and raw cedar shingle, rolls of tarpaper, loose piles of sandy earth, and a blue dumpster overflowing with packaging and unusable scrap.

Phil cut the engine. The laborers stirred and rose listlessly from their seats on cinderblocks and stacks of lumber, strapping on their tool belts and walking stiff-limbed over to the truck for their coffee. They were still sipping it when Beekman pulled up in his black Hummer. He sat for a moment finishing a conversation on his cell phone, then got out and strode over to the crew. He was a tall, burly fellow with tiny eyes and a ferociously ruddy face, a Fortune 500 CEO with the carriage and attitude of a man accustomed to getting his own way. Kevin gave him a friendly nod as he approached, which Beekman predictably ignored.

"Late start today, Phil?"

The foreman shrugged. "I had to swing by the airport to pick up Kevin here, then to the lumberyard to order some Tyvek." He glanced at Kevin, who nodded solemnly to confirm this little white lie.

Beekman gave a low grunt and glanced suspiciously around the site. In another life he might have been a baker, Kevin thought, with a sudden vision of the aproned CEO bursting out of an antique Bavarian storefront to shake his rolling pin at some poor, hungry kid who'd made off with a loaf of bread. Beekman couldn't seem to find anything wrong, so he allowed his face to relax into a smile of snakelike amiability.

"Well, I'll let you fellas get to it, then. Give me a holler if there's anything I can do to speed things along, okay, Phil?" He climbed back up into the Hummer and spun its tires as he drove away, leaving the crew wheezing in a cloud of dust.

To supplement his construction income, Phil worked as a caretaker for a few dozen summer homes. Often, he would spend the middle part of the day, after he'd gotten everything started at the Beekman place, driving around the island to complete various small repair and maintenance jobs. Usually he left Kevin in charge at the site, but the laborers were putting up sheathing today—extremely straightforward work—so he invited Kevin to come along. They drove to a cottage built on the sand dunes at the northwest point of the island to repair a screen. From there they went back into town to adjust a chimney flue in a nineteenth-century whaling mansion, and finally to the Overlock place, a sprawling, cedar-shingled house on the bluff overlooking the harbor, where they had to measure the "flower-arranging room" for a new set of tiles.

"Unbelievable," Kevin said, when Phil told him what the room was for.

Phil grinned. "These ladies take their flower-arranging seriously. I've seen whole outbuildings dedicated to it. No joke."

Kevin shook his head, incredulous. He'd never seen the inside of a house like this, with its immense floor plan and carefully crafted woodwork, and its unthinkably valuable collection of art and antiques. And this was only a summer home. One thing he knew for sure: if he ever had this kind of money, he wouldn't spend it on a flower-arranging room, nor on hiring someone like Phil to do things he could easily do himself. But then experience had taught him that rich people were, for the most part, pretty helpless. They would call someone in to fix a flat tire, or to rake a few leaves. Probably they rationalized their laziness as generosity, as an excuse to toss a few coins to peons like Phil and Kevin.

After they'd eaten their sandwiches, Phil left Kevin ripping up the old tile while he went to the lumberyard. Kevin was an efficient worker, and the job didn't take long, so he had time for a self-guided tour of the Overlocks' home. It was a sprawling, well-built place: tightly seamed trim, hardwood floors and cupboards, no cost cutting on materials or technique, even the invisible stuff that was obvious only to a carpenter. Most of the rooms were decorated with a nautical theme: antique lamps crafted from astrolabes and old ships' compasses, a collection of weathered mermaid figureheads, oil paintings of whaling captains and storm-tossed ships, plenty of scrimshaw lying about.

Kevin was especially taken with the scrimshaw. His old man had been a night-shift lathe operator at a furniture factory, never around much, asleep all day most days and fond of his liquor when he wasn't sleeping. But he and Kevin had gotten along all right, especially when the old man told stories about Kevin's great-great-grandfather, who'd crewed whaling ships out of New Bedford. Like many whalemen, their ancestor had spent the empty hours at sea etching finely detailed pictures into whale teeth. Some of these pieces had stayed in the family until just before Kevin's birth, when they'd been sold off to pay a debt.

The old man had always regretted that move, and he'd remained fascinated with scrimshaw throughout his life. For him, Kevin had later come to understand, the art form was so important because it represented the legacy of illiterate men, strong men of great spirit and small means who'd had no way to express their humanity beyond the things they made with their hands.

One gray January morning when Kevin was eleven years old his mother had awakened him with the news that the old man would not be coming home. He'd been killed the previous night, along with a few dozen others, because there'd been a fire at the furniture factory, and some idiot manager had locked the emergency exits. She was already sick at the time, and seven months later, she too had died. Kevin had gone to live with an uncle. His most treasured memories of his father were tied up in the stories of his great-great granddad the whaleman, and the Saturday afternoons Kevin and the old man had spent together in New Bedford, combing garage sales and pawnshops for scrimshaw. They'd never unearthed much, and what they had found they mostly hadn't had the wherewithal to buy.

The Overlocks obviously didn't have that problem. They were collectors. Scrimshaw could be found throughout in the house, artfully scattered on mantels and side tables, propped up in niches and glass display cases, accenting the expensive built-in bookshelves of the mahogany-paneled library. Kevin could see that these were authentic works of art, too—real antiques, literally hundreds of them. The old man wouldn't have believed his eyes.

The commutes that evening and the following morning were less turbulent, but not enough to put Kevin at ease. On both flights he ground his teeth and clutched the arm rests until the plane landed. When they arrived at the Beekman compound, Phil turned off the Ford's ignition and tossed Kevin the keys. "Feel like going freelance for a while?"

"Sure." Kevin eyed him. "What does it entail, exactly?"

Phil picked up the clipboard he kept on the sun-cracked seat and used a pencil to scan the list he'd written there.

"Well, summer's coming, and my caretaking jobs are starting to pile up. I have to go up to Providence next week to help my brother build a deck, and I think I should spend more time here at the site before I leave. Yesterday these bozos measured the windows wrong, and I'm pretty sure we're going to have to re-sheathe the entire guesthouse. If Beekman gets wind of it . . ." He trailed off, looking sheepish, as if being under the gun were something to be ashamed of.

"Consider it taken care of," Kevin said reassuringly. "I won't let you down." Truth was, he liked the idea of driving around the island by himself. The camaraderie of a construction crew had never done much for him—all the sex talk and the crude banter left him feeling awkward and sour—and the fact that Phil thought well enough of him to let him work unsupervised was a boost to his ego. It was nice to be trusted—and rare, in his experience. Over the last few years, he'd come to understand that when it came down to it he was not someone people felt all that comfortable with. This had become undeniably clear on his last two jobs, from which he'd been dismissed with the almost identical non-explanation that he just wasn't "a good fit."

Easing the old truck down the rutted sand driveway of the estate, he was filled with a pleasant sense of purpose. He would get the work done quickly and expertly. He would make both Phil and himself look good.

He started with the small jobs: checking the air conditioning at a secluded mansion near the lighthouse, tightening the hinges on the back door of a guesthouse near Silversides Point, replacing a few rotten boards on a deck south of town. He drove to the lumberyard to pick up the Overlocks' tile and some shiplap pine he needed to panel the hall in the attic leading up to the widow's walk. That and the flower-arranging room were part of an overall effort to make the house more "presentable," Phil had wryly informed him. Kevin shook his head in disbelief every time he thought about the Overlocks.

By four, he was done laying tiles, and he decided to take another look around the house. He ended up in the library, gazing at a piece of scrimshaw he'd noticed the day before, which sat on a shelf in front of a three-volume biography of Winston Churchill. It was a small piece—insignificant really—a polished, slightly yellowed, blunt fang of ivory etched with a pair of crossed harpoons. When he picked it up it felt smooth and substantial in his hands. As a joke, he slipped it into the pocket of his work pants, where it settled as a cool weight against his thigh.

He could keep it easily, he mused. Surely the Overlocks would never notice. The scrimshaw felt natural where it was, hammocked comfortably in the bottom of his pocket with the curve of the tooth nestled against his thigh as if it belonged there. And in a way it *did* belong there. After all, even if it wasn't his ancestor's work—and who was to say it was not?—he surely could claim a closer tie to the lonely whaleman who'd etched those realistic-looking harpoons than the Overlocks could, this faceless, pampered, absentee family who paid a caretaker to do their simplest chores.

He would just hold onto it for now. He could always bring it back tomorrow, or the day after.

The next Friday, Phil invited him out to the houseboat for lunch. It was a crystalline spring day—a few wispy clouds, sky and ocean the same pale, hopeful shade of blue. The air smelled pleasantly of brine and rotting seaweed, and a light breeze ruffled the water as the skiff motored past the empty moorings of the inner harbor. Phil cut the engine as they approached the houseboat, a squared-off barge about forty feet long with blackened particleboard siding and a rusty stovepipe sticking out of the roof.

Ursula came out on the narrow deck and Phil threw her the bowline, which she tied expertly to a cleat on the aft gunwale. She was younger than Phil, somewhere around the same age as Kevin, with a head of curly-blond hair and a slightly bruised look about the eyes, like a silent-movie actress. Kevin had met her a few times before, and he'd never thought of her as a particularly attractive woman. Today he found himself revising that impression. Maybe it was his mood, or perhaps it was that the houseboat was her home environment, but Kevin could barely keep himself from staring. She was big-boned and slightly overweight, but she had full, sensual lips, and as she moved around the deck setting out sandwiches and bottles of Heineken, he couldn't help but notice the way her breasts filled out her white-cotton Oxford. The shirt had flecks of blue paint on it and she wore it untucked, with the sleeves rolled up to reveal strong, well-tanned forearms.

When Phil got up to use the head, she looked into Kevin's eyes and smiled. "Is something wrong? You keep staring at me."

"Nope," he replied, taking a swig of beer to cover his embarrassment.

She gazed at him insolently, still smiling. The water lapped against the flat hull of the houseboat. After a moment there was a hydraulic flushing sound and Phil emerged. "Ready to go, Kev?"

"Sure," Kevin replied. Ursula continued to hold his gaze as they both got up from their deck chairs. Phil leapt into the skiff and bent down to start the motor. Kevin was about to follow him when she gripped his arm.

"Nice to see you again, Kevin," she said. Her gaze was intense and full of unspoken meaning. He felt his ears reddening.

"You too. Thanks for lunch."

"You're very welcome. I hope you'll come again."

"I'd like that."

Kevin stepped down into the skiff, and Phil steered them back to the fisherman's wharf in silence, with the wind sifting his white hair and a peaceful expression on his dark-skinned, boyish face. If he'd noticed the chemistry between his wife and his employee, it didn't appear to have bothered him.

Kevin was a perfectionist on the care-taking projects. His focus was craftsmanship: measuring twice before cutting, beveling and sanding exposed corners, taking care not to leave shavings or sawdust or spots of paint or plaster. So far he'd seen the interiors of more than a dozen houses, and from each he'd borrowed a small souvenir. Nothing major; just a simple, finely wrought object that was not likely to be missed: a soapstone rhinoceros; a pewter crab; a piece of scrimshaw, if he judged that the homeowners had enough of it. On the windowsills of his Hyannis walkup, he kept a large and growing collection. He'd made a point of writing down the original placement of each piece, so that he could return them before summer if that became necessary—but he doubted it would. Even if a few of the knick-knacks *were* missed, there was a parade of workers going through these houses in the off-season—plumbers, electricians, cleaning maids, landscape crews, decorators—so there was no real way to trace it back to him, or to Phil. He thought of the objects as tokens of the homeowners' gratitude for his flawless, anonymous work. A small price to pay, really, considering that he was risking his life twice a day just getting to and from the island.

Often, as he worked, he found himself thinking about Ursula—her dark, expressive eyes, her full lips, the pressure of her grip on his forearm. He'd never been much of a womanizer (not for lack of trying), but he *had* been married once, and he knew enough about women to understand that the electric current of desire crackling between them had not existed in his imagination alone. What he was unsure of was whether he'd received an actual *invitation* under the radar, or whether she'd merely been engaging in some heavy flirtation.

Soon enough, that mystery was resolved. On Wednesday, five days after the lunch on the houseboat, she happened to sit beside him on the morning plane. She'd been to Providence, she said, visiting Phil and his brother. They were making progress on the deck, but Phil would be gone for at least another week. Kevin politely pretended to listen, but as the plane taxied down the runway he was consumed by the usual terror. Ursula chattered away, seemingly oblivious to the turbulence and to Kevin's white-knuckled silence. As they touched down, she invited him out to the houseboat for lunch, and he accepted, gritting his teeth and smiling to hide the strain the flight had caused him.

She met him at the fisherman's wharf with the skiff and they rode out to the houseboat. At first there was an awkwardness between them, but after a few beers he began to relax. Before long, the conversation turned frank.

"Kevin," she asked, casually, as if she were offering him another beer, "would you like to fuck?"

Nothing like this had ever happened to him before. She took him by the hand and led him to the cabin. Her fingers were strong and rough with calluses; life on a houseboat must not be easy, he reflected, especially during the long Atlantic winter. There were books stacked all over the dimly lit room, which was cluttered and smelled of rosewater. She undressed in silence, then knelt on the bed with her face pressed into the pillows. The half-globes of her buttocks glowed palely in the gloom. He fumbled with his belt to ease the pressure in his jeans, but something made him hesitate.

"Come *on*," she urged, her voice muffled and hoarse, almost angry-sounding.

"What about Phil?" he asked.

She sighed heavily and turned to face him, breasts dawning in the murky light like enormous, strawberry-nippled moons.

"Your loyalty is admirable," she said dryly. "But don't worry about Phil. He knows what I'm up to."

"He does?"

"Well, not *exactly* what I'm up to. Let's put it this way. We have a kind of unspoken agreement. Is that okay with you?"

Kevin thought for a moment. She made it sound so easy, so harmless. Why shouldn't he oblige her? He undid his belt and his jeans slid to the floor.

On the evening flight home, he surveyed the sweep of an ocean that was glassy and calm, pink-hued and glittering in the late April sunset. It was such a beautiful sight, he forgot his usual panic. He felt better than he had in years. It was if he were being rewarded for not giving up, for working hard, for making the effort to get his life under control. Two months ago he would have been gripping the armrests as the plane hurtled through the dark, too wracked with dread to appreciate the stars outside the window. Now spring was here, the sun was retiring in all its red-gold glory, and he felt, for the first time in his life, that his destiny was finally in his own hands.

Friday morning Kevin knew Phil was back, because when he came out of the terminal, the blue Ford wasn't in the parking lot where he'd left it the previous evening. Ten minutes later the foreman pulled in—the battered old pickup misfiring, his crazy white hair flickering in the breeze through the open window. Kevin watched him carefully for some indication of a change in their relationship, but the older man was as easygoing as ever. It was a relief. On some level, Kevin had been preparing for a confrontation.

While they waited for coffee at the pharmacy, Phil asked about the caretaking jobs. "Have you run into any of the homeowners? They usually start showing up around now."

Kevin was surprised. "This early?"

"Quick trips, usually. They sometimes like to air out the houses, get psychologically prepared for the season."

"Well, no, I haven't run into any yet. I'll start knocking on doors, though, before I go barging in."

"Good idea. And I hope you haven't been moving anything around at the Overlocks'. Furniture or anything. Mrs. O. is seriously anal about her décor."

Kevin's heart skipped a beat. "I don't *think* I have," he said. "But maybe I should go back and check."

Phil waved his wallet dismissively as he paid for the coffee. "Don't bother. She'll get over it."

When they pulled into the site Beekman was already there, leaning against the door of his Hummer with his arms crossed, his face a mask of irritated ill humor.

"Uh-oh," Phil said, revving the engine a few times before cutting it. He glanced at Kevin and mimicked Beekman's uptight expression with such cartoonish accuracy that for the rest of the day, Kevin had to laugh out loud whenever he thought about it.

He didn't see Ursula for almost a week, so he had to assume that it had been a one-time deal. In a way, this was a relief. Despite what she'd said, it just didn't feel right to be having sex with the wife of a man he considered a friend, and one who'd put so much trust in him. But he couldn't help thinking about her. He would relish the opportunity to see her again, but he wasn't about to push things. Not with Phil back.

The foreman kept him on caretaking duty, which he continued to enjoy, and everything might have continued on a more or less even keel had he not found the note stuck in the door of the Riegles' house, where he'd been re-grouting the bathtubs in all three guest suites. "Will be here 2:30," the note said. It was not signed, but it was heavily scented with rosewater.

Grouting was an unpleasant, undignified job, and it was a relief, as well as a pulse-quickening thrill, when he heard the front door open and close. He wiped his hands on his jeans and went downstairs.

"How did you know I'd be here?" he asked.

"Never mind," she replied, all business. She led him up to the master bedroom and they did it there, with her on top, on a king-size canopy bed with a sweeping view of the harbor and the candy-striped lighthouse in the distance. He fantasized that this was their house—his and Ursula's. Just another lazy afternoon in the life of the very rich.

"Does Phil know you're here?" he asked afterward. He stretched out languidly on the bed, still naked. She stood in front of Mrs. Riegle's full-length mirror, reapplying her lipstick.

"Stop worrying,," she replied without turning around. "It's only sex, you know."

She came by the next afternoon, too, and they undressed each other hungrily. Afterwards they took a proprietary stroll through the house together, ending up in Mr. Riegle's den. They stood at his desk, admiring the model of a tall-masted frigate. It was large for a model, and whoever had built it had spent years on the details: decks and masts carved in teak, a tiny mahogany ship's wheel, furled sails of realistically weathered fabric, moveable gun ports with tiny brass cannons. Kevin had noticed the piece before, and he felt gratified that Ursula seemed to appreciate it as much as he did. The craftsmanship that had gone into every millimeter filled him with awe. "How much would you say it's worth?" he asked.

"No idea," she murmured, gazing at it. "Quite a lot, I bet." She sat in the desk chair to examine it more closely while Kevin poked around the den. On a bookshelf he spotted a piece of scrimshaw he hadn't noticed before: a fine arctic scene etched with polar bears, an igloo, and a whaling schooner anchored beside an iceberg.

"What are you *doing*?" Ursula had looked up in time to see him slipping it into his pocket.

"Don't fret," he said casually. "They'll never notice it's gone."

She stared up at him from the desk chair, wide-eyed.

"Seriously," he said. "I mean *look* at this place." He gestured around the den, at the cherrywood paneling, the customized porthole windows, the model frigate and the antique grandfather's clocks and the built-in bookshelves lined with vintage model airplanes. "Do you think anyone this rich is going to miss one little toy?"

"Please tell me you haven't been stealing from Phil's summerhouses."

He felt his face redden. "I wouldn't exactly call it *stealing*."

She continued to stare up at him, horrified. After a moment, she said quietly, "Do you have any idea what this could do to Phil? He's been caretaking on this island for *decades*, Kevin. He's built a reputation. People trust him. If somebody discovers something missing—"

"There are dozens of workers coming through," Kevin put in. "There's *no way* they could—"

"Are you sure about that? It seems to me that Phil would be the most logical suspect."

"Okay. Okay." Kevin held up his hands, feeling his defensiveness threatening to slip into anger. He removed the scrimshaw from his pocket and set it back on the shelf. "But if you're so worried about Phil's welfare, how come you still haven't told him about *us*?"

It was her turn to blush, and suddenly he understood that what he'd been afraid of all along was true. "There's no 'agreement,' is there? Phil wouldn't be okay with what we've been doing, would he?"

Her eyes blazed defiantly for a moment, then seemed to lose their focus. Kevin stared at her, incredulous. For her to object to his pocketing a little piece of scrimshaw on the grounds of the damage it could do to Phil seemed laughable in comparison to what else they'd been doing. Not that he was innocent, either. A part of him had known all along that this wasn't going to be as straightforward as she'd made it sound.

"Listen," he said. "No harm done, okay? Let's just forget it happened and go about our business."

They went downstairs together. He walked her to the door, where she paused and gave him a worried look.

"What?" he asked.

"You haven't been . . . 'borrowing' anything else, have you? From the other houses?"

"Of course not. This was just a whim; a one-time thing. I was just being an idiot. I have no idea what I was thinking."

"Good. Because Phil's worked so hard. It's not as easy as you think to make a living on this island."

"Don't worry," Kevin said, unable to keep a note of irritation out of his voice. "I'll make sure Phil stays out of trouble. He's *my* friend too, believe it or not."

She gave him a sad look. "With friends like us, who needs enemies, right?"

"Yeah," he agreed. "But from now on, that changes."

She held out her hand, and they shook on it. But the look that passed between them was full of mistrust.

The next day was Friday, a gusty, rainy day. The morning flight was especially rough, as if Kevin's personal demons had been gathering strength while his attention had been diverted. His heart pounded; he held onto the seatback as the Cessna bucked and shivered through the unsettled air. As they began the descent, the plane hit a pocket and dropped suddenly, causing the other passengers to gasp. Even the pilot looked tense: white-knuckled hands gripping the stick; crew-cut head with its big earphones straining forward to see better through the gloom. Kevin's whole body ached, and he worried that he was going to have a stroke. The minutes stretched on like hours.

At the terminal, he went straight to the lavatory and stood in front of the mirror for a long time, not caring what all the men coming and going thought. He needed to pull himself together. It was doing him some kind of grievous damage, this twice-daily encounter with his own terrifying mortality.

Phil was waiting out front, the Ford idling. Kevin looked for the angelic smile, but the windshield was beaded over with rain, and all he could see of Phil was the brown oval of his face and the blur of white hair. When he climbed in, he could feel the difference. There was no greeting, no eye contact.

At the rotary they turned right, toward the Beekman compound.

"No coffee today?"

"I'm taking you off caretaking," Phil said coldly.

Kevin nodded and stared out the window at the drenched moorland. He felt his weight pressing down into the cracked vinyl seat, as if the Earth's gravitational field had suddenly been turned up a notch. There was no need to ask what had changed.

He spent the next few weeks pounding nails. Phil had arranged for him to take a taxi to and from the Beekman compound, the excuse being that both of them could get to work earlier that way. But Kevin knew the real reason: Phil could no longer stand the sight of his face. The older man was hardly ever on site, and when he was, their conversation was limited to curt exchanges about window installation or the next delivery of shingle pallets.

Back on the mainland, he ate Lucky Charms and frozen pizza and watched endless hours of sports on cable TV. The days felt repetitive and unreal, a series of waking dreams punctuated by the terror of the morning and evening flights. He missed Ursula—her company, not just the sex—and he missed the vicarious fantasy-life of caretaking. He was certain that he smelled bad, though he showered both morning and night. Mornings were especially difficult. Often he was too full of dread about the coming flight to finish shaving or brush his teeth. It drove him to drinking again—only a pre-breakfast swallow or two from a flask he kept in the medicine cabinet, for now, but if experience was any guide, the habit would quickly begin to take on its own momentum. Above all he felt ostracized, as if something he had done, or something he was, had cut him off from the mainstream of humanity. Maybe it was simply his selfishness. Maybe that was the hidden quality people recognized after they'd known him for a while; the quality that prevented him from being considered a "good fit."

Finally, one morning in early May, he could take it no longer. He called one of the West Indians on the crew to say that he had the flu and wouldn't be coming in. He gathered up all the scrimshaw and other well-made objects and packed them in newspaper in a duffel bag left over from his two-year stint in the Coast Guard. Having everything together in one place revealed the true extent of his problem:

the duffel was as heavy as a bag of driveway gravel. He drove down to the ferry dock.

The ferry was crowded with tourists and returning islanders; it was a Friday morning and the summer season was fast approaching. Once the big boat was underway, he climbed to the main cabin and got in line at the bar for coffee, with the heavy duffel slung over his shoulder. It was a long line, looping around through the booths and tables on the interior deck. He stood in it for ten or fifteen minutes, inching forward toward the bar. But the line seemed to stall, and glancing down at the nearest booth he was surprised to see Mr. Beekman. Kevin looked away quickly, but it was too late; he'd been noticed.

"Shouldn't you have taken a flight?" Beekman demanded suspiciously, folding the newspaper he'd been reading and putting it down on the table. He regarded Kevin over half-moon reading glasses, a quizzical frown on his broad red face. "Aren't you missing a whole morning of work?"

Kevin felt the heat traveling up his neck and spreading to both his ears. He opened his mouth to say something, but no words came.

"Why don't you answer me? What kind of game are you playing, fella?"

Kevin let out his breath in an unintentionally vocal sigh.

Beekman shook his head wonderingly, and took out his cell phone. "I'm calling Phil. You'd better have a damn good explanation for this."

Without stopping to think, Kevin snatched the phone out of the CEO's doughy hands, let it drop to the floor, and ground it to rubble with the heel of his work boot. Beekman's jaw dropped; his face darkened to a dangerous shade of purple. In the nearby booths, conversations trailed off.

"You're going to regret *that* move," Beekman assured him, but Kevin was already walking away, the scrimshaw clinking faintly in the duffel at his back. Fuck Beekman, he thought. Fuck them all.

But his rage was already bogging down in despair. Phil *had* been his friend, sort of, hadn't he? Kevin didn't have many of those. In fact, he was hard-pressed to think of a single one.

Out on the upper deck it was a breezy morning, warm for May, with a soft light filtering through a diffuse Atlantic haze. Looming over the southeastern horizon was an oblong blue cloud, and below that, a thin horizontal gap and a platinum stripe of sunlit water. As he watched, the cloud lifted, the gap widened, and the bright line on the surface of the ocean faded to burnished silver. He leaned against the railing, hawked, and spat, watching his saliva hit the water and disappear in the ferry's churning wake. He couldn't get Beekman's purple, Bavarian-peasant face out of his mind. The man was a captain of industry. When he gave orders, people jumped. But he didn't seem any more intelligent than Kevin, or Phil, and he certainly wasn't better looking. Why was it that some people got to run the world, while others had to lick their boots?

Making a sudden decision, he slung the duffel over his shoulder and walked back down to the interior deck, where he was greeted by a tense silence. Beekman stood by the bar, next to a uniformed member of the ferry's crew. Both men stared at Kevin with cold alertness as he approached.

"Here," he said, tossing the duffel hard into Beekman's chest. The big CEO's arms closed reflexively around it; he staggered a little under its weight. "These are from the summerhouses Phil takes care of. It was all me. My bad, okay? Phil had no knowledge of any of it." He spun on his heels and started for the stairs again.

"Wait," Beekman called after him, but Kevin didn't look back. He leapt up the stairs three at a time. At the railing he took a deep breath, heart beating wildly. The haze-refracted sun cast a cheerful glint over the sound. In the ferry's wake, white sea-foam bubbled up from the dark-green water, fizzing like ginger ale and falling behind the boat in a long, wavering line. He stepped back, grasped the cool, metal bar with both hands, and vaulted over the railing. When he hit the water, he let himself plunge, holding his breath for as long as he could. Then he rose to the surface and began to swim.

Diamondback Mountain

Henry takes the stairs three at a time, balancing a tray with a pot of coffee and two of the lodge's signature blue-enamel mugs. An inch of fresh powder frosts the windowsills, and the light slants in to illuminate the framed mountainscapes that line the stairwell. On a normal day he might stop to admire these photographs—shadow and light, black crags and windblown snow, all the danger and beckoning allure of the great alpine summits: Mont Blanc, Wildspitze, Matterhorn, Weisshorn, Dents du Midi—but today he has reason to ignore them. At the Edelweiss Suite, he knocks and waits. The door swings open, and Celia appears in a dressing gown of sky-blue satin. Her eyes are charmingly swollen with sleep. A loose strand of mahogany hair caresses one flawless olive cheek.

"*Buongiorno*," he says, doing his best to replicate the pronunciation he's learned from Benny, the lodge's Swiss-Italian chef.

Celia laughs delightedly. "*Ciao*, Henry. *Come stai*?"

He shrugs, helpless, because his reservoir of Italian vocabulary is already depleted.

"*Cos'*è questo?" She points to the tray.

"This? I brought you coffee."

"*Caffè*," she corrects him."

"*Caffè*," he repeats.

"*Molto buono*, Henry."

They stare into each other's eyes. An odd weightlessness comes over him, the distinct sensation of floating a few inches above the floor. He doesn't consider himself star-struck—they've had half a dozen conversations by now, and a game of checkers in the great hall the night before—but it remains a struggle to believe that such a girl can truly exist in the three-dimensional world. Moreover, and miraculously—if he's not mistaken—in the brief time they've known each other, a strong connection appears to have sprung up between them, a current of mutual attraction that exerts its magnetic pull despite logic and the social and cultural barriers that conspire to keep them apart.

"Good morning." Her father has appeared in the doorway beside her. An award-winning cinema director rumored to have close ties to Mussolini himself, he's a handsome, older man, aristocratic of bearing, of medium stature and somewhat delicately boned, with close-cropped salt-and-pepper hair.

"Breakfast is served in the Great Hall, sir, whenever you're ready. Meanwhile, Mr. Peggett asked me to bring you this."

"I'll take it, Papa." Celia reaches for the tray and favors Henry with a radiant smile before disappearing into the suite. Her father stands with his arms crossed in the doorway, a grim-faced sentinel.

"Anything else, young man?" He speaks in a less pronounced accent than Celia's, a good deal more British than Italian.

"No, sir," Henry replies, "just the coffee. And the news that breakfast is served."

"Thank you." The Italian nods curtly and closes the door. Henry takes the staircase more slowly on the way down, savoring the aftermath of his interaction with Celia, and mostly undaunted by her father's forbidding attitude. He's well aware that the prospect of anything coming from this flirtation is unlikely. Celia is a motion-picture actress—not a household name outside of Italy yet, but a rising star, by all accounts—and he is a low-paid hotel employee. The expense and difficulties presented by an ocean and two thirds of a continent, not to mention the accelerating conflict in Europe, appear to present insurmountable obstacles. And yet, somehow, the future is unimportant. It is the present that concerns him.

In the seconds before awakening that morning, he dreamed of New Hampshire in summer. Warm air currents scented with fern and peat; golden-green sunlight filtering down through hemlock boughs to highlight a ground covered in moss and bare tree roots and smooth gray stone. The air alive with dust motes and gnats spiraling around the half-dozen boys gathered at the edge of the cliff overlooking the deep granite quarry. Lloyd was there, and some of the old crowd from Sugar Glen: hairy-chested Swoop Holcomb, saucer-eared Grinny Miller. "Don't be afraid," Lloyd said.

"I'm not," Henry replied, staring down at his toes and the edge of the cliff, and far below, the roughly rectangular pool of black water. But he was.

A breeze picked up, and the shadows of the hemlock boughs skittered over the roots that gripped the granite like bony fingers. Lloyd was down in the water now, so far below that his head was like a tiny cork bobbing at the center of a target made by his expanding, concentric ripples. He was shouting something, but Henry couldn't make it out. The words reached him, but they were garbled, nonsensical.

He turned to ask the others, but Swoop and Grinny had vanished. Looking back into the pit he was disturbed to see that Lloyd was also gone. The water was frozen flat. Wind whipped ghostly patterns of snow over a surface of dull black ice.

After breakfast, the party assembles on the main deck for the first filming expedition. It's a clear Rocky Mountain morning, the sky bright blue overhead and darker, almost bruised-looking, over the backlit cockscomb of the Animas ridge to the west. The frozen air smells of woodsmoke and pine needles. Last night's snow is so fine that the slightest puff of wind explodes it off roof angles and ponderosa boughs in perfectly conserved flakes, creating the illusion of snowfall from the cloudless sky. He notices Celia shivering in her fashionably cut wool jacket, and he wishes he could go over and wrap his arms around her—but of course such a public gesture would be scandalous. She'll warm up quickly, he knows, once they get moving.

He sets off to pack a trail in the meadow that slopes up into the aspen glades above the lodge. Trail-breaking is heavy work, but Henry revels in it. As he moves up the slope, he appreciates the landscape anew, through the guests' eyes. The fathomless sky above the burnished-silver aspen trunks. The long blue fingers of shadow vaulting across the unbroken snow. Behind him, the procession stretches back, their cane poles creaking in the snow as in scrubbed cotton fiber. He imagines himself at the head of a party of Vikings, or a squadron of Hannibal's troops crossing the Alps. The thought of the war getting underway in Europe crosses his mind, but he quickly dismisses it. If people on the other side of the ocean are foolish enough to kill each other for abstract ideas such as empire-building and national pride, that's their own affair. He wants no part of it.

A little later, cutting a switchback on a steep hillside, he startles a snowshoe hare, which bounds off into the shade of the spruce forest like a white-on-white ghost. Three ravens ride the wind over the black treetops, rising and falling in unison. One lets out a parched *kruk, kruk,* like two hollow sticks tapped together. For a moment he imagines that the bird is speaking to him directly, though he has no idea what it could be trying to say.

At the first overlook, the party stops to admire the view. Mr. Peggett passes around a thermos of coffee, and

Celia's father sets up his tripod. He wants a still shot of the region's presiding summit, Diamondback Mountain; of its flanks cloaked in black conifers; of its barren gray crag rising up serene and colossal like the tombstone of some forgotten pagan king.

The party moves on. Henry's brother Lloyd takes his turn breaking trail, and Henry lingers behind, pretending to adjust his bindings as Celia's father puts away the tripod. "A good day for shooting?" he asks.

"Too bright."

"Maybe the afternoon will be better?"

"Maybe so." The film director's eyes remain hidden behind his smoked lenses. His expression reveals nothing of his feelings about Henry, though of course there is no reason to believe that these have softened since the morning.

The party continues along a snow-choked cart track left over from the gold-mining days into the perpetual shade of the spruce forest. Dozens of switchbacks and three steep herringbone climbs take them up to the alpine meadows beneath the southern cirque of Diamondback Mountain. Celia's father sets up his tripod in the lowest meadow, intending to film each member of the party as they ski past.

In the highest meadow, the party gathers. Mr. Peggett passes out Triscuits and summer sausage while Henry and Lloyd go around collecting the guests' climbing skins. Henry cinches down his bindings and sets off first, Mr. Peggett having instructed him to wait at a spot halfway down the run to ensure that everyone makes it to the lowest meadow. The hickories cut soaring arcs through the virgin powder. A red-tailed hawk calls down to him from its gyre: a savage, resounding shriek. The clean scent of balsam fills the air. Millions of snow crystals glint in the sunlight like stars in a universe of gently rolling white. Henry's pulse throbs in his ears, and he's possessed by an urgent instinct to embrace the beauty of the moment; to internalize it fully before it has a chance to end. He glides to a stop between the middle and lower meadows, at the entrance to a kind of chokepoint between two fir copses through which everyone will have to pass.

One by one, the party flies by: his brother Lloyd, the everpresent cherry-wood pipe clamped between his teeth; the more clumsy but passable Mr. Hermon and Mr. Fish, Hollywood producers who are long-time associates of Celia's father; and finally the hotelier, Mr. Peggett, Henry and Lloyd's employer, a compact widower with close-cropped, silver hair and deep wrinkles radiating out from under his smoked lenses.

But where's Celia? Henry waits, scanning the conifer-populated meadow. The others have disappeared over a roll in the slope below the chokepoint. He starts herringboning uphill, and in the next moment she comes into view, frowning with concentration, skiing defensively but with a graceful, Austrian-style technique. She plows to a stop just above his spread ski tips and he notices that her woolen headband is dusted with snow. "Everything all right?" he asks.

"Oh, yes!" She leans forward on her poles, gasping for breath. "More than all right, Henry. It's so beautiful!"

He laughs aloud, delighted by her enthusiasm.

"You go ahead and ski down, Henry," she says. "I need to rest."

"I'll wait. I'm supposed to go last, anyway, and I want to stay behind you in case you fall again."

"How did you know I fell?"

He reaches up to dust the snow off her headband, but she catches his hand. She uses her teeth to pull off his leather glove, brings his palm up to her mouth, and traces a warm circle with her tongue. He gasps, shock-waves of desire surging through his body. Laughing, she pushes his hand away, throws the glove as far uphill as she can, and pushes off with her poles to propel herself down the slope.

It's snowed all night, and dense flakes continue to fall. The conditions are not good for shooting film, so the party skis in the fields near the lodge, making use of a rope-tow Mr. Peggett has rigged up using an old Model-T engine. Although the run is not long, it can be repeated endlessly. All day the shadowy figures flicker through the whiteout like a company of speeding wraiths.

Henry looks for a chance to be alone with Celia, but her father is ever-present. He finds solace in the powder skiing, which is giddy and exhilarating, like waltzing down a tilted cloud, a precisely controlled free fall through a medium as weightless and frictionless as air. He revels in the muted *whoosh* of the hickories as they slice through the snow; in the falling flakes that sting his cheeks and enclose him in a fast-moving tunnel; in the snow-burdened ponderosas that loom out of the blizzard and then fade back like spectral watchmen.

Time slows to a crawl. The day blurs at the edges, becoming an indeterminate period of all-encompassing whiteness that could well stand in for eternity.

That night, a lodge tradition: the Masquerade. The guests combine with the hotel employees in a festive group of around a dozen attendees. They spend the afternoon plundering the costume closet and the staff decorates the great hall with crepe paper, linen tablecloths, and a multitude of candles stuck in empty wine bottles. Mr. Peggett brings out his Magnavox and his collection of dance records: Tommy Dorsey and Glen Miller and Artie Shaw. Outside the lodge the snow has stopped, but the wind has become an intermittently savage howl. Inside, the fire crackles merrily, the clarinets and trumpets weave their intricate melodies, and the whiskey flows.

Celia, a gypsy in a bandana and hoop earrings and a long, red flamenco dress, is much in demand. She dances with her father—dressed as Wyatt Earp in a black Stetson hat and sheepskin chaps with fake pistols and a sheriff's badge—and with Josiah Fish, the Hollywood lawyer, comically overstuffed into an old pair of Mr. Peggett's lederhosen. She dances with Allan Hermon, the producer, who is dressed like a pirate, and with Lloyd, in a plaid skirt and a blond wig and a well-stuffed bra under his old Dartmouth sweater. She dances with Mr. Peggett, in a black cape and a Venetian doctor's mask, and with

Lloyd again, grinning and whirling in his skirt with the cherry-wood pipe clenched between his teeth. Henry, a Plains Indian dressed in fringed buckskin and a braided wig, sits by the bar under a framed photograph of the Jungfrau and gazes out on the proceedings with increasing gloom. Celia is impossibly beautiful. He's observed the way she bathes her dance partner in the radiance of her full attention—how her gypsy eyes flash as she laughs—and it makes him wonder if he's been mistaken all along to assume there is anything unique about the way she's been treating him. Perhaps it's her practice to make every man she meets feel as if he could be the one. Perhaps she simply enjoys making strangers fall in love with her.

He pours himself another whiskey. The liquor settles like embers in his gut. The seconds tick by at an alarming rate, but he's helpless to do anything about it. Lloyd appears beside him at the bar and pours himself a tumbler. "You okay, Sitting Bull?"

"Never better," Henry replies.

"We've missed you out on the dance floor."

Henry grunts, taking another swill of whiskey.

"Want to get some air, brother?"

"Sure." He follows Lloyd out to the deck. The wind has swept the remaining clouds from the sky, leaving a brightly spattered canopy of stars, and the frigid night is bracing after the close heat of the great hall. Lloyd reaches down under his skirt for his tobacco pouch and fills his pipe. He strikes a match to light the bowl, and the flame flares up to illuminate his handsome face.

"God, you make an ugly woman," Henry says.

"Don't I?" Lloyd grins, puffing on the pipe. "Celia's something else, isn't she? Don't worry," he adds hastily, responding to Henry's sharp glance. "I'm just making an observation. I appreciate her the way a man appreciates any masterpiece: avidly, but from a cordoned-off distance."

Henry sighs, leaning against the trail. "I can't remember the last time I felt this way about a girl, Lloyd. It's almost as if . . ." he trails off, embarrassed.

"Yes? Come on, spill it."

He shakes his head. "It's silly. I'm pretty sure it doesn't matter anyway."

"Come on. Have you forgotten who you're talking to?"

"Okay. Let's just say there's this animal, the last one of its kind. The only living remnant of his species. Are you following me?"

"Sure." Lloyd suppresses a smile, and Henry presses on.

"All right, so this animal lives among the other animals in the forest, never quite understanding what it is about himself that's unique. But then a new animal comes into the forest, a female, and she's very beautiful, but that's not the main thing. It turns out that he recognizes something in her. He understands that for the first time in his life he has met another animal from his own species. This comes as a surprise to him—because remember, he never really saw himself as different. But now he sees that he *is* different. What's more, he feels that the connection he has with this new animal has always existed, and always will, no matter how much time passes, no matter what happens to the forest or the other animals. Do you see what I mean?"

"Jesus. You're pretty far gone, Henry, aren't you?"

Henry colors. His words sound ridiculously naïve in his own ears, especially after the revelation of watching her on the dance floor.

"Well, my condolences." Lloyd taps the pipe on the railing, leaving a pile of red embers that blaze for a moment before flying away in the wind. "But don't tie yourself in knots over it, okay? This may be hard for you to hear, because you're in the grip of a powerful infatuation. I know how that feels; believe me. But in her own country she's a *movie star*. You, brother, are an underpaid hotel worker. And she's only here for, what, another three or four days? Then it's off to New York City, and from there, back across the ocean to Europe. Where, in case you haven't been paying attention, there's a big war in the process of breaking out."

A blast of music reaches their ears as the doors to the great hall swing open. It's Celia, exquisitely flushed from the exertion of dancing. "I told them I was going to have a cigarette. Why are you being so cold, Henry? Why won't you dance with me?"

"I thought you—that is, I didn't know that you—"

Lloyd shakes his head, smiling, and takes out a box of Choward's Violets. Out of politeness he offers it to the couple, but they don't notice, and he judges it best to leave them alone.

The new snow has restored the upper meadows to their virgin state, an unbroken expanse of sloping fields guarded by the snow-blanketed figures of sleeping conifers. Henry breaks trail up to the base of Diamondback Mountain's horseshoe cirque, where the party unloads the gear and prepares for the morning's motion picture shoot. He takes off his skis and postholes through deep snow to help Celia remove her climbing skins. She smiles fleetingly, but there is a sadness in her dark eyes that brings an aching constriction to his throat. He drops his gaze and kneels in the snow to peel the climbing skin from the bottom of her ski. "Everything all right?"

"It's just that I hardly know you. And we have to *leave* soon."

He doubles the skin on itself and stows it in his rucksack. "Don't think about that, Celia. Not yet. Let's make the most of the time we have."

"I can't *help* thinking about it."

He peels off the second skin and folds it slowly—once, twice—crouching over her boots in the snow. Perhaps later in the day they will find a way to be alone together. Her departure still seems abstract to him, as if it doesn't matter; as if the entire universe is made up of the lodge and the wild Colorado landscape that surrounds it; as if nothing exists outside of it; no politics, no economics, no war, no ocean, no differences in their lives and social positions, not even time. Just these few days: nothing before, nothing after. It's a crazy thought and he knows it, but it nevertheless strikes him as, in some way, undeniably true.

The party spends a few hours skiing and shooting in the meadows. At midday, Lloyd, Henry, and Mr. Peggett boot-pack a flat area and spread out the lodge's oversized oiled-canvas tarp. They unload the rucksacks and assemble a picnic of cheese, summer sausage, canned peaches, Hershey's Bars, and four bottles of fine Italian wine from the Lodge's cellar.

During lunch, Celia's father becomes intrigued by what he says is a natural ski run bisecting the central bowl of the horseshoe cirque. He offers to film Lloyd and Henry skiing down it. The brothers gaze apprehensively up at the bowl, but after a moment's hesitation, they agree to give it a try. Celia looks alarmed, and Mr. Peggett shakes his head. "We don't generally go up into that sort of terrain this time of year," he tells the Italian director. "It could be unstable, especially with all this new snow."

"As you say," Celia's father replies. "But these young men seem eager to try it."

Henry catches Lloyd's eye. "Eager" is not the word he would use, but the truth is that Celia's father has issued a challenge, and for his own part, he doesn't feel like he has much of a choice. "You could send the footage to the newsreels," he says to Mr. Peggett. "If it's good enough, this could put the lodge on the map. After all, when it comes to the scenery, Sun Valley has nothing on Diamondback Mountain."

In the end, Mr. Peggett agrees to let them go. Henry and Lloyd attach their skins and start breaking a trail toward the cirque. Glancing back at the tarp, he waves to Celia and smiles in a way that he intends to be reassuring. She puts a hand up to her mouth, her face pale with worry.

The slope steepens at the foot of the bowl, and the brothers shoulder their skis and use their boot-toes to kick a trail. It's a slow and difficult climb in the deep snow. The plan is that when they reach the top of the bowl they'll put on their equipment, and when they're ready to go, they'll signal Celia's father to roll the Cine-Kodak.

The sun pierces the high clouds in such a way that the light is both bright and flat, making it difficult to distinguish contours in the snow. But on the laborious journey up the bowl, there's no mistaking the steepness of the pitch, and Henry becomes increasingly nervous. As they mount the final cornice, he experiences a knee-weakening attack of vertigo. The slope beneath them falls away so abruptly that their boot trail is hidden from view. Dread hovers around the edges of his consciousness, shadowy batwings flickering in sync with his pulse.

Lloyd presses onward, up along the ramp-like ridge. He's heading for the most photogenic spot, a high point in the cornice above a broad, funnel-like chute. Because of the light, he's begun to look slightly unreal to Henry, like a ghost image in a double-exposed photograph. A strong westerly wind funnels down from the mountain, peeling off a sheet of snow and sending it sifting down into the bowl. Beyond Lloyd is the summit crag, rising up out of the snow-covered saddle. It looks especially sinister from this angle, a colossal shelf of barren, charcoal-gray bedrock.

They boot-pack a platform for themselves a few steps back from the lip of the cornice. Far below they can see the dark brown picnic tarp, like a postage stamp in the middle of a white plain fringed by the ant-like bodies of the filming party. Squinting, he can make out Celia—just a hint of that bright white headband—and two dark figures standing a little away from the tarp, which must be her father and Mr. Peggett with the tripod. "Want me to go first?" he asks, shouting to be heard over the howling wind.

"As you prefer," Lloyd calls back.

Henry raises his hand. After a moment's delay, one of the stick figures repeats the signal. Henry adjusts his glacier goggles and lowers his hand. The figure below lowers his hand. Lloyd gives him a thumbs-up, and Henry pushes off. The hickories slide across the wind-blasted snow, gaining speed as they approach the cornice lip. The ski tips find empty air, and he plummets.

After a moment of imbalance, he finds his center. The hickories become precise instruments on a slope this steep—gently flexing extensions of his feet—and the snow yields to them, hissing and billowing over his chest and face as he floats downhill in rhythmic sine curves across the fall line. The footage will be excellent, he thinks. The bowl is protected from the wind, and other than the hissing, everything is dead silent. The snow is as light and airy as smoke.

Faint shouts from below reach him. A quick downward glance catches the figures around the tarp, jumping and waving their arms, their enthusiasm oddly excessive, almost hysterical. In the next moment the snow all around him shudders and ripples like a bowl of milk on a shaken table, and that's when he begins to understand.

Adrenaline shoots through his limbs as he stops turning and points the hickories down the fall line, reasoning that if he can gain enough speed, he may be able to outrun it. But he's too late. With a thunderous crack, the entire slope dissolves in a field of careening white blocks.

It's strange how slowly it all unfolds. The initial sensations are almost pleasant. The snow is soft at the beginning, and he's buoyed along in the middle of it as in a cataract of dry whitewater. But as the avalanche gains momentum, it compresses, becoming a force of surprising brutality. It plunges him into darkness. It pummels his ears and rips off his woolen cap. It punches the breath out of his lungs and bends his body into impossible positions, like a child experimenting with a doll. He tries to swim up to the surface, but the hickories act like sea anchors. Twice he reaches daylight—quick glimpses of a wildly whirling sky—but each time he's snatched down again into the punishing depths. His left ski comes off, but the other remains attached, twisting his right leg until the knee gives out with a sickening pop.

The avalanche grinds to a halt. He finds himself suspended in an airless darkness that is like a womb of frozen concrete, with an immense weight pressing in on him from all sides. At first he is frantic, but he can't move more than a twitch, and gradually a feeling of serenity washes over him. When he thinks about it, he's known for a while that this or something like it was coming. In a way, the pressure of the snow is soothing.

A dream or a memory comes into his mind: he and Lloyd at sunset, standing on a hill above the lodge, gazing up at the alpenglow on the summit crag of Diamondback Mountain. The peak glows like a massive, red-gold ember against the black conifers on the mountainside that cradles it. The dying sunlight illuminates every detail, every crack and fissure in the stone.

A blue-black Steller's jay stares down at them from a ponderosa bough. Its sidelong glare feels strangely familiar, and it opens its heavy beak to utter what sounds for all the world like a phrase in English. Henry feels that he should know the words, but their meaning escapes him. The jay repeats the phrase again and again, and Henry feels that he's right on the verge of understanding. But he never does.

The next image is of Celia stepping down off the train, hands plunged into the pockets of her wool jacket. Her face is vaguely troubled, as if she's lost track of something, but can't quite remember what it is. Her eyes search the platform until they come to rest on his, and then she smiles.

The Foreigner

At a quarter to seven, James locked up the darkroom, grabbed his camera and tripod, and went out to shoot the procession. There had been a light rain, and the air was perfumed with flowers and melting candlewax. A crowd was forming in the Plaza de la Primavera—no good vantage point for the camera—so he kept walking, tracing the route the celebrants would take along the cobbled street through the Sacromonte. Eventually the crowd began to thin, and the street dwindled to a footpath winding out through the valley toward the Vírgen de la Esperanza chapel. He found a spot that would have a good view of the procession—atop a stone wall at the base of a steep hillside planted with rows of olive trees—and set up the tripod.

To his left and right, and indeed all along the path, onlookers had built small pyres using scraps of cypress and olivewood, and at a precise moment just before dusk—by what pre-arranged signal, James could not guess—the pyres were lit, filling the valley with flickering orange light and a haze of fragrant smoke. The onlookers were subdued, only the occasional outcry of a child rising above the murmur of conversation and the hiss and crackle of the fires. A Spaniard standing on the wall next to James tapped him on the shoulder and held out a *bota*, but James shook his head. The man raised his eyebrows and offered the wineskin again; when James declined again, he shrugged and pointedly turned his back. The mood was not festive, as a stranger might expect, but solemn, almost grim.

Soon dissonant music came echoing down the valley, the out-of-tune horn march and steady drumbeat familiar from the bullfighting season. The murmur of the onlookers rose in volume, and James stepped behind the tripod to peer through the lens. He felt the tension within his chest dissipate somewhat as the role of photographer filled him with a sense of competence and directedness.

The music was louder now, and the first of the secret societies rounded into view, men dressed in white robes and high conical hoods, disturbingly reminiscent of the Ku Klux Klan. "*Cofradía de los chapineros*," the Spaniard who'd offered him the *bota* intoned. He'd turned to face James again, and was staring with a curious intensity.

James adjusted the shutter and aperture to compensate for the celebrants' white robes, which were surprisingly bright in the smoky half-light. He already knew about the *cofradías*, which had their roots in the ancient trade guilds. That the city was home to a network of secret fraternities was a strange and faintly unsettling concept.

Several more *cofradías* filed by—red robes, black robes, one especially striking combination of royal blue and gold—and then came the procession's centerpiece, a float or palanquin bearing the ancient wooden statue of the Vírgen de la Esperanza. The float appeared top-heavy and unbalanced, loaded with an array of tall candles, Easter lilies, silver chalices, and reliquaries, as if at any moment it might tumble off the suffering shoulders of the bearers and into the tangled ravine below the footpath.

Next came a few more floats, one bearing an enormous gilded reliquary in the shape of an ark, which James guessed housed the bones of a martyred saint. It was on this float, perched atop the swaying ark, that a small boy dressed in rags sat and seemed to wave at him. He zoomed the camera in on the urchin, who was thin and extremely pale. And yes, it *was* James the boy was waving at, or someone close behind him on the wall. He turned to look for the Spaniard who'd offered the *bota*, but the man was gone. James peered through the lens again, but the boy had left his perch and was nowhere to be seen. How strange, he thought, that the urchin had picked him out of the multitude lining the path; normally he felt all but invisible in a crowd of Spaniards. And the man with the *bota*—who had been staring at him so avidly just a moment before—where had he gone?

At the tail of the procession came the marching band, brass section silent now, as if vanquished by the mournful beat of the drums: *doom, doom, doom.* The whole valley shook with the sound, so regular and predictable that it seemed to have been hovering in the air for weeks. As the musicians passed, the crowd swelled and filled in behind them, choking the footpath and pressing up against the wall where James stood. Fearing that the human river would soon overflow the wall, he collapsed the tripod and dropped into the procession heading back to the city. Night was closing in. Everything blurred together in the flickering firelight: the crowd, the drumbeat, the treasure-laden floats bobbing ahead as if carried downstream on an undulating, slow-motion torrent. Nearing the Sacromonte the crowd pressed in closer, and James's uneasiness slipped into a strange feeling of disembodiment—as if he were watching the procession through someone else's eyes, or through the lens of the camera now slung over his shoulder. This, too, was a familiar sensation, and an unpleasant one, reminding him forcefully of his longstanding distaste for crowds.

By the time the procession reached the Plaza de la Primavera it was impossible to move in any direction not dictated by the press of murmuring bodies. He saw flashbulbs ahead and caught a glimpse of a group of tourists standing on benches at the south end of the plaza, by the riverbank—a quick vision of glistening white teeth hinting at the skulls behind the faces. Spurred by panic, he shouldered his way through the crowd in the opposite direction and ducked into a narrow alley opposite the northern end of the plaza.

The alley was dark and climbed at a steep angle, becoming a cobbled staircase that led up into the heart of the Albaicín, the old Arab quarter. He sat on one of the steps, panting dejectedly. Down in the plaza, the crowd continued to stream by. Beyond him, on a hillside visible through an opening between the buildings, the Alhambra loomed in all its glory, high walls and turrets lit by golden floodlights. It was what the tourists came for, and what James himself had originally come to see and to photograph: the largest Moorish palace in the world, a masterpiece of architecture commemorating seven centuries of Arab rule in Spain. He leaned back, with his elbows on the stairs, and closed his eyes. What was troubling him? Nagging at the edges of his consciousness was a simple fact, one that he thought would explain everything, if only he could remember what it was.

When he opened his eyes, there was a woman. She was supporting herself against one of the stone buildings at the alley entrance, breathing heavily as if she'd been running or dancing—or perhaps, like James, escaping her claustrophobia by fighting her way out of the crowd. She wore a black dress gathered tightly at the waist, with billowy, multi-flounced skirts like those of a flamenco dancer.

"*Buenas noches*," he said, shyly curious.

"*Buenas noches*," she repeated, in a teasing voice that was clearly intended to mock his American accent. He couldn't see her eyes—her face was hidden, backlit by the Alhambra and the flickering torchlight from the plaza—but he thought he detected a note of warmth in her voice, perhaps even a hint of flirtatiousness.

"Do we know each other?" he asked in his rudimentary Spanish.

She laughed, took out a cigarette, and lit it. The alley filled with the pleasantly astringent scent of burning cloves.

"May I have one?" he asked in English.

"May I have one?" she repeated, mocking him again. Then she flicked the burning cigarette his way and was gone. Acting on a sudden instinct, he got to his feet and ran after her, but it was no good. She'd disappeared into the crowded plaza.

Shaking his head, he strode back up to his cobbled step. He found the smoldering cigarette and picked it up. He examined it for lipstick stains, then put it to his mouth and inhaled deeply. The clove tasted good, cool and numbing, and it kept the woman's image fresh in his mind: the old-fashioned dress; the cascade of black hair; the impression, more felt than seen, of her scornful eyes watching him from the shadows. And yes, her body: the narrow waist, the suggestive swell of her bosom as she breathed. There had been something so bittersweet in the way she'd mocked him—a presumption of familiarity, as if she'd known very well who he was, and what it was that he wanted.

But perhaps that was only wishful thinking. What young Spanish woman would care to know anything about *him*, a solitary foreigner who spoke her language at a very basic level and lived in her city without a single friend or acquaintance—who existed, in other words, in a state of near invisibility?

James lived in a small apartment not far from the Plaza de la Primavera, in the heart of the warren-like Albaicín. He'd made a darkroom out of a converted storage closet on the rooftop terrace, and it was there that he spent most of his time. Early on in his stay, he'd made an effort to reach out to the Spaniards in his neighborhood. He still said "*buenos días*" or "*buenas tardes*" whenever he passed one of them on the street, but by and large they ignored him. He had no interest in Granada's expatriate community, and the feeling was apparently mutual; the Americans had organized a dinner party for Thanksgiving to which he'd not been invited, and there had been various other functions, over the months, that he'd gone out of his way to ignore. He had no idea whether the other foreigners even knew his name, although he supposed they probably did. Still, there was no way of knowing for sure, because he'd never spoken to any of them. His solitude was nearly absolute. This allowed him to focus intensively on his work, but that too was problematic. He couldn't seem to get beyond the hackneyed tourist shots. He had no interest in producing postcards, yet that was basically what he was doing.

Still, he kept at it. In a way, shooting photos was the only method he had to prove to himself that he was real—not a figment of someone's half-remembered dream.

He spent the day after the procession cloistered in his darkroom. First he developed the shots of the floats, a few of which showed promise in a grainy, impressionistic way. The skinny boy atop the reliquary appeared in none of them, which was a surprise, because James remembered framing him several times, and the float he'd been sitting on had come through clearly enough.

He turned his attention to a series of shots he'd taken several days earlier, three rolls of a church façade carved playfully in the plateresque Renaissance style. He'd spent an entire morning shooting it, and the photos were remarkably clear, conveying the warm texture of the sandstone, the lyrical curves of the human forms, and the whimsically inventive shapes of the grotesques—dragons; mermaids; various half-beast, half-human composites.

One of these was especially interesting, a figure with the body of a winged serpent and the face of a man. He'd used up half a roll on that figure—from different angles, adjusting the aperture—and when he hung the photos up side by side he noticed something strange about them. A closer examination revealed the source of the problem: the expression on the figure's face appeared to change from frame to frame. It was subtle; each of the changes took place over several shots. But in the end—James had to close his eyes and open them again and again—there was no mistaking it. The expression changed. The face was that of an elderly man, with stern brows and an imperious hawklike nose, a face like a Roman philosopher's. The tight-lipped face gradually went from disapproving to sardonic; then bored; and finally, in the last few shots, it began to grin with dawning delight.

James stared at the photographs until they began to blur. Then he put away the chemicals, turned off the crimson overhead light, stepped out of the darkroom, and bolted the door behind him. He leaned his back against the door and massaged his eyes with his fingertips. Mystery solved. He was losing his mind.

Strange as it may seem, the new insight into his condition improved his mood. He slept unusually well that night, and the next morning he got up early and ascended the stairs to the rooftop terrace with his camera. It was early April. The air was warm, and suddenly the buds on the caper vines had burst into flower—little yellow stars cascading down the wall of an adjacent terrace. The sun threw long shadows over the roofed hillsides of the Albaicín, whose antique charm was only slightly marred by its spiny jumble of television antennae. The Alhambra sprawled along the high ridge across the valley, its massive square towers almost frighteningly medieval in the soft-hued morning light.

A pigeon fluttered down to rest on the terrace. It pecked around for a while on the chipped cement floor, then flapped up to the wall and cooed softly just behind James's head. He scooted his chair around to keep the bird in view, but it grunted and flew off. He moved his chair back to its original position facing the Alhambra. A light gust of wind blew a leaf across the terrace. Following it with his eyes, he noticed a face peering at him over the terrace wall. He stood up quickly, his heart pounding.

The man nodded curtly. He had slicked-back white hair and alert aquiline features that were familiar from somewhere—the open-air market, James thought, or perhaps the small photography store in the new town where he bought his supplies. A neighbor, obviously, though he'd never seen the man out on the terrace before.

"Beautiful day, is it not?" The man spoke excellent English. His accent was upper-class: noticeably Spanish but educated, with more than a hint of Oxbridge.

"Yes, it is." James struggled to regain his composure. "You spooked me a little there. Just showing up like that."

The older man frowned. "So sorry. I should have announced myself. But you looked so . . . unhappy. I did not wish to intrude."

"It's no intrusion, really. Always good to meet a neighbor. James Levin." He thrust his hand over the wall, and the man took it.

"Eusebio Romero de la O. Very pleased." His grip was firm. They gazed at each other over the wall, James wracking his brain for small talk, feeling more awkward as the seconds passed. The old man appeared content merely to stare.

"So you live here?" James finally said. "In the building, I mean?"

"I worry about you, James," the old man said. "Do you not know who I am?"

James shook his head, feeling embarrassed and inexplicably frightened. The old man's gaze was intense and unrelenting, and he couldn't for the life of him figure out where they might have met.

"I worry about you, James, because you insist on spending your time alone.

"Oh, I don't mind *that*," James explained. "Actually, I *like* being alone. It's one of the professional hazards of being a photographer."

"No, my friend." The elderly man shook his head slowly, brows knit over the prominent arc of his nose in an expression of grave concern. "You're not *just* a photographer. And you should not be alone so much, not now. There is an establishment I know. I'm going there tonight, in fact, and I have come to ask you to accompany me. Do you consent?"

James shrugged uncomfortably. It would be rude to turn down such a direct invitation, but he generally hated the idea of going out. He usually read a little, studied his Spanish, and went to bed early. It was a soothing routine.

And yet, if he thought about it, how could he say no? He had, in fact, been feeling guilty for not taking part in the famous Spanish nightlife. Often his slumber was interrupted at three or four in the morning by singing and drunken carousing under his window. Now, during Holy Week, the nighttime streets were alive with noise: guitar music, laughter, screams, young Spaniards roving the streets in gangs, clapping their hands in complex, inescapable rhythms that annoyed him and thrilled him and kept him awake until he had to cover his ears with his pillow.

"All right," he said, letting out his breath. "What time should we meet?"

"I'll come to your door at eleven," the Spaniard said. His face broke into a broad grin and James's stomach dropped, because suddenly he knew why the old man was so familiar. He bore an uncanny resemblance to the figure from the photographs now drying on their line in the darkroom. The figure with the expressive and subtly changing face that had been carved into golden sandstone more than four centuries before.

That evening he went out to witness another procession, this one known as "El Silencio," because it took place in total silence. All the celebrants held candles, which lit up their faces so that their heads appeared to float freely, unattached to human bodies. The vision filled him with dread.

He went back to the apartment and tried to read, shivering on the couch under a heavy woolen blanket. He didn't know whether Eusebio Romero de la O had been a real person or just some spectral vision concocted by his disturbed imagination. He hoped the old man was imaginary, because the truth was that he had little desire to go back out tonight.

Eusebio did come by, as promised, at exactly eleven o'clock. Together they walked down to the Plaza de la Primavera, and from there westward on the narrow street that followed the valley between the two steep hills that made up the old part of town, with the Albaicín above and to the right, and the spot-lit Alhambra looming up implacably on the hillside to the left. The air was cool, and by the time they arrived at the entrance to the establishment—a shadowed doorway three steps below street level in an unlit side alley—James was fully awake.

Eusebio gave him a companionable wink as he pushed open the riveted oak door, and a murmur of conversation and clinking glassware drifted out. It was an old wine tavern, a vaulted bodega lit by candles and torches bracketed to the brick walls. There were polished, antique mahogany tables and a hewn-oak bar. It was crowded with Spaniards of various ages chatting and laughing, their faces gleaming in the yellow light, their shadows dancing on the low brick vaults of the ceiling.

He turned to Eusebio, but the old man had melted into the crowd. James felt a wave of indignation that his neighbor would dump him so unceremoniously after having invited him out in the first place. He scanned the crowd for familiar faces from the photography shop or the open-air market, but he recognized no one. He found it striking, though. He could sense that the people in the bar were acutely aware of him—although no one would meet his eyes directly—whereas normally he felt invisible in a crowd. Here it was just the opposite, as if he was the most visible person in the room. Feeling conspicuous and painfully self-conscious, he crept through the crowd to the bar, where he sat on an antique-looking metal stool. Suspended from the ceiling behind the bar were a half-dozen sweating hocks of mountain ham. Beneath them was a broad cutting board stacked with baguettes, powdery links of dried sausage, and several bulky rounds of Manchego cheese. The barman put down a small tumbler, which he proceeded to fill with a clear yellowish liquid. James rarely drank alcohol, but with a newfound feeling of recklessness, he decided to take a sip. It was some kind of chilled sherry, and he found it uncommonly delicious: dry, refreshing, nearly bodiless. The barman watched him with an expectant smile. "*¿Bueno*?"

"*Excelente*," James replied, raising the glass to toast the barman before taking another sip.

The barman winked companionably and returned to the cutting board. He came back a moment later with a small plate, which he laid on the bar in front of James. "*Buen provecho.*"

The plate held a crescent of green figs and several paper-thin slices of ham. James didn't normally eat air-cured ham—it had a chewy consistency and a fleshy odor that he found disconcerting—but to please the barman he rolled one of the figs in a slice and popped it in his mouth. It was surprisingly tender, a delicate blend of flavors reminiscent of woodsmoke and mountain air. He closed his eyes, savoring the taste.

When he opened them, the barman was gone. A woman had taken the neighboring stool. She was facing away from him, and he took advantage of the moment to admire her shapely back, which was exposed to great advantage by a low-cut black dress. Her skin was of a warm olive complexion, and her raven-black hair fell down over her shoulders in loose curls. At the base of her left shoulder blade was a small diamond-shaped scar. James was gripped by a desire to touch it; to spin the woman around by her shoulders and kiss her on the lips.

She turned suddenly, and he just managed to look away in time. In his peripheral vision, he could see that she was now leaning against the bar, with both elbows resting upon it, gazing out at the crowd. It was the woman from the alley, he was sure of it—the one who'd made fun of his accent.

He agonized for a moment, and then slid the tapas plate down the bar for her. She shook her head and smiled sardonically, fixing him in her gaze. Her eyes were almond-shaped, green-flecked hazel, light as a cat's eyes but warmer, and luminous in their intensity. *Say something*, he urged himself silently, wracking his brain for an intelligent line. The barman placed a glass of red wine on the bar behind her, and she turned to pick it up.

"Are you a friend of Eusebio's?" he asked in Spanish.

She gave him a scornful look. "Am I a friend of who?"

"Eusebio Romero de la O," he replied sheepishly. "That's who I came here with. I thought you might know him."

"I have no idea what you're talking about," she said, still holding him immobile with the hypnotic intensity of her gaze. Her voice was slightly hoarse, simultaneously cultured and crude in the way of certain Spanish women. He caught a whiff of her scent: jasmine mixed with peppery clove. She was perhaps ten years younger than him, in her late twenties. He felt himself gripped by a sudden, powerful infatuation.

"May I kiss you?" he asked. He was shocked that he would come out with such a thing—the sherry was evidently impairing his judgment—but it was too late to take it back, and the truth was that he didn't *want* to take it back. For the first time in recent memory, he was actually enjoying himself. Yet there was something dwelling beneath this new sense of abandon, an unspeakable terror that clutched at his throat. It took all his concentration to stamp it back down into the darkness. *Not now*, he begged it; *not now*.

She gazed evenly at him and there was a long, painful silence. Then she simply picked up her wineglass and walked away. He got up and tried to follow her, but his passage was blocked by an uncooperative thicket of tavern patrons. Several of them hissed as he tried to shoulder his way through, and twice he was elbowed roughly. Finally he made his way to the exit, pulled open the heavy door, and climbed the stairs into the street, where he found Eusebio in animated conversation with three other elderly men. As he approached, the discussion died. They all regarded him politely.

"I'm going home," he declared. Eusebio gave a vaguely sympathetic nod, but did not urge him to stay.

When Eusebio knocked on his door the next night at eleven, James did not hesitate. In fact, he'd been dressed and ready to go for hours and was quite anxious to get back to the wine bar. They walked through the dark streets in silence, and when they came to the sunken doorway, James was neither surprised nor annoyed to find that the old man went in and left him alone without a backward glance. It was all part of the arrangement, apparently. James had concluded that the events of recent days were like real-time scenes in a play being put on for his benefit—a kind of vast street-theatre experiment of which he couldn't yet see the point, but in which he was an ever more willing participant.

The woman wasn't at the bar, so he sat and drank several of the exquisite *finos* while he waited. The barman gave him a tapa of deliciously cured hard sausage, sliced paper thin. After half an hour or so, as he'd expected, she did come, luminous in the black flamenco dress, with those extraordinary light-hued eyes, and the scent of jasmine and cloves. She sat next to him at the bar. They talked. She laughed at his Spanish. Occasionally her knee brushed against his thigh, and once, she reached out to squeeze his forearm, a surprisingly tender gesture that set his heart racing. After an indeterminate amount of time—it must have been several hours, though they flew by like minutes—she asked him to walk her home. Her name was Soledad. She lived deep within the Sacromonte, on a cobbled footpath where gypsies had dwelled for centuries in the hillside caves their ancestors had carved out of the soft volcanic rock. Conventional wisdom held that it was dangerous for a foreigner to walk in the Sacromonte at night, but when he mentioned that to Soledad, she said scornfully, "That's just a rumor we spread to keep the tourists out."

At her door she let him kiss her. Her lips were warm and dry. Her breath was cool and smoky, with a hint of clove.

The next night there was a Moroccan band playing at the wine bar. The music was strange and primal, complex percussion rhythms and high, trilling Arabic wails. One could hardly call it music at all in the sense to which James was accustomed, but it was strangely seductive. He'd never liked dancing—it made him feel exposed, as if he were naked in public—but with Soledad there, he got caught up in it. At first he danced tentatively, watching his feet to make sure he didn't step on anyone's toes, but soon the intricate rhythms possessed him, and he began to spin loose-limbed around the floor, an aimless marionette puppeted by the drums and the trilling voices. Soledad danced in front of him with graceful, flamenco-inspired moves, watching him the whole time with a serious, almost grave expression. Such prolonged scrutiny would normally have made him intensely self-conscious, but every so often the hint of a smile would come into her face, and he would speculate with rising exultation that this was the face of true love.

And then a wild feeling overtook him, a feeling utterly foreign to his experience. It was a floating up, a surrendering of self, a sense of joyous communion with the shadows whirling across the vaulted brick ceiling of the tavern. Soledad and the other dancers blurred and disappeared, replaced by flickering beams of pearly white light that spiraled and pulsated in synchrony with the complex drum rhythms. There was something terrible about this vision—a fearsome power—but it was also staggeringly beautiful, as if each dancer had taken on the concentrated essence of the aurora borealis.

The beat changed, and he lost sight of the vision. He stopped dancing and pressed his eyes shut, trying unsuccessfully to summon it back. When he opened his eyes he saw that he was standing alone. He made a full circuit around the dance floor looking for Soledad, and shoved his way through the crowd to the women's *aseo*. He waited by the door, but several girls and women came and went, and it became obvious that she was not inside. Feeling increasingly claustrophobic and desperate, he found the exit and ascended the stairs to the darkness of the street. She was waiting for him there, her clove cigarette a glowing ember in the shadows by the wall of the tavern.

"I was afraid you'd left," he said.

She flicked the cigarette onto the street. "No. I was waiting."

"Do you want me to walk you home?"

"No. Not home."

"Okay. Where to?"

She strode off into the darkness, and he hastened to follow. She led him down to the river, across the bridge toward the Alhambra, then uphill—he struggled to keep pace—into the vine-choked network of aqueducts and walkways that crisscrossed the hillside below the vast Moorish palace. It was a warm night, more summer than spring, and the uneven cobblestones still radiated the heat of the day's sun. Gentle breezes wafted the distant smoke of burning olivewood, blending it with the more intimate scent of blossoming caper-vines.

They climbed until they came to a stone footbridge, an old Moorish arch spanning a deep-cut ravine. The only sound was the chatter of a streamlet from the shadows under the bridge. Soledad stopped halfway across and sat on the waist-high stone railing, flipping the skirts of her gypsy dress so that a fold of it draped playfully over the edge.

He sat beside her on the wall, his heart pounding, a cool rivulet of sweat running down his chest. They kissed. Her lips were soft and yielding, pleasantly spicy with clove, and when he lifted up the dress she did not protest, but giggled into his mouth, and then she began to moan softly as he made love to her against the railing.

Afterwards he held her close, one hand resting on her narrow waist and the other luxuriating behind her neck among the silken curls of her hair.

"Do you adore me?" she asked softly, the words just audible over the gurgle of the streamlet beneath the bridge.

"Of course I do," he replied. "I practically *worship* you."

She put her hands on his shoulders and shoved him back, then slapped him hard across the face. "What the hell?" he exclaimed in English. "Why did you do *that*?"

"What the hell? Why did you do *that*?" she mocked, the exaggerated syllables echoing up and down the ravine.

And in the next moment, she was gone.

In a state of shock and growing anger, he made his way back to the tavern. Eusebio was standing at the bar in conversation with three cronies. "Where is she?" James asked.

"Where is who?" Eusebio looked annoyed at the interruption. The other men stared calmly.

"You know very well who I mean. Soledad, the woman I've been spending so much time with for the last few nights."

"I don't remember you with a woman. Usually, you sit alone at the bar." Eusebio glanced at one of the other elders, who smiled thinly and inclined his well-groomed, white-haired head.

"Come on. You must have noticed her. She has beautiful eyes, like a cat."

Eusebio gestured dismissively and turned back to his

companions. James was infuriated by this rude treatment; the old man seemed to have thrown aside even the pretense of friendship.

He caught the barman's eye and signaled for his usual sherry, and when the drink was delivered, he asked if the barman had seen the woman he'd been talking to. The man gave him a funny look. "I don't remember you with a woman. Usually, you sit alone."

James quaffed the sherry. It was acrid. "So you're in on it, too, then," he said. "What's it all about? Why me?"

The barman raised his brows and shrugged. James slammed the tumbler down and walked out, furious. He sensed all eyes on his back as he pulled open the heavy door and exited to the street. He wandered for hours through the filthy unlit alleyways of the Sacromonte, not returning to his apartment until well after dawn.

After sleeping into the late afternoon, he walked up to the Alhambra to shoot a few rolls of film. At the keyhole entry arch he hesitated; it seemed important to go in, but he felt shaky and nauseated, and in the end he just couldn't make himself do it. It was as if a truth awaited him inside the palace, and it was a truth he wasn't ready to confront; a truth that filled him with sickening fear. So he made his way downhill on the network of cobbled paths, hunting in vain for the footbridge where he'd made love to Soledad.

Back in his apartment, he waited until well past midnight for Eusebio, and when he was sure the old man wasn't coming, he walked down to the wine bar by himself. Standing in the recessed stairwell, he stared at the riveted oak door for a moment, breathing in and out to calm his racing heart. When he pushed the door open, the tastefully lit interior was gone, replaced by shiny modern décor and harsh fluorescent lighting. Rows of video slot machines lined one wall, and a juke-box played American top-forty music. A scattering of customers sat on polished chrome barstools: there were no familiar faces. Even the barman was a stranger.

He fell into a numbing haze of despair. The days ground on in a colorless routine. He carried his camera wherever he went but it always remained zipped up in its case; the darkroom gathered dust. He went back to the wine bar several times, but the old décor never returned. There were no tapas, no suspended hams, and the new barman didn't seem to know how to keep his sherry properly chilled. James came to believe that the whole thing had been an elaborate fantasy concocted by his tortured imagination, as a lonely child peoples his nursery with imaginary friends.

Above all, he yearned for Soledad. Every night, he wandered the narrow streets and steep alleyways of the Sacromonte—a dangerous practice, he knew, despite what she'd said—but he couldn't help it. His only goal was to catch a glimpse of her.

One night in mid-May, he thought he spotted her ducking into a doorway near where he remembered—

but, of course, had been unable to precisely locate—her cave. Inside, he found himself in the midst of a boisterous crowd of red-faced German tourists. They were all shouting and clapping at a middle-aged woman in a black flamenco dress who'd just stepped out onto a low stage at the back of the cave. Off to one side, a fat gypsy sat on a stool, plucking a twelve-string guitar and crooning in an ugly, high-pitched quaver. Reeling, James fled, cracking his forehead against the lintel as he hurried out the door.

He wandered aimlessly through the maze of cobbled alleyways, relying on the numbing rhythm of his stride to keep the dread that dwelled deep within him at bay. It was an increasing strain. How much longer could he fend it off?

At a certain point—it could have been moments or hours later—he became aware of footsteps echoing on the cobbles behind him. His scalp prickled and he quickened his pace, glancing nervously over his shoulder. As far as he could make out, there were four or five figures trailing him. They kept to the shadows, and seemed to hang back at a constant distance. He saw, or imagined that he saw, a flash of white teeth—a quick, feline grin. Ducking into a tight-walled side alley, he glanced back over his shoulder again. The shadowy figures had gathered at the alley mouth as if to block his exit. With a surge of panic, he broke into a run; behind him, a sudden clatter of footsteps rang out on the cobbles, and it became a full-fledged chase.

At the next alley he cornered right, uphill toward the ancient wall that marked the upper limits of the city. His heart raced with a strange mix of terror and exhilaration. Behind him his pursuers were fanning out, hooting and whistling to each other, commando-style. Beyond the wall, he knew there was an open hillside overgrown with yucca and prickly pear. If he could just make it over the wall, he thought, he might be able to lose them.

The alley narrowed and steepened to a staircase; James was amazed that his lungs weren't bursting with the effort of running so fast, but he didn't even feel tired. Ahead loomed the broad, black mass of the wall. He sprinted toward it, reaching out with his hands to feel in the darkness for a gap or a chink that would give him the leverage to climb up and over.

Almost there, he stumbled, and the next thing he knew, he was being hoisted roughly and shoved against the wall. His assailants were panting for breath, and there was a long pause before anyone spoke. The stone felt cool and abrasive against his back, and the texture of it was oddly soothing. If anything, he felt a sense of impending closure and relief.

One of the men—a gypsy with a quick feline grin, the shape of which James could now see was the result of a pronounced harelip—pulled a knife from his belt and held it up to James's neck while one of the others turned his pockets inside out.

"Go ahead," James said helpfully. "Take it all, please. Take everything I have."

The gypsy scowled. His breath was spiced with clove.

"Did Soledad send you?" James asked.

One of the other gypsies barked out a short laugh. The harelip narrowed his eyes and pressed the knife harder against the skin of James's throat. James held still. The blade was a cool bar of pressure against his Adam's apple. He supposed that they were about to murder him. The thought should have filled him with panic, but it did not. The simple truth that had been lurking in the depths of his mind finally burst to the surface. "You can't kill me," he said. "I'm already dead."

When the harelip drew the blade across his throat he could tell that it was only an illusion, an echo from a previous life that he could only remember in vague flashes, as in a dream, or a loop of an old film montage playing with the sound turned off. There had been a trip to Granada, maybe various trips. He had been a photographer, and he had shot a Holy Week procession, or maybe more than one. He'd also shot a wall of Renaissance grotesques, where one figure in particular had attracted his attention, a face that appeared again and again on the wall—a self-portrait of the sculptor himself, perhaps. He'd gone to a candlelit tapas bar; he'd lounged on a private terrace in the sun. He'd walked across a footbridge on the vine-choked hillside below the Alhambra. He retained the memory of a sunset hour within the palace itself, with a camera, shooting the fountains; the city view; the high, airy Moorish ceilings. There was a woman—not Soledad, but a blond stranger—and she was laughing at him, and her face became worried as he climbed through a lacy Moorish window to a narrow balcony with the city behind and far below him . . .

Back in the Sacromonte, his view of the late-night alley had locked up, as a stopped film frame becomes a still photo. The shadows in the photo were bleeding toward each other across the frame, gradually closing in to a uniform, black nothingness.

He shook his head, and the shadows froze. He stamped his feet, and the shadows receded, reopening his view of the night scene at the wall. The gypsies were still there, gathered around him in a menacing knot and pressing him up against the wall. "What do you want from me?" he asked.

The harelip's face blurred and was replaced by that of Eusebio, with his slicked-back white hair and noble, hawklike nose. "My dear boy," he said softly. "We only want you to see the truth."

"But I *do* see the truth. It's that I'm dead, right? I've been dead this whole time?"

The old man smiled sadly. "That's *part* of the truth. But there's more."

James shook his head. Whatever it was, he didn't want to know. He glanced around desperately, looking for a handhold, a crack, a protruding stone, anything he might use to escape, get over the wall, resume his flight. But it was no good.

"What about Soledad?" he asked, with a faint stirring of hope. "Isn't she involved with this?"

"See for yourself, James." The old man stepped back, and a hooded figure stepped forward from the group to replace him.

"Is that Soledad?" James asked. The figure was silent, and he hesitated, but then he stepped forward, grasped the top of the hood, and tore it off. He shrank back in horror. There was no face, only an escaping spiral of flickering light, and the robe collapsed on the ground.

"Damn you," he said. He turned to Eusebio, but he and all the others were gone, their clothes crumpled like shadows on the ground. Bodies of diffuse light flickered around the wall for a few moments and then coalesced in a single, achingly bright column that pulsated, hummed, and began to move toward him. He pressed his back against the wall again, but it was no good. Finally, he understood. There could be no escape. The only thing left was to embrace it.

Keepers

Elliot made slow progress along the tier of black ballast rocks jutting into the harbor, pausing at the wider gaps between the tumbled boulders to search for footholds. A stiff northwesterly breeze whipped brine over his wading shoes and up around his bare shins, occasionally splashing his shorts and the mesh-bottomed stripping basket belted around his waist. It was the last day of his annual September break—the last fly fishing of the season for him—and although the ocean was warm, the air had gone cold, as if to emphasize the end of summer. The light too had gained a new clarity, swept in by the wind to suffuse the rocks and water with the cold glint of Atlantic winter. But there were other fishermen out, or at least one, a burly local in brown neoprene waders standing on a high rock several hundred yards from the beach.

"Any sign of life?" Elliot shouted into the wind.

"Nah." The islander spoke without looking up.

"I got a keeper a few days ago," Elliot offered. "A little further out from shore." The Nantucketer nodded and reeled in his line, his bearded face reflecting the green tint of the ocean. He lifted his rod tip and plucked the fly out of the wind—a chartreuse Clouser minnow, Elliot noticed—and hitched it to the fly-clip above the reel. Only then did he look up, his eyes flickering over Elliot's canvas wading shoes and bare legs before settling on his face. "Better be careful out here. Rocks'll be underwater with the high tide."

"Don't worry. This isn't my first time out here."

What the man had said was true. The exposed tips of the ballast rocks were already wet from the douse and suck of the swells, and the tide was coming in fast. But Elliot knew that the jetty was negotiable even when fully submerged. You just had to look under the surface for the bone-colored patches of barnacle, which were abrasive enough to give your felt-soled wading shoes a reliable grip. So he continued, his free hand outstretched for balance, stepping carefully so as not to lose his footing on the rust-colored fronds of kelp at the waterline. He could sense the islander's eyes on his back, a slight prickling among the fine hairs at the base of his neck.

His progress was delayed along the middle section of the jetty, because he had to wait for the swells to go down before he could see the barnacles. Then it was a question of summoning the faith that the bone-colored patches were indeed stationary beneath the surface, which shifted back and forth to create the illusion that the underlying rocks were also shifting. He stopped on an exposed rock to tie on his own chartreuse Clouser, poking the tippet through the eye of the hook and looping the line back over itself, twisting five times and threading the loop before spitting on the line to wet it and pulling the knot tight into a compact monofilament noose. The Clouser looked terrified, with its bugged-out barbell eyes and flume of chartreuse hair sweeping back over the hook.

He began to cast, bending the graphite rod to form the line into long, quickly unrolling loops, then letting it straighten and drop to the water. He counted to ten slowly, allowing the line to sink beneath the wind-tossed surface and into the stripers' feeding zone. In clear water you could sometimes see them, schools of three or more fish patrolling the submerged edges of the rocks, fin-tips glowing green against the eel grass, or profiled against the sandy bottom like the shadows of fast-moving clouds. For Elliot, these fly-fishing excursions were like pilgrimages into a sacred realm of wind and tide and current. Out here good instincts were the only important quality. Freedom was absolute, and the bewildering complexities of life receded before the absorbed mindlessness of a hunter stalking prey.

He stripped the line slowly—pause, strip, pause, strip—the fly imitating a wounded baitfish.

This morning he'd awakened with a breeze coming in through the screen window like cool breath on his face. Sarah had lain on her stomach beside him, snoring lightly. He'd slid carefully out from under the sheet so as not to wake her, and tiptoed over the creaking pinewood floor to the small bathroom. It was the worst feature of the old rental cottage, a cramped space with awkward angles and a slanted ceiling, so that standing over the toilet, you either had to crouch or lean back, limbo-style.

On his way downstairs to go over his fishing gear, he'd heard Zoe stirring in her room. Unable to resist tip-toeing up to peer in through her cracked door, he'd found her wide awake, lying on her side with her arms around her pillow and her eyes open, a characteristically solemn expression on her face as though she were pondering some deep philosophical question. All parents are love-blind, and Elliot knew it, but he couldn't help but wonder at the miracle of this small creature he and Sarah had created. She was an exceptional two-year-old: wise, sweet-tempered, and patient.

When he pushed open the door, her hazel eyes swung around to meet his—almost reluctantly, he thought—but when his presence registered, her face lit up in a broad smile. He came in and sat on the bed, and they grinned at each other for a moment in conspiratorial silence. He took her in his arms, her head reassuringly heavy on his shoulder as he carried her over the floorboards into the master bedroom. He pulled back the sheet and placed her on the bed next to her sleeping mother, gave her an exaggerated wink, and pressed his finger to his mouth. Zoe nodded to show that she understood, and Elliot tousled her downy hair, imagining Sarah's moment of confusion as she awoke to find her husband's bulk replaced by the tiny form of their daughter. Zoe would see the joke and giggle delightedly, and it was likely that Sarah would go straight into tickling mode. As far as family life went, he could conceive of nothing to surpass it: a whole morning spent laughing in bed with beloved, newly awakened females in their warm cotton nightshirts.

He wasn't going to be able to stick around for that, though—not today. The sooner he cooked breakfast, the sooner they could start packing. The sooner they packed, the more family time they would have. And the more family time they had, the more predisposed Sarah would be to grant him a few hours of fishing time before the ferry. On the walk down the hill from the rental cottage the harbor had looked like hammered steel, but now that he was standing out on the jetty, it looked molten: the slate-green surface glinting and swelling and nettled with sea foam. The wind etched capricious fingerprints that moved to and fro across the swells with alarming speed, and peeled hissing plumes off the tops of the waves. Casting in these conditions was difficult. There was no sign of fish, and Elliot made up his mind to turn back. It would be nice to give Sarah—who hated cutting things close—the pleasant surprise of an early arrival at the ferry dock. One more cast, he decided, and he would head in, buy them each an ice cream cone, and take their smiles as consolation for the looming reality of his beckoning daily life: gridlock traffic, computer screens, marketing meetings.

But when he'd stripped in the final cast, something made him shoot out the line once more. And that was when the fish hit. From the way it fought—an initial series of powerful, dog-like tugs followed by the high-pitched whine of the reel as it ran for deeper water—Elliot could tell it was a big striper. He turned the dial to tighten the drag and bent his knees, wetting his free hand in the water in order to press his palm to the bottom of the reel. But it was too late. Sensing freedom, the fish thrashed hard; the rod bent double for a second, then shook out straight; and the line, which had been humming with the spirit of a wild fighting animal, went slack.

He cursed and reeled in.

He reached into his chest pack for another Clouser and tied it on, hands shaking. The wind was increasing. Glancing up, he saw that a massive wedge-shaped cloud had blown in to darken the sky to the northeast. Over the submerged rock on which he stood flowed a foot of clear, fast-moving water. Schools of agitated baitfish streamed across it, bouncing off his shins like a volley of soft machine-gun bullets. His watch said 16:04. A few more casts would mean he would have to hurry to catch the boat, but that was nothing new; Sarah would expect it. He would hold himself to a strict turnaround time of four thirty, maybe four thirty-five, four forty at the latest. The steamship wharf was a ten-minute jog from Jetties Beach. He still time to spare for the five o'clock departure.

He clipped the Clouser to the cork rod butt and squinted at the swirling currents ahead. A mottled gray storm petrel sailed overhead, following the line of the breakwater like a shadow escaping to the open sea. The spine of ballast rocks was nearly submerged, and the water rushing in from the ocean side formed increasingly defined rips, the dull roar of the flooding tide playing a strangely seductive counterpoint to the high-pitched shriek of the wind. The closest rocks were difficult to see in the dark green water, but he could make out a bone-colored barnacle patch wavering under the surface a few feet away. Farther out there were some high rocks still exposed to the air, and if he could just cross the gap . . . .

He hesitated for a moment, then stepped into deeper water.

This morning, after a leisurely breakfast during which he'd done his best to suppress his impatience to get on with the day, they'd packed the bags, cleaned the cottage, taken out the garbage, and walked Zoe in the stroller down to the children's beach. They'd built a sand sculpture in the shape of a whale and played in the water until the wind had picked up; then they'd taken shelter behind an overturned skiff for a picnic of leftover swordfish. Zoe had fallen asleep on a blanket beneath three layers of beach towel.

He tried to interest Sarah in sex and from the full-mouthed way she responded to his kisses, he could tell that she was considering it, but in the end she dashed his hopes by removing his hand from its casual resting-place on the curve of her bikini bottom. They lay spoon-style with his face buried in her clean-smelling hair, the close-pressed warmth of her backside an enchanting contrast to the increasingly chilly wind. Somewhere on the island a heavy surf was pounding, the distant rumble of it accented by the hollow slap of waves against the hulls of harbor sailboats nearby.

Elliot had begun to feel restless. Sensing this, Sarah rolled over and glared at him in mock disapproval. "*Go*. But don't be late for the ferry."

He got to his feet and helpfully began to stuff the leftover picnic supplies into a plastic shopping bag. "I'll be at the wharf by four-thirty."

"Sure you will. You're always so punctual when you've been fishing."

He grinned. "Don't worry. I'll be there."

"If you miss the boat, Elliot, you may as well jump in with the fish. Because you'll have to swim pretty hard to reach the other side before Zoe and I drive home without you."

"Zoe would wait for me," he said.

"Not with Mommy at the wheel, she wouldn't."

"You wouldn't *really* leave me behind." Elliot tried to imagine it: the Prius pulling out of the parking lot, Zoe's mournful little face pressed against the rear window as she scanned Hyannis Harbor for a glimpse of her backstroking Dad.

"Why don't we *not* find out, okay?" Sarah said.

Elliot kneeled on the blanket to kiss her lips—the lingering promise of unfinished business, perhaps tonight back at home—and he kissed sleeping Zoe on the forehead. Then he set off for the cottage to collect his gear.

"Happy hunting," Sarah called after him, but her words were lost in the rising howl of the wind.

Before he could gain purchase on the barnacle patch, a chest-high surge knocked him over. Holding his fly rod out of the water, he searched with his feet for something to stand on, found a flat surface slick with rubbery seaweed, was buffeted by another surprising swell, and slipped, his free hand scraping painfully over a knife-edged rock toothed with barnacles. For a moment he was adrift, flailing, pulled by the undertow into the savage dance of the open water. In a fit of panicked determination, he let go of the rod and thrashed back to a rock white with cormorant guano, which he hugged tightly while his feet probed for traction. At length he was able to wedge the sole of his wading shoe firmly into a crevice between two rocks, and he finally had a moment to collect himself. The guano let off a strong ammoniac tang. His heart beat wildly. After the initial shock of immersion, the water felt surprisingly warm. "You *idiot*," he said, surprised by how frightened his voice sounded. "That was a four-hundred-dollar rod."

The wind whipped salt spray into his eyes. It had started to rain, warm drops drumming his scalp. The tide alternated between buoying him up on the swells as if to loosen his grip on the rock, and dragging him down as if to suction him into deeper water. Then he saw it: a huge green wave, the wind ripping spray off the top as it came. A glimpse of the lacy pattern of foam on the concave wall of water, and he was plunged into a deafening green silence. When the wave receded, he concentrated on trying to catch his breath. He now perceived a dull pressure in the arch of his right foot, a small ache that hadn't been there a moment before. When he tried to work the foot out of the crevice, he realized that he could not: it was stuck. Was it possible the rock had shifted?

Another wave came in, and he swallowed brine. When the sea receded, he gasped for air, gripped by a renewed onslaught of panic, a tingling in his limbs and a quick flurry of spasms in his groin. Looking up at the horizon, he saw a squall advancing from the northeast, a wall of rain and wind that blurred the sky. In the next moment the squall hit, a sizzling haze of blown droplets. The wind was a steady scream punctuated by moments of absolute silence as Elliot held his breath beneath the latest swell. It occurred to him that his fly rod might not be the only loss that day. Perhaps he had succumbed too blithely to his primitive urge, which might have been something like the predatory instinct that drew a striper to a pinch of bucktail tied to a stainless steel hook. Only he had to admit that, in his case, the action hadn't been quite so automatic. He'd known all along that he was making a choice, and taking a risk.

Between immersions he got a look at his diving watch: 16:32. In his mind's eye, the ferry was already leaving the dock. The Prius was pulling out of the parking lot on the other side. He could see the determined frown on Sarah's face as she drove home through the parade of taillights on the highway. She wouldn't report him missing, at least not right away. She would wait for him to call her, to apologize for the worry and inconvenience he had caused. He concentrated on working his foot out of the crack, deliberately at first, then back and forth in increasingly frantic jerks.

The foghorn blast signaled the ferry's imminent departure. Sarah sighed, lifted Zoe and the canvas day-bag, and followed the line through the light rain to the boarding ramp. She stopped to give the man her ticket and glanced over her shoulder one more time, hoping to see Elliot jogging toward her through the puddles on the steaming asphalt of the parking lot. The rain had been short-lived but heavy, blown almost horizontal by the wind coming in through the mouth of the harbor. That had worried her, especially when the downpour had turned briefly to hail: marble-sized pellets whitening the pavement and the decks of the boats at their moorings. But the squall had passed quickly, and it was true that she worried too much: among their friends and extended family Elliot was famous for making it just under the wire, and for his good luck.

She walked up the ramp as slowly as she could, glancing back several more times before she had no choice but to board. In the crowded main cabin, summer families and college kids sprawled out among the booths, their black labs and golden retrievers pulling on their leashes, and a few weathered old islanders read newspapers or dealt out hands of solitaire.

"He likes to push it," she told Zoe, setting her down on the fake-leather seat of one of the few unoccupied booths. "It would be funny if it weren't so maddening, sweetie, wouldn't it?"

The little girl nodded solemnly.

"He says life's too short not to make the most of it. Well, *always* trying to make the most of life isn't a good way to reduce stress, is it, sweetie? It's a way to *increase* stress." She took a coloring book and some crayons out of the canvas bag and laid them out on the table in front of the child, who stared thoughtfully at the cover of the book for a moment before opening it up to a particular page. The air inside the main cabin reeked of damp clothing and snack-bar hot dogs, and the windows were already fogging up. Elliot could take a bus back to Hartford and call her from the station, Sarah thought with a surge of frustration. It would serve him right for not being there to help her move their heavy luggage, put gas in the car while she fed Zoe, talk to her and keep her awake on the long, dark drive home. But beneath the frustration was an increasing undertow of worry.

"What do you think, Zoe?" she said, bending to rescue a crayon that had rolled off the table. "Should we be worried about your useless, irresponsible Daddy?"

When she sat up, the little girl was gazing wide-eyed over Sarah's shoulder. Sarah's heart skipped a beat and she spun around, half-expecting a grim-faced Coast Guard captain or some other uniformed messenger of death. But it was only Elliot, his chest heaving with the exertion of running, his clothing soaked and dripping on the soggy industrial carpet of the enclosed deck. "It's about time, for the love of *God*," she said, putting more emphasis on the last word than she'd really intended.

He smiled weakly. His hair was plastered across his forehead as if he'd been swimming, and there was a bloody gash along his left hand and wrist.

"Jesus, honey, what happened? Are you okay?"

He glanced down at his legs, which were also leaking blood from several cuts and still puckered from the water. His smile was uncertain, as if he still couldn't quite believe he'd made it.

"Damn it, Elliot—" But she stopped short, not wanting to alarm Zoe. He nodded, acknowledging the justice of the criticism. There was a hint of barely suppressed fear in his sun-bronzed face, and Sarah noticed that his eyes were different. Slightly wider, perhaps, the fine wrinkles around them more pronounced.

Zoe stared up at her father with her delicate little eyebrows raised. Her expression was tolerant and serene, like a miniature blond Buddha. Elliot knelt on the carpet in front of the booth and bent his head in an oddly submissive way—like a surrendering general, or an errant dog.

"Bad Daddy," the little girl said, patting him on the head. "Bad, bad Daddy."

About the Author

AUTHOR PHOTO BY DANIA MAXWELL.

Tim Weed is an avid outdoorsman in addition to being a writer, and has pursued a parallel career leading international education programs around the world for National Geographic and other organizations. Tim teaches at Grub Street in Boston and is the co-founder of the Cuba Writers' Program. He's the winner of a Writer's Digest Popular Fiction Award and his first novel, *Will Poole's Island*, was named to Bank Street College of Education's Best Books of the Year.

CPSIA information can be obtained
at www.ICGtesting.com
Printed in the USA
LVHW04s0357250818
587959LV00003B/3/P